STILL NOT OVER YOU

AN ENEMIES TO LOVERS ROMANCE

NICOLE SNOW

ICE LIPS PRESS

I'm SO over that gorgeous, scary, heartbreaking man who hates my guts.
   I'm just counting on him to save my life.

Never, ever fall for your brother's hot older friend.
   I flunked the test the instant I laid eyes on Landon Strauss.
   Tall. Ripped. Commanding. Irresistibly alpha.
   He gave a damn like no one else did.
   His soul-searing eyes saw me, not just a nerd girl next door.
   I had my idol, my destiny, and names for our future kids picked.

Then I read Landon's little black book.
   One nosy peek exposed the shock of a lifetime.
   His confession. His pain. His *plan.*
   The sweet boy I loved was gone.
   Hero-turned-villain-turned-bad-memory overnight.

Five years later, an insane slip of fate puts us under the same roof.

Sweet closure, I think.

I almost forget he hates me.

I almost think we'll talk like *normal* adults.

I don't expect the shirtless behemoth who comes barreling through my door.

Landon's grown up. All snarls, testosterone, and lethal chemistry.

We're in trouble, he says.

Oh, Landon. Oh, baby, don't I know it?

I: AT LEAST IT'S NOT BOX WINE (KENNA)

*N*ever trust a man who drinks Cabernet Sauvignon.

That's always been my rule and it's never steered me wrong. Cabernet Sauvignon is for men who have certain ideas about themselves, but not a damn bit of what it takes to back them up.

All slick and shiny on the outside. Inside, it's just empty promises and pointlessness.

No dreams. No heart. No grit. No soul.

Nothing like the man who set an impossibly alpha standard for every date I'll ever have. Right after he finished playing kickball with my heart. After the day that ended us, the one I swore I'd never fixate on again.

Welcome to my life in present day SoCal.

I'm not sure I'm going to find what I'm looking for out here in the plastic Ken-doll lineup of L.A. hotties, but I know Mr. New Money isn't it. Not by a Tinder mile.

I'm not sure why I gave him a chance once he ordered his Cab with that shallow, overconfident smirk.

Maybe it was those blue eyes.

Empty as a bottomed-out glass. But they reminded me too much of someone I keep reaching for even though he's forever out of my grasp.

Mr. New Money would've been easy, but I don't do easy. I need more.

Although I wouldn't mind Mr. New Money's sleek Mercedes to come cruising by and rescue me, right now.

Half a block. Just half a freaking block around the corner from Skofé's Wine Bar to my place, and I still managed to break a heel.

That's the kind of luck I have.

Kenna Burke, human black cat.

At least it's not Friday the 13th, or I'd be cursed double.

It's a choice between walking barefoot on beat up L.A. sidewalks or limping along in one broken heel.

I choose limping – and regret it by the time I make it up the stairs to my apartment. I kick my shoes off with a little extra spite for the broken one, sending it rocketing across the entryway, and step forward. My aching foot comes down on something cool; an envelope. I pick it up and flip it over.

My name's on the front, neatly handwritten. Land-lord's letterhead logo in the upper left corner.

Oh, crap.

Just another thing I don't want to open tonight.

I need something to fortify. Wasn't that the whole reason I went out, anyway? Not to meet some Cabernet-swigging wannabe Casanova.

I've been ignoring an email from my publisher all day. Subject line? "Re: His Royal Nuisance."

Pinch me. I sent the manuscript in over two months ago. Normally I get a response back within weeks. The silence has been deafening, and I'm afraid the email will be damning.

If I'm going to author-hell, I'll do it on a five dollar bottle of pink Moscato.

Never trust a girl who drinks Barefoot Cellars, either.

She's usually broke and chases her wine with straight up bad luck.

I drop myself on the barstool in front of the kitchen island, pour a glass, and toss it down. Courage comes in pink fizzy form.

I close my eyes, letting the tingles go to my head until everything feels a little floaty. Sweet distance. That's what I need. That muting layer of mild intoxication that makes everything feel just a little farther away, and a little less likely to stab me in the heart.

Okay. Now for the envelope.

I slit the top with my fingernail, so not in the mood to care about my manicure. The single sheet of paper spilling out is obviously a form letter. The blue ink swoop of my landlord's name gives it away. So does what's supposed to look like a signature, but is obviously a rubber stamp smacked on by a tired secretary. A number in the middle of the top paragraph jumps out at me.

Two thousand dollars.

That's what they want to charge me for rent, starting in two weeks.

I can barely manage the eighteen hundred I'm paying now for an overpriced shoebox of a one-bedroom walk-up.

"Holy shit," I mutter to myself, the grim realization

setting in. Two thousand will push me from living on ramen to living in the cardboard box the ramen was packed in.

Defeat hovers over me like a guillotine waiting to drop, but that thread's not snapping just yet. There's still hope in the email.

All I need is a solid advance for His Royal Nuisance and I'll be able to handle the rent hike. At least long enough to keep from having to move *again* after the fifth rent adjustment in two years.

I top off my glass, take a sip for bravery, unlock my phone, and swipe the email notification.

And immediately feel my throat close shut at those horrid first words, "We regret to inform you…"

Those bastards don't regret anything at all. Not when they go on to list a litany of my faults, calling the book rushed with flat, unrealistic characters, incoherent sex, and zero chemistry.

I guess it's not enough to stick the dagger in my gut.

They have to twist it, too.

Mission accomplished because I can't even breathe.

Yes, I know I forced the book. But I thought I'd been doing this long enough that I had it in the bag and could at least rely on experience to push me through.

I haven't been shot down like this since I was a baby author sending my first query letters. Another brutal sign I'm off my game.

Mojo, lost. Everything's a disaster, and that disaster's name is McKenna Burke.

I'm ready to chuck my phone across the room when it buzzes in my palm. My brother's name pops up on the screen with the same cheesy cheerful selfie grin I'd set for his icon.

Steve, not now. Bad, bad timing.

I almost hang up. My head throbs, my heart hurts, and I don't know if I can stand someone else being happy right now while I'm so miserable. But I could use a little human connection, too, and one way or another...

Steve always makes things right.

I take another swig of Moscato, this time straight from the bottle, then wipe my mouth with a gasp and tap to answer the call.

"Hello?" It falls from my lips by reflex, when my mouth feels numb and my head is whirling.

"Hey, sis," Steve says. Perky as ever. With the way I feel right now, it's like being dead and hearing voices from the living. "Did you get my email?"

"Email? What?" I blink vacantly, and pull my phone away for a second. Oh, hell. There's like...ten other emails I'd ignored, including one from Steve with the subject "Gamma's birthday." But he's still talking, this tinny voice coming from the speaker, as I put my phone to my ear again. "Sorry, sorry, just looking now. I just saw it and haven't had a chance to open it. Sorry."

"No biggie! I was just asking about the card."

"Card?"

"Gamma's turning ninety, remember?"

"Oh..."

Ninety. Oh God. Oh hell, I...I completely forgot, and ninety's the big one. Ninety's the one where you know you won't have them for another decade, but you hope anyway and celebrate like it's not all downhill and scary from there. I'd wanted to pick out something really nice for Gamma's ninetieth, and yet I've been so wrapped up in my own mess that I *completely* forgot.

Add bad granddaughter to my growing list of faults, too.

"Sorry," I mumble, and the next thing I know the counter is blurry in front of me and my nostrils are burning and I can't make heads or tails of anything when everything inside me is constricting. "I'm sorry, I-I –"

And that's when the tears hit.

Snotty, sniffly, ugly-cry tears, slamming into me like a sledgehammer and coming out on a coughing sob. I cover my mouth, trying to whimper another apology, but all that spills out is these wretched, awful sounds. Steve makes a panicked noise.

"Kenna? McKenna, what's wrong? It's – Jesus, sis. It's just a card. You didn't murder anybody, don't worry, I'll pick one out for you if that'll help –"

"Steve, it's n-not th-tha..."

"Then what's going down, baby sister?" His voice softens. Calming. Soothing. "C'mon, Kenna. Talk to me. Let it out."

I take several breaths, quick and deep, trying to get myself under control until I'm not stammering and hitching with every word.

"Everything, Steve." I croak out finally. "My publisher just rejected my latest novel. My rent's going up. I can't meet a single man who isn't like some creepy carbon copy of Ryan Seacrest. I'm so cursed I might as well be a black cat, and my life is shit. It's just *shit* and I don't know what to do."

The last part is a wail that makes even me cringe, but Steve takes it all in stride. He always does.

He's older than me by a few years, almost thirty, but with his bright cheer you'd think he was the younger one. He's like a Labrador or Golden Retriever or something. Just scratch behind his ears and his world is all good. And if you're hurt, he comes running.

"You're not cursed," he says with more confidence than I could ever muster. "You're going to be fine. Everyone has bad streaks. The important thing is to make a plan and get through it. You're great at planning, remember?"

"Right. Just fabulous. The last time I planned a family vacation, we ended up sleeping in a stable in Nepal. With goats. Remember?"

"That was an AirBnB mixup, not yours." He laughs. "Look, sis, you need to recharge your batteries before you write your next book. So why not stop worrying about rent and get away to the beach?"

I snort. "Sure, I have beach money lying around. I'll just live on my wealthy rich kid trust fund for a few months."

"Okay, smartass," he teases gently. "But I'm serious. I know a place you can hang out. Look, it's just a few hours north of L.A., like twenty minutes north of the bay in Sausalito. You can drive there in less than a day. An old friend has this place on the beach where you can stay in the guest house rent free."

I tilt my head, eyeballing the bottle of Moscato. It's calling me, but I'm trying to resist its lure. It won't help me. Steve, on the other hand...

"No such thing as rent free," I tell him. "Where's the catch?"

"Nah, no catch. Friends helping friends, that's all. You remember Landon, right? My best friend? How we were always over at his place when Mom and Dad were traveling?"

I remember.

I remember hard enough to drop a stone on my heart, and the bottle of Moscato's suddenly in my hand like a woman dying of thirst while I take a deep swig.

Holy hell, Landon Strauss. I could live ten more lifetimes and I'd never, ever forget that name.

"Nope!" I say as soon as I swallow. "Sorry, Steve, but no."

Landon Strauss isn't someone I need to be around. He's just a dark memory.

But wasn't it that memory of blue eyes and how starry-eyed he made me feel that led to a completely foolish decision tonight?

Once upon a time, I had the worst crush on Landon Strauss. More than a crush, actually.

I was crazy mad in love with him, and how he'd spin me all around until I was ecstatic and floating, the next I was small and awkward and ready to crawl in a hole and die.

I don't want that feeling back. The nerd next door, glasses and all. Annoying baby sister tagging along everywhere.

I'm also not ready to revisit that unspeakable, unholy thing that happened the day my crush on Landon ended. That stupid, dark, soul shocking thing that transformed him into someone else right before my eyes.

Not just no. *Hell no!*

I've grown into myself and I'm now McKenna Burke, successful romance author.

But to Landon, I'll always be that annoying child who

stuck her nose where it didn't belong, and uncovered secrets I never should've seen the day I picked up his damn journal when he wasn't looking.

I'll always be the girl who knows something damning I can never believe, but that could ruin him if I ever opened my mouth.

He hates me. And I should hate him.

And he sure as hell won't want me living on his property anytime this century.

"Kenna? Why not? What's the big deal?" Steve asks, pulling me back from my memory-misted past and into my wine-fogged present. "Hey, it's not like he's going to invade your fortress of solitude or anything. You'll have plenty of free writing time. He won't even be there most of the time."

"Why not?"

"His security company's really taking off. He's a busy dude. Enguard, remember? That's the name. So, he's away on jobs most of the time. He's had a few beach bums and prowlers squatting on his property, I guess, and he said he needs to take care of the cats and make sure kids don't mess around. Really, you'd be doing him a favor. Keep an eye on the place, do a little writing, and soak up the beach without paying a dime of rent. No big scary neighbors from the past up in your space."

I make a noncommittal sound under my breath.

I can't possibly be considering this, but I have to admit, it does sound tempting. Life rent-free, a place to get my head together, away from the too-familiar rush of L.A.

If it's possible to get cabin fever from an entire city, I've got it.

Still, it's *Landon.*

"What do you say, sis?" Steve presses.

I sigh. "Give me time. I'll think about it, okay? It's not really as easy as packing up and taking off. Let's talk later."

Except it *is* that easy, if I want it to be, I realize as I hang up the phone.

It's exactly that easy.

It's not like I haven't done it before, only this time I'd be doing it without hungry landlords nipping at my heels. Hell, half my stuff is still in boxes from the last move. I never bothered unpacking because I didn't feel secure.

I can't possibly be considering this. But the opportunity is too good to ignore, and maybe...

Maybe I need closure.

Maybe he does, too.

I owe Landon an apology, at least. A few words to clear the air. I can tell him I'm sorry, purify the bad blood between us, promise him I've kept his secrets, be an adult and hope he's willing to be one, too.

As I go to bed, I tell myself I'm not doing anything on heartbreak and cheap wine.

But by morning, I've already left notice for my landlord that I'm terminating my lease, and I'll be back in thirty days for my things.

The next thing I know, I'm packing.

Sun, sand, and some time alone to screw my head on straight.

All I have to do is write the perfect book, and I'll be back in the game and able to take care of myself again. It's not like, if things go wrong with me and Landon, I have to deal with him very much.

Okay. *Okay,* I tell myself as I stuff a sports bra and yoga pants into a duffel bag.

Let's do this.

No hesitations, and no regrets.

I'm going to get over Landon and everything dark in my life, or else.

II: LITTLE MORE THAN A FIG LEAF
(LANDON)

I'm really not into animal cruelty, but right now, I'm ready to skin a cat.

That's because one just dropped down paws-first on my sore, bruised stomach. Among their other talents, cats are experts at concentrating all their weight onto one paw and then drilling it down into you like they're trying to puncture through to an exit wound. And one of those sweet little assholes – Velvet or Mews, I've only had them two months and I can't tell them apart – is currently doing a Russian army march right over the freshly purpled bruises I picked up during a rough night.

Whoever said love is pain was clearly a cat owner.

The cat on my stomach meows. Loudly.

Mews, then. A fitting name if there ever was one.

I groan, but don't open my eyes just yet. I've got a headache from hell I was hoping to sleep off. Just five more minutes for the first time in what feels like years.

Cats, however, don't really care about my beauty sleep. Or my blood pressure.

They care that I have opposable thumbs and can work a can opener, and the fact that I'm not doing so right this second.

I groan, dragging a hand over my face. "Fine," I mumble into my palm. "Okay, okay. I'm up."

Actually, I don't move.

A soft, velvety forehead butts against the back of my hand, followed by a rusty-sounding purr. Even if I'm ready to string the little monster up, I can't stop myself from scratching between his ears. He closes his eyes in sheer delight and thrusts against my fingers.

This is how they get you. Food for love.

Don't think for half a second this fuzzy little jerk means it.

A thump and weight pressing on the end of the bed tells me I have about five seconds before Mews has a dance partner on my aching body. It's that more than anything that gets me to roll out of bed, pausing to stroke between Velvet's ears before dragging a robe on against the faint, wet morning chill blowing in off the ocean. Downstairs the sun is bright through the kitchen windows, scraping at my bleary eyes.

Coffee. I need a strong, paint-stripping cup.

And then it's back to business as usual.

I'm still shaking off my 'fun' from the night before. A Mayor's campaign downtown brought us in, extra security for their fundraiser. The rabble rousers who showed up made good on their promise to make a scene after tensions flared. One of the assholes broke the police line, managed to land a blow to my gut and another to my jaw, before I had him by the throat and on the ground, holding him until the cops took over.

I remember why I don't like politics, even when it pays.

I leave a pot to brew and dump out a couple fresh tins of foul smelling food in the monsters' bowls. Grain-free or something, but it's just meaty and heavy and enough to make me retreat while they shove their faces in with hungry, messy sounds.

At least they're easily pleased.

Wish I could say the same for the fucksticks jerking me around lately.

A few of said fucksticks whine nasally from my voice-mail as I plop my phone on the counter and set it to play back on speaker while I do something about breakfast. Both voicemails are pure bullshit, and both are from agents of the same client.

Milah Holly. The next big starlet manufactured by a Hollywood sound studio and fed the lyrics they've decided will be the voice of a generation. She's high-profile. Big money. A good contract.

And she's driving me out of my mind, when the job hasn't even started yet.

These voicemails alone are full of scheduling issues. I might start working for Milah in a few days, or in a few weeks.

I don't know. She doesn't know. No one knows, and I halfway think they need to hire someone to get their shit straight long before they hire a security firm.

But I can't afford to let this slip through my fingers. It's too big an opportunity for Enguard.

Ever since I turned over my old man's company, Crown Security, to Dallas Reese – grade A asshole, son of dad's former and currently incarcerated partner, Reg

Reese, and the jackass who's been playing a one-up game with me since we were fucking twelve – I need *every* leg up I can get to keep my own company thriving.

Enguard's seen rapid growth and won a solid piece of the market, but if I let my guard down too long, then Dallas and Crown Security will swoop right in and snatch Milah – plus the prestige this contract nets me – right out under my nose.

I sigh, once again adjusting the dates in my phone's calendar, and settle to pour a cup of strong black brew. As I set the carafe down, though, a hint of motion flashes in the corner of my eye, out of place among the gently wafting trees framing the house.

I glance out the window. Someone's skulking around the beach house again.

Fuck. I bet it's those goddamned kids again, or someone casing the place for a possible break-in.

I've had enough.

Slamming the carafe back into the brewer, I stomp to the door, yanking it open. I've got to get the drop on them this time.

Before they've seen me coming, and run off before I catch their faces on my phone, or collar them before calling the cops. This isn't the kind of security I do, chasing down idiots on my property, but that doesn't mean I can't use my skills to make sure they get what they deserve for trespassing and potentially breaking and entering.

I duck into the trees, staying out of sight, and take off at a ground-eating run.

I hurt all the fuck over, but I don't care.

I'm pissed, thoroughly sick of this, and pure rage and

adrenaline are pumping enough endorphins to numb the bruises and devour my pain. I don't even stop when a branch catches my robe and rips it half-off, the belt coming loose and the robe falling down one arm.

I'm past caring if these assholes get an earful and an eyeful.

I come bursting out of the trees like a juggernaut, barreling toward the front door. Before I lay a hand on it, though, it snaps open – and a petite figure steps out.

At first I don't recognize her. Not when this slim, leggy young woman is nothing like the awkward little thing with huge frames who used to followed me around like a lost puppy.

McKenna.

Kenna Burke.

Reb.

Standing there all poised and prim and sexy as hell, her green eyes wide and startled behind the kind of librarian glasses that make you wonder what she'd look like with all that chestnut hair pulled free from its tail and rippling around her face and shoulders.

Fuck. *Again.*

Even though she's clearly surprised, poised like a faun ready to bolt, she's still completely put together and gorgeous in a pair of slim jeans and a loose, pretty silk tank top that clings to her in ways that promise things those dreamy eyes can't quite follow through on. Kenna's always been a bit of a dreamer, lost in the stars, and she's wearing that look right now.

Almost like she's seeing other worlds when she looks right through me.

And I'm standing here half-naked with my robe torn

up, leaves in my hair, cock practically falling half out of my boxers. She opens her mouth to speak, but then closes it a second later.

This is off to a great fucking start.

* * *

WE'RE JUST STARING at each other for what seems like forever. Her lips stay slightly parted like she still wants to say something, but the shock tore the words from that glistening pink mouth.

I'm no better, breathing hard from running, standing here with my jaw hanging like a damn fool. For a minute I'm teleported back five years ago, and all this anger comes boiling up inside me again. I haven't seen her up close like this since the day I cursed her name.

Not since little Reb became the only other human on the planet to know what I was planning.

I don't know what to do. That's rare.

I'm sure as hell not going to unload on her just yet. Not when she's already mumbling something like an apology, a nervous strain in her soft, low words.

I can't even look at her.

I can't fucking have her here.

So I turn my back on her, dragging my phone from the pocket of my loose robe and pulling the terrycloth up to belt it securely around my body again.

This is Steve's fault. No mistake. When my best friend said he had the perfect person in mind to handle the house, I had no idea he'd gone this fucking loco, sending Kenna here as if he didn't know exactly what he was doing.

I'm already pulling his number up in my contacts, ignoring the faint, flustered sounds behind me.

First, I'm going to murder Steve.

And then I'm going to send McKenna Burke packing. Right back where she came from.

III: YOU HAD ME AT HELLO (KENNA)

his wasn't how I wanted our reunion to go.

I thought I'd have time to prepare for something a bit more formal in a setting where there were appropriate social rules and conventions to keep this from blowing up in my face.

Like a brunch on the patio or something. Objects between us to create proper distance and remind us to be polite, instead of stabbing at each other with words and butter knives and possibly a breakfast fork or two.

Instead, I have *this.* This insanity.

This behemoth of a man charging out of the trees at me like freaking Tarzan, half-naked and his eyes lit up with crackling electric blue storms.

He's thicker than I remember. All corded muscle bulking out his frame. Writhing with more tattoos than I remember. He looks like the devil himself with his chin bearded and scruffy, and nothing like the boy I'd once idolized.

That boy sure as hell hadn't been this much of an *asshole.*

He's practically in a tantrum, giving me his back and snarling under his breath as he stabs at his phone and then waits, this bristling mess of raw male energy and thorny irritation. I'd bet what little is left in my bank account that he's calling my brother.

If I could, I'd double that bet when the call ends without picking up. He just growls and tries it again.

I sigh, hands on my hips.

Sure, Landon caught me off guard, but this is ridiculous. He could have at least tried to be civil, instead of treating me like unwanted trash.

Does he expect those fierce glares to make me afraid of him?

Does he think I'm the same little girl who'll be disarmed with *that* look?

Like hell.

He hasn't managed to frighten me away yet, and I've seen him at his worst.

Known him at his darkest, and his most depraved.

I march right up to him and take a firm grip on one of his shoulders. Obviously, I can't budge a titan as large as Landon, but at least he won't ignore me.

And he doesn't. Ignore me, that is.

He whirls around so quick it makes my heart stumble, and jerks back until I'm no longer touching him. He's in full beast mode, upper lip curled in something between a snarl and a sneer, his glare cutting into me.

I lift my chin, pride more than anything making me brave. "The word you're looking for," I bite off, "is 'hello.'"

The word he gives me instead? "Fuck."

And then he says, "Are you out of your mind? What was Steve thinking, sending you here?" Those brilliant blue eyes narrow. "Or was this your idea?"

I scowl. "It wasn't. Steve was trying to do you a favor, if you'd let him."

"A favor," he scoffs. "Like sending you here is helping me gain anything besides a headache. You can't be here, Kenna. It's absolutely ridiculous. You and I, we don't –"

"Don't what?" I demand. Anger, right now, is easier than the ball of hurt knotting in my chest.

He goes still. There's something strange in his eyes, before they ice over and he looks at me oddly, remotely, distantly. More standoffish than I ever could've expected.

"Just don't," he says, as if that's the final verdict.

He's written me off with a snap of his tongue. Not even a chance to talk things out.

I'm not the little girl I was back then, but all he sees is a nuisance sent to disrupt his orderly life and expose his secrets. But if I'm not that little girl anymore...

Then I'm not afraid of him anymore, either.

Not like I was then.

Back when his Dad died.

Overnight, Landon became a different person. A person I didn't recognize. A person who terrified me, terrorized me, and ran me off with a promise never to come back.

Well, I'm back now. And I didn't show up just to go full circle.

Yes, it's his property. His place. His life.

He's the one who needs *me* – this glorified housesitter-catsitter thing I signed up for. If I have to, I'll go crash on

Steve's couch and leave Landon to deal with his problems on his own.

"Now look," I say firmly. "If you're done with your little roid rage explosion, how about we try talking about this like two rational adults?" I square my shoulders. "It's just a job. I didn't come here to screw up your life, Landon. And I didn't come here to dig into old wounds. I'm helping you, you're paying me with room and board, and since you'll be gone soon, we don't even have to see each other. All I need is a week or two to handle my affairs. By the time you get back, I'll be ready to leave."

It's a tight timeline. Two weeks to produce a novel, instead of a month?

Ugh. But maybe the pressure will light a spark under me. If anything, it'll just give me more incentive to get it done so I can get away from this asshole as soon as possible.

I let Landon Strauss break my heart once.

I won't do it again.

He's still watching me with that same measured look. Assessing every second.

I feel like I'm suddenly in hostile territory, and he's sizing me up as the enemy. Like he's back in his military days and I'm just another obstacle to overcome with tactical assessment and a little strategic finesse. But just as quickly that look fades, leaving him looking almost bewildered, and then annoyed.

He grunts something under his breath, then looks away, staring across the sand to where choppy waves have turned to lead under the storm blowing in, the sky all steel and silver-shot lightning.

There's something dark in his eyes.

Something haunted.

Something damaged.

The boy I knew doesn't live in this hardened, scarred beast. Not anymore.

Landon's fists clench. He drops his phone into his bathrobe pocket.

"I'll think," he mutters, a drawling rasp darkening his sultry, deep voice.

Then he turns and walks away, leaving me standing alone on the beach. The first mist of storm spray washes in, kissing my cheeks in cool beads that feel like the tears of the little girl I refuse to ever be again. Not for him.

I don't know what kind of mess I've gotten myself into, but it's already hurting like hell.

I almost want to laugh, give my throat something bitter and jagged. Whatever it takes to dislodge the lump forming there.

God, I really can't control anything in my life, can I? Not even one confrontation with a wild man who still holds the map to all the wounded places in my heart.

I've never been in control of anything. Why should this be different?

Because I want it to be. Just this once.

Because my heart feels like it's cracking, splintering in two, going back to a dreadful place I swore I'd left behind.

But this time, there's a difference: I've gotten pretty damned good at taping it back together.

IV: LOVE TO HATE YOU (LANDON)

*S*omehow, I'm not surprised Steve's still not picking up his phone.

He may be a complete prick for putting me in this position, but he's got a sense of self-preservation.

It's been hours. At least a dozen phone calls.

Half a dozen voicemails before I quit wasting my voice and just hit redial until I got sick of it, chucked my phone across the desk, and settled back in my chair to stare out my office window.

I've been watching her all day, catching hints and flashes. Glimpses of her moving through the windows. A ghost I thought I'd chased away years ago, who shouldn't even be here.

She's not quite the same, true. This Kenna is older, more collected. That awkward young thing blossomed into an adult with that first entirely enticing, entirely maddening blush of new womanhood clinging to her like some heady perfume the second I got in her face.

Too bad the little things about her body language are

too much the same. Still familiar enough to jolt me, until all day I've been out of sorts, close to making mistakes every time someone on my crew checks in with me about setup for the Milah job.

Skylar, my lead and logistics manager, tells me the singer wants us helping her entire entourage of stuck-up groupies. Whatever, I say, as long as Milah Holly understands we're security and not their damn servants. Skylar drops off as soon as she catches the edge in my tone.

The one Reb put there without trying.

Fuck. This isn't going to work.

She's already got me off my game, detached from my job, and I hate it.

I hate how grown-up she looks.

How her eyes, behind her sleeker, thinner glasses, are still the same clear, liquid green that seems to expect something more from me. Hate how it's the same pool I could lose myself in too long. Hate how one phone call from Milah's manager, later, tells me I have no choice but to rely on Kenna when Milah needs me in Sonoma by Saturday afternoon, and it's Friday now.

I fucking *hate* everything about this. About her. And about the demanding brat signing my next six figure check.

I've tried to come up with a work around all day, but it's just not happening. I'm backed into a corner, and I can't even get my head around what's happening now.

Not when I keep remembering. Reliving what happened years ago – on the day I truly met the girl who shouldn't be here tormenting me.

* * *

Ten Years Ago

SOMETIMES, teenagers can be complete and utter pricks.

That's the first thing I think when I see her crying. I barely know her; she's just a shadow who hangs around my best friend now and then, someone I vaguely identify as his little sister, McKenna. Kenna, right?

I probably shouldn't even be talking to her. I'm eighteen, close to graduating, and she's this dorky fourteen-year-old freshman.

But she looks almost afraid of me. I find her out behind the bleachers on the football field after school, sobbing her eyes out. Like someone hurt her and she thinks I've come to deliver the killing blow.

Something about that look makes me want to fix it, even if I'm not the one who fucked it up. It's not my business, true, but for some screwed up reason I want to make it mine.

She's curled on the grass, leaning against a post. I sit down on the other side and rest my back against the wood. That way she doesn't have to feel like I'm looking at her, judging her.

"You want to talk about it?" I ask.

"No!" she forces out, sniffling, her voice thick.

"Okay. Whenever you're ready, I'm here."

For some reason, that sets her off crying again. I just wait and listen.

Sometimes people just need someone to be there with them when they're sad, but I hope I'm not embarrassing her and making it worse. Thankfully after a while there comes another sniffle, and her breathing sounds easier.

"Sorry, it's just…" she mumbles. "Thanks. I guess."

I look over my shoulder. She's taken her tear-streaked glasses off to reveal the largest, widest green eyes I've ever seen, swimming and nearly glowing with their wet sheen. She's busy stretching her bulky, ill-fitted shirt out of shape trying to clean her lenses before she darts a quick glance toward me, then reddens and looks away.

"Not here to make fun of you," I say. "It's okay to talk. Really."

I think she'll clam up again, when she lowers her eyes to her suddenly motionless hands. But she lets out a lifeless shrug and whispers bitterly, "Just boys being boys. Assholes, I mean. And I'm an easy target."

"Did someone hurt you?"

"No. Maybe?" Another shrug. "Just my feelings. Jonah McMillan thought it would be funny to –" Her voice hitches as if she'll breakdown again, then smooths as she clears her throat and continues with a touch of stiff pride. "He pretended to invite me to Homecoming. Big fancy fake letter and everything. And when I went to ask him if it was a joke or something…"

"He humiliated you," I guess, a slight growl curdling my voice. "Like a fuckstick with nothing better to do.."

"In front of half the girls in my class!" she finishes with a touch of ferocity, her eyes sparking. "God. I tried to say I knew it was a joke, a stupid one, but he was too busy telling everyone how pathetic I was…thinking he'd ever go out with me. Like I'd be interested in him."

"Real cute," I offer, an awkward attempt to get her to

laugh. It works, even if it's just a kind of quick throaty hurting chuckle hidden behind a pinched smile.

"He's an asshole, is what he is," she counters, but a bruised smile lingers on her lips. Slowly fading. "I just...I don't even know. Now, they're all calling me Princess. Like I think I'm too full of myself when they're actually all too good for me."

"Princess?" I curl my upper lip. "Like you're somebody's yappy fucking purse dog? That's a shit name. And they're shit people. Here, I've got a better name for you." I stroke my chin, wondering if I should really put it out there like this.

She eyes me warily. "...what is it?"

"Rebel," I say, and grin. "Let's make it 'reb' for short. That's what you look like to me, telling these kids where they can stick it. And I bet that's what you'd like to be."

Her eyes widen. Her blush returns. I eye her a second longer, deciding she's kinda cute in a weird dorky little sister way. Of course, freshmen aren't something I'd be caught dead messing with – especially when she's Steve's own flesh and blood.

"Hmph," she says faintly, tilting her head. "I don't know. I'm not really that much of a rebel."

"Bull. You saw through their crap, yeah? You're too smart for this high school circlejerk, and too good for Jonah McMillan. He's a limp-dick bully who probably gets off on hurting girls. You did the right thing serving up what he deserved. The world's full of dudes like him."

She wrinkles her nose. "Great. I'm glad I have so much to look forward to."

"Just telling the truth." And if that's what I'm really doing, it makes me weirdly happy when she lets out this embarrassed little laugh, looking at me, then looking away again, bringing a hand up to scrub at her tear-streaked face.

"Hey. Look. I've been through four years at this shit-hole school. I'll tell you right now that if you try to be someone you're not, it's just gonna chew you up and spit you out in pieces on the other side. So forget being royalty. Be the rebel you are. This smart, gorgeous girl with rocking glasses. You'll have so many boys begging for you they'll be lined up the whole west coast to Seattle, babe."

I've never seen someone blush so red in my life, right up to the tip of her pert little upturned nose. She ducks her head, tucking her loose, frizzy hair behind her ear.

"You're just saying that because you're Steve's friend. Trying to make me feel better."

"Wrong. I'm saying it because I mean it, Reb." I reach over and ruffle her hair. "C'mon. Your bro will kill me if I don't give you a ride home."

I have no idea, when I offer my hand to help her up, what I've done on this day.

I've earned a friend, an admirer – and made one of the worst mistakes of my life. I have no idea, on this sunlit afternoon, that one day my life will go to hell when my father's mistakes get him killed, and there's nothing left for me but bitterness, but pain...

And the vicious disappointment of pushing her away.

* * *

Present Day

SOMETHING IS CHEWING on my fingers.

I'm dreaming about Gremlins, the old horror-comedy movie. In the dream, one of them is chewing on my fingers. Its teeth are sharp, its mouth wet and slimy, and its breath smells familiarly foul. Just like that awful, meaty cat food.

Velvet.

Goddamn. I wake up groggy.

Velvet's still chewing on my fingers, standing on the desk gnawing at me like I'm a human chew toy. Mews is prowling around restlessly, letting out his typical high demanding yowls while bumping up against the chair.

Yawning, I push myself upright, pulling my hand free from Velvet's mouth and wiping my fingers on my thigh. I fell asleep in my chair. I couldn't have been out long enough for them to start screaming for their dinner, though.

I see why when I glance out the window. Toward the burning orange glow of sunset over the ocean.

Except that glow isn't the sunset.

It's fire, licking up out of the windows of the beach house, curling against wood turned black by flames, giving off sooty streams of smoke that plume into the sky.

The beach house glows like the mouth of hell roared open against the early nighttime darkness, a raw ember of crackling death.

My mouth dries. My heart stops. My stomach ices over, and before I can stop myself, I spring up, bolting for the door with only one thing on my mind.

Kenna.

V: FLAME-BROILED (KENNA)

There are few things that can't be fixed by a Godzilla burger.

If you've never had a Katsu Burger, then you have no idea what you're missing. It's this weird Japanese-American mish-mash cuisine with grass-fed Kobe beef breaded in panko crumbs and piled with so much weird stuff, like wasabi mayo and coleslaw and ginger and even a fried egg, if you want it.

It's massive. Messy. The perfect thing for a bad day when you don't want to think about anything but trying to get more of the spicy mayo on your mouth than you do on your shirt.

I've got a stomach full of Katsu Burger chased by a green tea smoothie, but it's not the massive double-decker that's got my belly feeling heavy.

It's the miles counting down between me and Landon.

I'd rattled around the beach house all day, beating myself up left and right. If I wasn't guilting myself over shoving myself into his life in the first place, I was guilting myself over losing a desperately needed writing day to what was basically just biting my nails.

Worrying myself into an anxiety attack. I needed to get out, clear my head.

But now I've got to go back. I can't exactly sleep in my car, and this time of night, it's a little late to pack everything up again for the six-hour drive back to L.A.

I can head home in the morning, if I have to. This late, Landon's probably either asleep or out on a job, so if I just hole up in the beach house until morning, we don't even have to see each other again.

Still, my stomach bottoms out. I'm suddenly regretting every bite of that grass-fed Kobe beef when I turn onto the long drive leading to the guest house. I can taste it in the back of my throat, courtesy of one hell of a case of nerves.

He won't be there.

He won't be standing in the door with those cold, cutting blue eyes tearing me open, asking me what I think I'm doing on his property and banishing me from ever coming back.

Yet, as I round the bend, coming into view of the beach, my stomach drops for a different reason.

At first I can't really process what I'm seeing. It's too surreal, like I'm in an episode of Buffy and no one told me there was a convenient corner Hellmouth in the neighborhood.

Flames glow orange against the night, throwing harsh light out on the sand, turning it into a garish nightmare. Smoke plumes up into the sky. Mostly from one side of the house, an accusing black finger stabbing into the night.

The guest house is on fire.

Holy shit.

And I must be in shock, because my first numb thought is *Thank God I haven't unpacked my car completely yet.*

My second thought is *Oh. Fuck. Landon's going to kill me.*

There's a little more real fear in the notion than there should be.

I screech my little Smurfberry-colored Prius to a halt and stare, fumbling for my phone. Calling 9-11 is raw instinct, but before I can even press the first button I'm captured by a sharp, erratic motion next to the leaping flames.

Landon.

He's out here, flinging himself against the door to the beach house, shouting something I can't quite hear through the car's insulation.

But it sure sounds a lot like *Kenna. Kenna. Kenna!*

The sound of sirens wailing shocks me from my daze. Oh, thank God, Landon already called for help. I tumble out of the car without thinking, the sound of my name floating toward me in desperate cries that sure as hell don't sound like the voice of a man who hates me with every fiber of his being.

The firelight casts Landon in stark, violent shades until he looks like the darkly devilish thing he is, a demon against the leaping fire, smolderingly handsome.

Every muscle in his body straining. Sweat darkening in clinging spots against his shirt.

He throws himself against the door one more time with a ragged call – *Kenna!* – a call that cuts my heart and tears it into ribbons. The door splinters inward under the impact of his shoulder.

Then he pulls himself back, readies himself to charge again, latent energy bristling in every hard-cut line of him.

"Landon!"

My turn. I call his name, then stop, faltering, hovering a safe distance away. Not from the flames.

From him.

He can hurt me more than any fire. His looks can sear deeper than any burn.

He goes so completely still it's like he's been cast in stone. Then he lifts his head, staring at me, his eyes wide and haunted and stark, his face haggard.

I'm so confused I could pass out dizzy – torn between the adrenaline, the shock, the fear of the primal animal response to fire...and the charged, trembling emotions of my primal animal response to *him.*

He takes one step toward me. Reaches out a hand. "Reb." A nickname I haven't heard in years, a single syllable with the power to crush me.

And then the fire trucks come flying in, ambulance not a foot off their bumper, and there's no room for words. There's only the rush of the firefighters unspooling their hoses, turning roaring arcs of spray on flames.

The emergency responders swarm both of us, a buffering layer of humanity asking questions I don't quite process, but still manage to answer. No, I'm not hurt. No, there's no one else inside. No, I didn't inhale any smoke.

Landon's getting the same interrogation, but he's also getting hustled away from me when his shirt peels off over the powerful, tapered sculpture of a hard-chiseled chest marked in scars, revealing the livid red bruise he'd made on his shoulder trying to break down the door. His hands, too, are a mess, knuckles scraped raw from smashing at the beach house. *For me.*

He did that because he was worried for me.

I don't know how to feel. I just know that the distance between us is like a stretching thread, and I don't want it to snap. I want to be near him, suddenly, even if it hurts.

So I edge through the cloud of EMTs guiding him to sit on the edge of the open back of an ambulance, while a man in a blue uniform looks over Landon's bruises and scratches. I make myself unobtrusive, tucking myself against the open back door of the ambulance, less than a foot away from Landon. Close enough that I can feel his body heat. Close enough that every hair on my body prickles, as he stares into me, as if he can see right down to the center of my chaotic heart.

This whole time, he never looks away.

But he says nothing. So I don't say anything, either. We're locked in this heavy, heavy silence.

Together, we just watch, while the firefighters put out the flames. Water cools their glow, until the night is night again, and the only thing left burning is me.

IT TAKES A WHILE TO FINISH, after the fire seems to be out.

I'd never really thought a sustained blaze can take an hour or more of intense effort to completely put it out. It looks like it's only the kitchen that's damaged, though. The flames are contained before they spread to the rest of the house.

Did I do this? I'm just waiting for Landon to shake himself from his daze and start pointing fingers.

I've been known to be a bit of an absentminded klutz, especially when writing. I never lived down the shame of setting my dorm kitchenette on fire in college because I was so busy on a term paper I forgot the ramen I'd left in the pot. The pot boiled down and the ramen turned to char, and then turned into a little stinking glop of burning crud, setting off the fire alarms and forcing the entire dorm to evacuate.

Had I left the stove on when I went out for my burger? I'd made a pot of tea to calm myself earlier, but I was pretty sure I'd shut off the burner. I retrace my steps throughout the day, but there's nothing. Nothing I did that would've caused this.

I didn't even plug in my laptop, so I couldn't be the culprit behind an electrical fire. If that's what happened, then anything with faulty wiring was there before I showed up.

It's not my fault, I tell myself. *It can't be my fault.*

And even if it is, it's not like Landon can hate me more.

He hasn't said a word, not even after the EMT patched him up with gauze across his knuckles and a slather of salve on his bruised shoulder, and let him put his dirtied, sweaty shirt back on.

He's just alternated between watching the flames with a pensive look and watching me with something completely unreadable in his eyes. I've kept my gaze fixed on the beach house, ignoring the pounding of my heart.

When he speaks, it hits hard as a gunshot in a silence that isn't silence at all, filled with the sounds of rushing water and calling voices and crackling radios, but somehow between us, the stillness is so absolute that breaking it is like shattering glass.

Shattering me.

"Come on," he says. "We're just in the way now."

He prowls to his feet in a powerful flex of flowing muscle, the rear of the ambulance bucking upward as his solid weight leaves it, and turns to trudge toward the house, the set of his shoulders grim and weary, his crudely beautiful, large hands hanging helplessly at his sides.

I swallow hard, fighting the sensation that Landon's helplessness is my fault. And I'm frozen, not sure what to do. Unable to believe he's actually inviting me up to the house.

But finally, I shake myself and scurry after him.

Back to being the tag along little sister, always trailing unwanted in the big boys' wake.

He lets us in through the kitchen door. The house is the kind of massive thing I'd never have expected from him when we were kids, but it's fitting for the owner of a prestigious company. It's somewhere between Mediterranean and Doric. Really open and spacious with a floor plan that avoids feelings of claustrophobia, feelings of being shut in – arched doorways and large windows and white marble tile flooring give a welcoming sense.

That, I think, suits the Landon I know.

He wouldn't be able to live in a dark, closed house that made him feel caged.

The kitchen itself is all white marble, granite, and pale honey wood tones. I tentatively slide myself onto a high bar-style kitchen chair in unvarnished pinewood, leaning my arms on the cool surface of the kitchen island.

"Listen," I start, swallowing against my thick, fumbling tongue. "I...I don't know what happened. I never touched anything. I made a pot of tea, but I *know* I turned off the burner before I left. I should've just...I should've –"

"Stop." He cuts me off with the single cold, clipped, forbidding word.

My words dry up, my tongue rooting itself somewhere in the back of my throat. He braces his hands against the edge of the counter, leaning on them hard, staring down at the thick granite slab with his eyes stark. Strange. Intense.

He grinds his jaw back and forth, then bites off, "You've got the job, Kenna."

I blink. "Pardon?"

He shoots me a glare bordering on resentful. "I *said* you've got the damn job. You don't have to leave."

"Oh."

"That's all you have to say? *Oh?*"

"I – sorry, I'm..." I'm fumbling. Cursing myself in my head.

Whatever happened to my vow to not be afraid of him? *Damn it, damn it, damn it.*

I take a deep breath, soothing my nerves, wishing my heart would stop flitting around like a butterfly in a glass jar. "I'm still trying to process all this. That's all. When I left, you wanted me gone. When I came back the beach house was on fire and now you want me to stay. It's a lot to take in."

"I'm stuck," he admits grudgingly. "And this little fiasco just drove home how stuck I am. I'm heading out to Sonoma for the weekend soon. Big job. Imagine if that fire happened here in the main house, and no one was around to call 9-11."

I don't want to. Clearing my throat, I look at him, promising I won't look away.

"You've got a security system," I point out, then mentally kick myself for undermining my own case. I don't know when I started *wanting* to stay here, but I'm not helping myself right now.

He shoots me a fiercer glower. "And the security team won't get here fast enough for them."

He jerks his chin toward the windowsill – toward the two near-identical slate gray, velvet-furred cats sprawled there, both staring attentively out the window at the small, distant figures of the firefighters still working around the beach house.

Now, I get it, and I kind of wish I didn't.

Landon could be a hero in one of my books.

Snarly asshole with a soft spot for his pets.

And just like one of my heroines, I'm going all wibbly inside over it. Sometimes, it's the clichés that get a girl when she isn't looking.

Damn, I know this trope. I write it. I should know *better* than to fall prey to it.

Hell, I make my heroines smarter than this, don't I? And I'm smarter than my characters!

Then again, old history and dangerous men have a way of making a girl weak, too. Pair them up with a bad cliché, and it's a drama cocktail on the rocks.

I keep my eyes on the cats. Not on him. I feel like if I look at him, he'll be able to tell all the weird stuff going through my head. "Well," I say neutrally. "I mean, taking care of the cats isn't a huge problem, I guess."

"Good." It's harsh and tight like he's back in the military and I'm one of his soldiers, and he's just finished detailing a mission. "You'll stay in the guest room. Don't get me wrong, Kenna, this is a trial run. Just for the weekend. We'll see how you do."

Right. Trial run.

Because the Landon who screamed my name while tearing himself up to get to me is gone, and cold, angry, hateful Landon is back.

And cold, angry, hateful Landon can't be caught *dead* actually giving ground. Especially not to me.

I close my eyes. "Trial run," I repeat, trying to force the words around the knot in my throat. "Got it. Promise I won't let you down."

"I don't want your promises. Just feed and water the cats, and try not to let this house catch fire."

I wince. I know he's not deliberately trying to say it's my fault, but right now, everything hurts way more than it should. Even if I wasn't in the fire, the whole thing is catching up to me in a rush of trauma. Cold shock.

My emotions are all poisoned on one raw nerve, and he's scraping on it just by breathing in my space. Which is why I shouldn't say anything else. Just accept it, and try to hunker down for some sleep.

I already know it's a bad idea to open my mouth, and yet I do anyway, asking, "Since when do you have cats?"

Silence. It's an innocent question, one that shouldn't mean anything, but I can feel the tension bristling.

I risk a glance at him, and there's nothing there. I see flesh, I see the shape of a man, I see a hard, forbidding stare, but there's nothing there to make him a person anymore. It's all walled away inside, completely shut down, and the only thing I get from him is a sense of expectation that says he doesn't want me to be here.

Fine. I slide off the barstool, turning my back on him. "I'll go. Better see if my stuff survived the fire, and get my other things from the car."

"Guest room's the second door to the right off the stairs. I'll be gone by tomorrow afternoon," he grinds out.

I start to answer, but there's a sudden rattle, a hard slam. I look up in time to see the chair he'd crashed into toppling back into place, and his back as it disappears through the open arched doorway into the rest of the house.

How does this situation just keep getting worse and worse?

I stand there in the kitchen for long moments, heartsick and heartsore, then drift over to the cats and let them sniff my fingers. "Hey, little guys." I offer a weak smile. "Guess we're spending the weekend together. Maybe at least you'll like me."

One of them meows. Loudly.

As in, so loud it almost hurts, but there's something about it that startles a laugh from me, especially when the loud one butts up against my hand, followed by the other swarming in for attention.

Suddenly I'm super busy. Two hands, two cats, and if there was a third, I'd be in trouble because they want all the love right now. I spend a few minutes finding soft spots under their jaws. Then that little sweetness right behind their ears that makes them melt.

When Landon's willing to speak to me again, I'll have to ask their names.

Thinking of Landon, though, sobers me up. Reminds

me I should get moving. I don't want to piss him off more by coming back to the house late enough to wake him when he's probably got a busy morning ahead.

I let myself out through the kitchen door and head down the path to the beach house. The flames are completely gone, but the firemen are still moving in and out of the house, probably checking for structural damage. I hope it's safe to go inside. Doesn't look like the bedroom or living room where I'd left my things took too much of a hit, though I hope my stuff doesn't reek like smoke.

My heart sinks just looking at it, even though it isn't mine. The whole place will need big repairs.

I'm trying to figure out who I should talk to for permission to go in, when I overhear two of the firefighters talking.

"Anything we should note on the report?" one of them asks, glancing at his partner, a woman with soot smeared down her cheeks and dotted on her baggy, oversized fire-retardant uniform.

"Nothing important," she says. "Looks like the fire was started by some brush nearby. Probably another rich asshole who didn't get the bulletin about clear-cutting with the weather this dry."

Part of me wants to jump in to defend Landon. He's not an idiot.

He wouldn't be so careless. He'd know California is such a wildfire haven, even this close to the ocean. One little spark and a pile of dry leaves is all it takes to burn down half a county. But I keep my mouth shut, duck my head, and slink toward the door.

Why bother? Why do I want to defend a man who hates me, anyway?

If the situation were reversed, he'd throw me to the wolves.

And maybe he'd be justified.

VI: LIKE PULLING A CAT'S TAIL
(LANDON)

*I*n the words of my esteemed and late father, "This is some bullshit."

I don't know what's pissing me off more. This entire situation, or the fact that I have multiple options to choose from when defining what, exactly, is pure and utter bullshit that I don't have time for right now.

Kenna. In my goddamned house. I don't want her there. I don't want her alone with the possibility that, no matter what the firefighters or police say, there's someone prowling around trying to get cute by playing arsonist.

I don't want the weird feeling that got all knotted and crazy in my chest when I started to come back into the kitchen, watched her getting cozy with Velvet and Mews, and hung back like a soppy idiot. Just staring with her completely oblivious while the cats crawled over her like I'm starting to want to.

No. *Fuck no.*

I'm not a cat. I don't need those pretty little hands petting me. Or doing anything else.

And I sure as hell don't need to be out here at the crack of midnight, kicking through the debris, all that's left of half my goddamn beach house.

I'm going to need to put some kind of protective covering up. Not that it ever rains a ton this time of year, but there's still wind, sand, animals, little rich kid shits who like to play with lighters.

I just don't quite believe the official verdict: no foul play.

Mainly because I keep my turf clean, and there weren't any bushes planted close enough to the house to cause a fire. With the house half-on, half-off the sandy beach, there's nothing but grass ringing the backside.

If there was enough loose brush to set a fire, could someone have put it there?

Maybe drunk kids would be that stupid, especially after I've chased them away more than once. But something doesn't feel right.

This might be more than just kids.

Which makes the idea of leaving Kenna here alone even worse.

Tomorrow. Tomorrow, I'll brief her. Fill her in on my thoughts, let her know what to do in the event she feels unsafe. Hell, I might not even take my whole team with me to Sonoma.

Maybe it'll be a good idea to leave one of my guys behind on call. Milah Holly's not the only one who needs protection.

And if I'm willing to admit it to myself, I care a hell of a lot more about Kenna's safety than Milah's.

Whatever happened between us, she's still Steve's little

sister. And even if I want to murder Steve right now, I'd never let anything happen to Kenna.

I glance back toward the main house. The light's still on in the upstairs guest bedroom, but I know her. I know her better than I want to admit, and I'd bet she fell asleep with the lights on, probably still fully dressed, a book half over her face.

I see I'm ninety percent right, once I go back to the house and head upstairs. The guest bedroom door hangs open as I pass. I can't not peek inside.

She's sprawled sideways on the bed on top of the covers, her shorts riding up to expose the slender smoothness of a pale, soft thigh, her shirt twisted in clinging layers against her waist. The overhead lights are on, bright as day. But the book's not over her face.

It's underneath her cheek, and I think she just might be drooling on it and ruining the ink.

That weird feeling is back in my chest again. I don't like it.

I *hate it* because it comes with the world's worst case of blue balls. I haven't had a woman in months. Too busy. And I can't remember the last time I shoved my raging dick between the legs of a woman worth the fuck.

I whip my eyes off her shorts before I wish they'd burn right through them. Having Kenna Burke a few rooms away is already torture.

It'll be a special kind of hell if I start thinking too hard about my hands on her body, tearing off her panties, taking those pert, teasing tits in both my hands until she whines real sweet.

Fuck!

Sighing, I shift my pants and then lean into the room,

just enough to flip the lights off. Then I quietly shut the door and hate-march myself to my bed.

* * *

I'M up again before the dawn.

Too much trouble sleeping all the way through the night, and my head always seems clearest in the dark hours before the sun comes up.

My morning swim helps. I slip into the cool dark waters, ignoring the throb of my bruised shoulder, pouring everything in my bones into it. I do this every morning it's warm enough; it's why I built my house on the beach, so close to the sand.

I feel more at home in the ocean than I do on land. Fighting the strong pull of the currents keeps me in shape, and suspended underneath the waves with the world submerged into the crash and call of the sea I can feel like...

Like I'm weightless.

Like the insane stress and worry my life has become is gone, and I can just float until my mind clears and my thoughts buckle and I can start the day with a clean slate.

I feel a little less like destroying everything in my path by the time I pull myself out of the waves, towel off on the sand, and head up to the house. The sun is just breaking over the horizon, turning the pale grays and whites of my home into a multicolored canvas of pinks and blues and purples and golds.

I'm not expecting company when I let myself in through the kitchen door.

And I'm certainly not expecting Kenna, sitting right

there at the kitchen island, her legs crossed primly in another pair of those damnably short shorts, her fingers busy with a pen, scratching across the pages of a little black book in scribbled dashes of ink.

I hadn't realized she was an early riser, too. Also didn't know, last night, the implications of giving her free run of the house while I'm still in it.

She's so completely focused she doesn't even realize I'm there, though she's got a hand free for Velvet in her lap. The cat shamelessly prostrates himself for her idly stroking hand. Mews prowls around the legs of the barstool, pushing himself up to rub against her little bare feet, occasionally being rewarded by a distracted scrunch of her toes between his ears.

Little traitors.

All it takes is one soft touch, and they're fraternizing with the enemy.

If she keeps being nice to my cats, it'll be that much damn harder to tell her to fuck off and leave once I come back from Sonoma.

I linger in the doorway, but as I step inside Velvet perks up, jumping from her lap and trotting toward me, Mews on his heels. I've suddenly got two lumps of fur twined around my ankles, plus a pair of wide, startled green eyes watching me, looking so lost it's not hard to tell she hadn't even realized I was here.

Tearing my gaze from hers, I bend to stroke between the cats' ears and down their backs, up to the tip of their tails. When I look back she's watching me with a sort of quiet fondness.

Something I *really* don't need right now.

Especially because the last time I saw her with a little

black book in her hands, she was prying where she didn't belong.

Everything inside me hardens, the tension I'd sloughed off in the pool cutting through me again to leave me bristling. She blinks at me, then falters, her head bowing, a shamefaced flush across her cheeks.

She remembers, too. She doesn't need to say it. The guilt in every line of her body speaks for her.

She remembers what she did. I made sure she'd never forget.

"Sorry," she mumbles. "I haven't had much inspiration for a while, and it just hit this morning. I didn't realize you'd be here."

I don't want to talk to her, all of a sudden. But I need to.

It's business. And I need to keep it strictly business, yet there's a hard knot in the pit of my stomach that's thinking of anything but keeping professional as I close in, watching how her hair falls across her face.

She's never been able to keep it wholly in a ponytail, soft chestnut strands always slipping free like they just can't keep themselves from touching her irresistible lips and playing against her cheeks. Those tumbling sweeps of hair shadow her downswept eyes, now, and there's an itching in my fingers that wants to brush her hair back, skim it across her brow, lift her chin until she looks at me with those eyes that always seem so innocent no matter what happens to her.

She's not innocent, I remind myself sharply. *There's nothing innocent about her.*

I clear my throat, shifting to lean against the counter, looking for that perfect neutral distance between too close and too far. Hell, even being in the same house with her is too close, but I can deal until I ship out for the gig. I rest my elbows on the counter and tell her, "We need to talk."

Her head flies up. Her eyes widen. She's so damned transparent, so guileless, that I can tell what she thinks I mean. That I want to talk about what happened back then, years ago.

She's flat out wrong. If the day ever comes when I'm ready to talk about that, shoot me first.

Before she opens her mouth, I cut her off. "About the fire," I clarify. "Something doesn't feel right."

Her brows knit together. "What do you mean?"

I don't say anything for several moments. I don't know how to say this without either panicking her or sounding like a paranoid asshole, and I'm already in bona fide grumpy old man territory with my temper seething every time I have to chase those goddamn kids off my lawn.

Finally, "This isn't the first incident," I force out grudgingly. "It's just been little things. People fucking with my shit. I wrote it off, blamed those rich brats screwing around on the beach, but this was dangerous. This fire could've *hurt* someone. That, to me, says foul play. And motive."

She goes pale. "What kind of motive? Why would anyone ever –"

"I don't know," I bite off. "But it almost feels like someone's trying to send a message."

Kenna frowns. She doesn't say anything, but she looks away, her gaze shuttering, and it's not hard to tell she's trying not to look frightened in front of me; trying to look tough.

It's not hard to tell that she's scared, either. Not with the way she wraps her arms around her shoulders. I don't think she even realizes she's doing it, but I've learned to read people's body cues, the language of flesh that speaks louder than words.

It always gives intentions. Feelings. Fears. When people wrap their arms around themselves like that, they're creating a defensive barrier and covering any places that feel exposed, vulnerable. They're trying to make themselves small so they're less of a target.

Right now, she's trying to make herself so small absolutely nothing can hurt her.

Not like I did before.

I try not to shake my head openly. I don't want to keep thinking these things, much less feeling them.

Especially not guilt.

It's *not* my fault. None of this is, and a pair of big green eyes and soft dark lashes aren't going to fucking change it.

I look away with a snarl. If I don't look at her, I don't have to feel this way. "Look," I growl. "You don't have to stay here alone. If it's too much, you can pack up and go the fuck home. I'll even pay for your tank of gas."

Her breath catches. "No! Landon – I'll be fine. It'll be okay. Really. You've got your security system and if the alarm goes off I'll just call the cops and hide. It's just a bunch of dumb kids anyway, I'm sure. If I come out shrieking like a banshee they'll probably pee themselves and run away screaming."

My mouth is doing this thing. I don't really like it.

It's gone all twitchy, trying to curve upward like I actually want to smile at her visual, arms flailing and eyes wide, careening out my front door and at a bunch of terrified, screaming rich kids who think they're heirs to the universe.

A low growl bubbles up in my throat. I fold my arms over my chest with a grunt and force the corners of my mouth to turn downward. "Don't know. This whole thing is probably a bad fucking idea. Let's be honest."

"How bad can it be?"

"You don't want to know." I blow out an explosive sigh. "Fine. Whatever. Stay. But first, you're going to memorize the security access code and the location of *every* intercom panel. I'm going to drill you before I go."

"K. Am I supposed to salute, sir?"

For some unholy reason, my dick throbs, right before I remember this is no joke.

"Don't be a brat. Listen." I fling her a glare, but she's smiling in that impudent-yet-shy little way that makes her such a fascinating mess of appealing contradictions. "Every intercom has emergency police call buttons. I'll leave one of my guys from Enguard, too. He'll do regular patrols a couple times a day. If you're really convinced you want to do this."

She squares her shoulders and lifts her chin. It's not hard to tell she's still nervous, a little tick of her pulse against her soft, vulnerable throat, but there's pride flashing in her eyes.

I don't want to admire it, but I can't help myself. Can't help how I linger on all her soft bare skin, stretching from the soft hollows beneath her jaw down to her collarbones. How those collarbones dip down toward –

I jerk my gaze away.

Not again.

Her eyes are up there, Landon. Those tits, the ones I badly want to suck, might just be out of this world.

"I'm convinced," she says, so seriously you'd think she was swearing in before a judge seats her. "I've got this Don't worry."

Little Reb. Always so earnest, always putting her heart into everythi –

She's not Little Reb anymore, idiot.

She's a pain in your fucking ass, I tell myself, *and she knows too much.*

I tear my eyes away from her again. I'm so done with this shit, and I have too much to do to be wasting more time here with her.

I can't even say anything else; I just turn around and walk away, stalking toward the stairs and my bedroom.

I can't believe Reb is back in my life like this. Fucking up my business again. Must come naturally.

Worst part is, this time, I've invited her.

VII: OLD FAMILIAR NAMES (KENNA)

I don't know what the hell I'm doing.

Okay. Not quite.

I *do* know. I'm close to hyperventilating. But in the broader sense, I have no freaking clue what I'm doing in this situation.

To be fair, I don't really know what I'm doing in most situations. I'm a pantser, not a plotter. I dive in and let my muse have the driver's seat.

But this isn't one of my books. It's real life. And I can't just delete a part that isn't working and then rewrite it in my favor.

If I could, I'd rewrite my entire history with Landon Strauss. No question.

Of course, that isn't possible. We can only write new pages, new chapters, and what's staring at me in ink as dark as the feral lines on his body?

Messages. Signals. Warnings that say things aren't as cut and dry as they seem.

Part of me says he hates me. That part of me is

currently screaming toward a panic attack of self-recrimi-nation and guilt, wondering why I didn't just pack up and go after our first catastrophic run-in.

But the other part of me remembers the wild look in his eyes by firelight. The frantic desperation in his move-ments. The fervor, how viciously, desperately, and beauti-fully he battered at the door to the beach house lashed by flames.

The way he shouted my name.

That part says, *he hates me not.*

It sends shivers through me even now. No one's ever tried to save my life before.

There's probably something messed up about me that it gets under my skin, but I can't forget the dark tattoos gleaming on the sweat covering his body, the tight ripple of muscle, that strength focused into pure animal frenzy. That bestial savagery. That bravery leaving no doubt he'd have crawled through the worst of the fire if he'd had to.

It does something to a girl, seeing a man willing to destroy every inch of his powerful body for her sake. Something compelling. Something heady.

Something I can't possibly have, much less hang onto, which is why I'm pouring it all into my Work-in-Progress.

At least he's given me words.

I thought I'd struggle to fill up the page after the death blow my publisher dealt my ego, but I feel like I'm fresh and new again. Back when I first started writing, I'd loved the craft so much – even if I wasn't always that good at it and had to work night and day to refine my skill.

What I lacked in experience, passion made up, but somewhere along the way the ratio reversed until the work part dominated.

Somewhere along the way, I guess I lost the fire. It became routine. A never ending battle against writer's block and creative inertia.

Funny that it took a *fire* to get my spark back.

We'll chalk it up to that.

Certainly not the embers cooling in my blood from the way Landon looked last night.

Or this morning, drawing his body through the ocean like a dark leviathan gliding sleek and dangerous through the deeps.

He has no idea I saw him during his swim.

When I'd come down for coffee, I'd caught a glimpse of motion on the strip of beach backing the house and thought it might be a prowler, or something. I'd peeked out the window instead and caught sight of water glistening on burnished skin, chiseled muscle.

My stomach dropped like an elevator. Without thinking, I'd hidden myself to one side of the window frame, everything inside me bristling.

Landon was everything I remembered and nothing I knew.

Before, his body had been lean. Hard. A smug, sexy Peter Pan with mischief in his eyes and power in his bones.

Now, it's been punished by life. Beaten into a vastly bigger, better shape – like forging and tempering a steel bar into a sharp-edged sword. It's incredible what years in a war zone and then becoming a private mercenary can do to a human body.

Battle-worn is too gentle a term. Each and every one of his new tattoos was a war wound turned into a scar, the one on his shoulder blotted and darkened by the bruise he earned last night, a badge of combat.

I couldn't quite make out what the ink was, but the designs were as compelling as music turned into art. Like, if I could trace them with my fingers, they'd sing dark, dangerous, beautiful hymns. Entirely disturbing things in the chorus of muscle and strength and power and broken, wounded, defiant things.

Watching him swim was enthralling. I lost time, lingering on the grace of his movements, the way he cut the water like soft butter. A rare, strange glimpse of a wild beast in his habit, and the urge to do so much more than just gawk, even knowing he'd turn at any moment and savage me to bits if I tried.

Landon Strauss is as dangerous as any feral animal – because he's as unpredictable as one.

I don't know him anymore.

I don't know what he could do to me.

I don't know what kind of trouble my own two eyes could get me into with him, if I kept letting them feast, imagining his full, fierce weight holding me down. Driving in. Filling and so *fulfilling* it hurts.

And that's why, when I saw him rising out of the waves like Poseidon announcing himself to awestruck mortals, I scrambled to fling myself onto the barstool and start writing.

If he'd caught me watching, he might have put me out on my ass.

It's strange how much I don't want to go. Not anymore.

I want to stay here. Just for a little while.

I want to help him, and if that means staying alone and

watching for creepers, so be it. I also really don't want to go crawling home to L.A. defeated. Life's handed me a few too many kicks to the teeth lately, and if I crash down after this one it'll be a while before I pick myself up.

Plus being here has inspired some of the hottest sex scenes I've ever put into words.

We'll just call it a coincidence that my smoldering, dark-haired hero is a complete and utter dominant beast in the sheets. And on his yacht, his car, his private jet, her parents' house – damn near everywhere I have him all over my very happy heroine.

I wonder if I'll give my hero some tortured secret, too. If he'll look at the heroine with melancholy blue eyes that remember the past.

Just like Landon did, this morning.

I lean against the railing of the spacious balcony off the kitchen, tilting my head back to stare up at the brilliant blue California sky, and sigh. It's late afternoon.

He didn't have to say a word this morning to cut me open with that look and tell me exactly what he was thinking. It's like we're both living the same memory in real-time every moment we're together.

No, we don't have to say a single thing to each other to know we're both re-living the same exact moment.

A place I don't want to travel back to, yet I just can't shake it. Has it really been five long years since we lost ourselves somewhere in hell?

Five Years Ago

IT'S BEEN A WHOLE YEAR, and I still can't believe Micah Strauss is dead.

It's weird how people die. How they're there one minute, gone the next. Making you question the when, how, and why of their existence.

That's what it was like when I heard about Mr. Strauss. I'd seen him just the night before his end, rushing into a black car with the people who'd hired him for a protection gig. Crown Security's portfolio of celebrities and famous politicians was only getting bigger.

He looked alive. Frantic. Determined.

Then the police found him the next day, just a cooling body dumped in the grass in a park downtown. Alone. The job went wrong, and that was the end result.

But even after death, life goes on.

Steve was a wreck. Landon leaving for the army did nothing to diminish their bond, and it's like my big brother shared his pain. Eventually, he bounced back like the puppy he is, but for a couple vile months, I'd never seen him so depressed.

I was upset, too. The Strausses were like second parents to me, with Mom and Dad traveling all the time. Dad's a legal attaché to an international firm, and Mom's his translator. They worked domestically for a while, until Steve and I were old enough to handle them being gone.

Suddenly, Steve became more like a surrogate parent, and Micah and Shirley Strauss were our gatekeepers across the street. Our friends. Adults we could count on.

It made them feel like family, too, and it tore me up to see Micah in a casket. My parents flew in for the funeral, then flew back out again, because business doesn't stop for death.

Everything went back to normal.

Except for Landon.

In the past year he's become someone else. Someone I don't recognize. Someone I don't understand.

Deep down, I think, he frightens me.

He's turned from my brother's charming dick of a best friend, that boy who ruffled my hair and told me I'd have boys lined out to Seattle, into this darkly brooding creature brimming with latent violence.

Not that I think he'd ever hurt me, even now.

I just wish I could still talk to him the way we used to.

Especially since he's supposed to be leaving soon. Iraq again. His last tour, counting down to his honorable discharge. All he does now when he's home is skulk around and smoke and glower and brush me off when I try to talk.

I'm worried about Landon.

Scared he won't come back.

That's why I'm out walking tonight. I tell myself it's just to clear my head with a good breath of crisp night air, but really, I'm circling the block. Trying to work up the nerve to approach their front door, knock, and hope Landon will open up without chasing me off with my ass smarting from that whiplash tongue of his.

We live right across the street from each other. We have our whole lives. Friends for years, with Steve in the middle, and me secretly hoping that we'd always be more.

I hoped he'd take an interest after I turned eighteen. If there was ever a chance, it was dashed the day Micah died, but I'm a patient woman. And I think he's a man worth waiting for.

It's just this year it's felt like he's worlds away. Grieving. He's entitled to his distance, his pain, his need to heal.

I must be on my tenth circuit of the block. *Must be.*

When I look at the house, I can't see any silhouettes moving against the window. No dark shape of a big prowling bruiser of a man peering through the curtains, wondering why the crazy girl from across the street is strolling past again with her eyes all wide like she's whistling past the graveyard.

But this time, as I'm passing, I catch a glimpse of something else. I hadn't noticed it the first five or ten times around.

A journal.

Sitting on the corner of the porch, pinned down by an empty beer bottle.

I don't even have to look at it to know it's his. I've seen him with it before on one knee; battered, black, and leather-bound. Clutched in his big hands. Protectively close.

I stop. My tongue dries to the roof of my mouth.

It's like staring into another world. How Alice must've felt gazing down the rabbit hole.

In that journal is everything he won't say to me.

I shouldn't.

Sweet Jesus, I shouldn't. It's a violation of his privacy, a betrayal, and completely against everything I am, but my heart hurts too much today. If I could just peek inside, see something that says...that says...

That says he doesn't *hate* me.

That he may be angry at the world, but he won't stay angry at me.

That he's going to be all right. He's going to get

through this. And maybe someday, however long it takes, he'll start grabbing life by the throat and realize he's strong enough to bend it any way he pleases.

My palms sweat. They're so sweaty I could probably use them to wet my mouth. Ew.

Ew, Kenna. Okay.

My brain is sprinting off on rabbit tangents. I'm being weird and I'm scared and my heart is bouncing between the back of my tongue and the pit of my stomach, but I drag myself up the walk.

There's no one around. Not even cars passing at my back.

No movement in the windows, though lights are on upstairs. I try to remember if the Strauss' front porch has a motion sensor light and can't. Cringing, my stomach twists when I rest my foot on the top step.

Everything stays dark.

I breathe out slowly, creeping toward the waiting journal like the world's worst cat burglar.

Slowly, trembling, I slip it out from under the beer bottle, then sink down to sit on the weathered wooden porch boards with my back against the railing, the leather warm as if it's alive in my hands.

I flip the cover open with my heart pounding so loud in my ears it's like a storm inside me.

There's so much on these pages. So much of his thoughts, so much of his heart.

All the things I've been missing, stretching back for years. Every little bit of inner turmoil. All those introspective thoughts swimming in dark, troubled blue eyes. The boy I'd missed is in these pages, laid bare one word at a time.

Until those words turn jagged and dark and angry.

Until I can see him changing line by line.

Until it's like this other self comes boiling out in black ink. This demon. This poison in his thoughts and in his veins, using him to write its furious words on the page.

I'm skimming my fingers under the lines to keep my place, the sound of my fingertips whispering on the paper, I'm moving so fast – until I get to the last entry.

Harsh, jagged lines, clearly written in anger, jerking up and down in black swoops of ink.

FUCK YOU FOR LEAVING, *Dad. Fuck your dirty laundry. Fuck your company. Fuck you for getting killed over nothing. And fuck your killer, too.*

SOMEDAY I'LL FIND *that asshole. I'll figure out who he is, and this time there won't be a body left to find.*

I'LL BE *the man you couldn't be.*

I'LL FINISH *what you couldn't. I'll give ma a reason to smile again – really smile – while I lie through my teeth about what you truly were. A selfish, arrogant, two-timing prick who put our futures on the line every day, and God only knows how many lives.*

GOD ONLY KNOWS *why you wound up loving money so bad*

you'd do the shit you did. And wherever God is, knowing, you're not with him now. You're in hell and you're never coming back.

MY HEART IS ICE, right now. Frozen so solid and heavy it can't even beat, but my head is spinning.

I don't understand what I'm reading.

Landon thinks his father was killed? Crown Security was dirty and...and...Landon hated *him?*

Enough to want to hurt him?

Enough to want him in *hell?*

But he loved him enough to kill his murderer?

Landon, the boy I know, the boy who's gone...

He's planning to kill someone.

The boy who shipped overseas and came home to a dead father is gone. There's a hardened, furious, would-be killer with a vendetta in his place.

I press my trembling fingers to my lips – and it's the only thing that stops me from screaming, instinctively clamping my hand over my mouth on a whimper, when the journal suddenly rips out of my hand, pages fanning violently enough to almost tear.

My frozen heart shatters. My blood goes electric. Terror. Shock. Agony.

I stare up at Landon, looming over me, his eyes lit with a glacial fury I've never seen.

"What the fuck do you think you're doing?"

The way he says it almost destroys me.

Instead of snarling temper and shouts, it's frigid and quiet and deadly, as if any part of him that cared for me at all is gone behind this mask of slow, calculating, murderous rage.

He's become a stranger, a man I've never seen before, and I think the reason my eyes well with burning, blurring tears is less out of fear of him, and more out of grief as I realize the Landon I knew really is lost.

Yet, there's a glimmer of something human there, too. Awful and familiar.

The betrayal.

And I hate that it's the only part of Landon left, and it's directed at me.

"Um, I..."

"You, nothing. I don't want to hear it." He snaps the journal closed with a finality that feels like a gunshot. "Save your breath, McKenna. I don't want to hear your apologies. Don't want to fucking hear anything else, not from you and not from Steve. Your brother's been up my ass for months. Everyone's walking on eggshells, treating me like damaged fucking goods, and the worst part is they're right. I've had enough. My life, my privacy, my shit, McKenna. Not yours or Steve's or anybody else's. Do yourself a heaping favor: get the fuck out and leave me the fuck alone. Say anything about what you've read to anyone, and fuck, you –"

My ears stop working. I'm trying to back away but I don't even know if my knees work.

I can't breathe. I can't feel.

My throat is so tight. Choking. I'm crying as much for him as I am for me, and I rise shakily to my feet. Some brave part of me wants to reach for him.

He's just a blur through my misting, fragmenting, blood orange vision, but I step closer to the dark shape he makes against the night. "Landon..."

"Are you listening? Leave!" He turns on me with a roar,

all kinetic energy and vibrant rage, radiating his own heat. The force of his voice hits me like a shockwave. It echoes in my bones. "What the hell do you think you'll accomplish? Last thing I need is some little girl sniffing around after me. Go fuck with someone your own age, McKenna. I don't need you. I don't need fucking anything. We're *done.*"

That's it.

Done.

That final word breaks me.

That word sends me stumbling away half-blind, tumbling out onto the sidewalk, fleeing home in a shaken stupor.

I don't look back. I don't want to see him.

I don't want to see the hate in his eyes again, when he looks at me.

But it's my last memory of him.

A few days later he ships out for the Army. I don't even get to see him one last time before he's gone. Just a hole in my life, and I don't realize how big a space he'd occupied until it's empty.

I'm not ashamed to admit I want him back. I miss my friend.

I want to talk to him, to tell him how much his words hurt me, to find some way back to normal. I even write to him – so many times, so many letters. I keep writing through my freshman year at college, sacrificing nights I should be out with friends or exploring myself. I give them up to pen him at least a dozen apologies and explanations, painstakingly crafted for days, with long, restless breaks in between buried in term papers and internships.

Landon never writes back.

Because he's *done*, he said.

And clearly, he means it.

Present Day

IT SHOULDN'T STILL HURT this much.

What happened to time healing all wounds?

My eyes are dry, but burning. How long have I been out here, losing myself in the past?

The ocean breeze tastes like sunset, and the sky is turning purple on the horizon, tinged with a touch of orange as the sun dips down like it might just set the ocean aflame. My chest is hollow. Aching.

It's awful. It's still so awful, like I'm that girl again, and he just ripped out my stitches, reminding me how useless I am and always will be. How I don't fit into his life, and never did.

Reminding me that he could have blood on his hands, and for some insane reason, I've kept his secrets all these years.

I don't know if I want to know if he was really able to go through with it.

Hell, I know I don't want to find out if he did.

I feel too out in the open, right now. Too exposed. Vulnerable.

I don't want to run into him, and I know he's in the house somewhere, rattling around and getting ready to leave for Sonoma in the morning. I risk a glance over my shoulder, then escape to my room.

One of the cats – Velvet, I think, still not sure after he'd tersely flung names at me a few hours ago – trails after me, a sweet blue-gray comfort twining around my ankles.

While the guest room is spacious, right now it just feels like more emptiness for me to rattle around in.

I hate feeling like a loose end. I should sit down, write, but I don't think I could even manage to sit still. I'm not exactly a Type A personality.

I'm more like Type ADHD, bouncing between wild periods of hyperactive multitasking productivity and long inert daydreaming sessions. When you catch me somewhere in between, it's nothing but disquiet.

What I like to call 'creative procrastinating.'

I need to do something to feel better right now, but my brain's still trapped in the dream.

Drifting to the bedroom window, drawn by the colors of the sunset, I let my eyes steal a little balm for my soul from the landscape. California sunsets are like pastel fires and dripping watercolors blended together, an arresting sight that helps take my mind off the lingering ache in my chest.

But the ache becomes a knife stabbing me as I catch motion on the beach again.

Landon.

He's standing on the sand, a change of clothes stacked on a beach towel close by. Only this time, he's naked. Brazenly, shamelessly nude.

Gorgeous, too, the setting sunlight gilding every edge of him until I could trace the poetry of his sculpted body in lines of glowing, gleaming light. His tattoos shape him, as if they're arcane markings binding this demon into the shape of a man.

From his broad, square shoulders to the trim line of his hips to the sinfully decadent dip of his Hercules crest, he's breathtaking. If he turns around, I just might die. If I see that secret part of him and start imagining all the terrible, wonderful, and wonderfully terrible things his cock can do to me...

No. Kenna, no, I tell myself.

Don't. Even. Go. There.

But my eyes do. It's like watching a wildcat move as he forges into the powerful push and pull of the waves. Mercifully before I catch a glimpse of everything.

I'm transfixed. Drunk. Watching all that compact, tight, dense muscle, working and flowing together in this brutally enchanting machine fueled by raw, primal masculinity.

Everything hurts.

Everything I am.

I've been horny before, like any red blooded woman, but this? It's on another level.

I'm suffocating with the force of this longing; my whole body prickles with the craving, the need, the wetness that has me pinching my thighs shut, my lips pulsing, my heart beating far too hard.

I'm all raw edges, and I don't know what I need more.

Landon's touch, or his forgiveness.

God. It really was stupid to ever come here, wasn't it? To ever think this was a good idea.

I can't go back in time and change what happened half

a decade ago. I can't take back finding his journal, snooping, and cornering him like an injured animal.

And I can't pretend I feel different.

I'm *still* obsessed with Landon Strauss.

That's what shreds the other *can'ts* into tiny little scraps of heart-sad confetti. That's what puts me in this unbearable situation.

Standing here with my heart on fire. Alone in a house that isn't mine. Desperate for a man I'll never have, once again invading a place where I don't belong.

VIII: MISS HOLLY (LANDON)

I'm not ten miles down the road to Sonoma before I already want to turn around.

I don't feel right leaving Kenna alone.

The sense of something wrong lingers, this weight in my gut – and that weight is slewed toward my house and the girl in it and the feeling I'm a fucking fool for not being there.

What if something happens? What if she needs protection?

I pound my fist on the wheel. The loud, jarring *thump* brings me out of it.

It's nerves, probably. I'm still too keyed up after the fire. Still in animal mode, reacting on pure instinct.

There's no reason I should worry.

She's got the security system, the cops, and Riker, the guy I left behind to do patrols. He was one of the first I hired for Enguard, and I'd trust him with my own blood.

If I had much family left, other than Steve, that is.

Hell, he's so close he might as well be my brother.

Except that would make Kenna my sister, and the deep

hungry pull in my gut doesn't see that woman in an ewww-family way at all.

Ten years ago, yeah.

Now?

Sweet fuck. I wish she hadn't grown up *so much.*

My dick springs to life, tormenting me a few miles, remembering how I walked in on her underdressed this morning. Her hair was tossed around, like she'd just lifted it off the pillow, and seeing that hair in its wild, natural state makes me think *terrible* things.

Far too close to how I imagine her chestnut mess would look in my fist. After I've left her lush body crawling up my bed. The sass, the tension, the hate-love curdling the air between us thoroughly railed out of her.

My balls throb. They're turning half-blue with unquenchable need when another sound chirps in the car.

My Bluetooth dash light flicks on with an incoming call.

The disquiet thrumming through me turns into irritation. My whole car – a late-model Impala that's pure Dean from *Supernatural* – is networked so I can handle work hands-free on the go, and the radio LED doubles as caller ID, flashing with a familiar number and the name *Reese, Dallas.*

Fucking Dallas.

It's no coincidence the second half of his name rhymes with 'ass.'

I'm tempted not to answer it. But there's an old sense of loyalty to my father's former company, a sense of duty, that says I'd better.

Besides, with Dallas as my main competition, I might

as well stay on top of his antics just so I'm not caught blindsided if he tries to steal Milah out from under me.

I press the dash button to activate the in-car speaker, then settle my hands back on the ten and two on the steering wheel.

"What?"

"You could at least say hello," Dallas' smooth voice echoes across the speaker, a smirk in his tone.

"You're the second person to say that to me in twenty-four hours. Again, *what?*"

"Really, Landon?" He clucks his tongue. "I was just calling to see if you were all right."

The bullshit concern in his voice takes me back to an earlier time. Dallas, standing on my parents' porch, shortly after my old man's funeral. His flimsy hand on my shoulder, a hand I never asked for, because he was the last asshole on earth I wanted sympathy from.

Not a memory I want. Or need.

"Why wouldn't I be?"

"I heard you had a little trouble at your place. Something about a fire?"

I narrow my eyes at the road. "How the hell do you know about that?"

"One of my team doubles as a volunteer firefighter. Word gets around. Frankly, I'm just glad you're all right. Lighten up, pal."

"Sure you are," I snarl, my throat turning into sandpaper.

"You *sure* have a talent for sarcasm, Landon." Dallas sighs, throwing it back at me. "Unfortunately, I did feel it was my civic duty to inform Miss Holly's team of the mishap. Business, you understand? In the event that you were indisposed and she needed a fallback –"

"*Civic duty*," I bark back, teeth clenched so hard my entire face hurts. "Fuck you. If you had anything to do with that fire –"

"Oh, come on! Must you be so suspicious? Have you ever thought I was trying to help you, Landon? This entire thing could've been arranged like gentlemen. So you were the reliable party who set up the fallback, ensuring Miss Holly was well cared for. Client satisfaction."

"While you get the fat paycheck, you mean." I'm so not in the mood for this.

"It's not about the money! How many times do I have to keep saying it?" He always sounds so calm, so smooth, every answer as prepared as a slick-dick politician's speech, and I hate it. "It's about your reputation. Enguard's reputation, I mean. Even if you're no longer with Crown Security, I can't help taking an interest in what you're doing. We're friends in the same industry. Quite a few people take an interest in what you're doing, you know. You're a person of interest now – and everyone in private security is watching and waiting for you to slip up on a job that's too big for your little outfit to handle."

Too big for me to handle?

I bet finding Dallas and wringing his fucking neck would give his sense of size a whole new meaning.

This smug, shitty asshole, pretending to actually give a damn about me or my company or my reputation –

But he's still talking. He's *always* talking.

Fucker treats the sound of his own voice like music.

"When it's too much for you," he says, "there's always a place for you at Crown. I hope you know it. Your father would've wanted it that way. He'd never have wanted you to lone wolf it, to leave the company he worked so hard to build."

There's a long, arrogant pause. Here it comes.

"Landon? Tell me one thing: why can't we just bury bad blood and work together? Partners?"

Not in this lifetime. Not in the next *ten*.

"Because I don't work with fucking vultures," I spit. "Fuck you, fuck Crown Security, and fuck the idea that you and I could ever work together. I'm not your friend, Dallas. And you weren't mine, even though you did a damn good job getting under my skin after dad was buried, and you thought I was all busted up, needing a shoulder to cry on. Go fuck yourself. I'd rather choke on glass than work with you."

"You'll certainly choke on that overgrown ego of yours if you're not careful." Smug piece of shit. There's always a comeback. "Remember, Miss Holly has a reputation for litigation. Not to mention, the star power – and funding – to eat you alive in court. Screw up, and you'll lose more than a contract. You'll lose –"

"My patience with this conversation," I interrupt. "Get to the point. Whatever you *really* called for, Dallas. Because it wasn't to play 'whose dick is bigger.' We outgrew that years ago."

"Am I really so transparent?" He sighs. At least when he speaks, this time, it doesn't sound mocking and trite; it sounds tired, and genuinely so. "Look, I'm not comfortable talking about this on an unsecured line, but we should meet soon."

I go still. There's only ever one thing Dallas wants to meet in person about. My entire body tingles with tension. It's too good to be true, especially when it's the very thing he holds over me, baiting my sorry ass into taking more of his calls. "You've got new intel?"

"Possibly. New details the police hadn't released before. It's best if we discuss it in person, Landon. You know that."

"Fine. When I get back from Sonoma. I'll call."

"Lovely. I really think we might be close to a break this time."

"That's what you've said every time." It's the closest to polite I can manage to be with him, when one more word will have me seeing red. My hands are aching, my knuckles white, from how hard I'm gripping the steering wheel, and if I'm not careful I'm going to swerve off the road just trying to unclench. "I'm driving and can't talk, Dallas. Gotta go."

He makes a sound that doesn't quite become a word before I slam the dash button, ending the call.

Shit. the last thing I need when I've got Kenna on my mind and in my house is Dallas planting seeds of doubt.

I've got this, though.

I've got this, and I don't need a massive security company behind me to make it work. Smaller is better. Lean. Tough. Focused.

That's how I built Enguard compared to the bloated beast that's Crown.

It means we can keep it tight and coordinate well with a trusted group of handpicked pros. Even before I'd left, Crown Security was starting to get sloppy. Careless.

Dallas is too ambitious, too focused on expansion, and

not even personally involved ensuring the job gets done right on every contract.

Dallas is the problem. *Not me.*

I have to remember that, and not let him get under my skin, or inside my head.

Especially not when he's sitting on intel that could point to my father's killer.

Information I've been after for five dreary years. And I'll be *damned* if that smug, bouncy, hyper-competitive asshole gets to the truth before I do.

* * *

Five Years Ago

AFTER DAD'S FUNERAL, flowers will always make me choke.

As long as I live, I'll always associate their bright colors, their perfumes, their circle-of-death arrangements with my old man's stiff face in the casket.

And the same goes for a few select fork-tongued words.

"It's all right, Landon, you shouldn't look so worried. My dad's talking to your mother right now. He's a good guy. We'll make sure you're both set for the rest of your lives and –"

"Fuck you, Reese," I snarl, tearing his hand off my shoulder. "If you think it's money that's got my balls in a knot, think again."

He sniffs, taking several protective paces away from

me. "Yeah. Sorry. I was being kind of an insensitive jerk, right?"

"It's cool," Steve speaks up, a few paces behind me. I whip around and glare, knowing he's just trying to keep the peace, and fucking hating it.

"Landon, he's just trying to help," my friend says, leaning to my ear.

"Fuck him again. I don't need –"

"Landon. Dude. Micah's barely in the ground. I know that's got you torn up, your head all kinds of bad, but the whole world isn't your enemy. I'm here. Your mom's here. So are my parents. And even that creepy kid you're not too keen on is just trying to lighten the load."

I grit my teeth. He's right, and I hate that too, along with everything else.

"I heard that," Dallas says, spinning around, tugging at that dusting of a blonde beard he's trying to grow on his face, red hairs sticking out of it.

Steve mumbles an apology. Asshole Dallas just laughs.

"Forget it, man. We're all entitled to our feelings. I don't expect to be best friends with either of you overnight. Just saying, don't be shy. I'm here to help. What happened to Mr. Strauss has got all of us on our backs. Only way we get back on our feet is if we help each other."

Sage advice. And so damn unwelcome right now, coming from him, I want to gag.

"Yeah," Steve says, always the peacemaker. "I'm sorry, again. We're all here for Landon and Mrs. Strauss. God. I can't fucking imagine."

Fortunately, Steve doesn't have to. I'm living the nightmare for him.

We're quiet, an icy truce between us, when the screen

door swings up. I hear mom sniffing loudly from the kitchen. I plod forward, ready to comfort her for the millionth time this week, only to slam into a wall of darkness and dense cologne.

"Shit, boy. Watch where you're – oh. Oh, no. Clumsy me." Reg Reese spins me around, helps me catch my balance, and then steps onto the porch past me. "Uncle Sam's really putting some meat on those bones, I see. Micah would be proud of you, Sampson."

I can't even manage an awkward grin. I don't know what the fuck my old man would think about anything happening right now. I'm not even sure I care.

Steve pulls the door open, following me into the house, and I hear a growl that makes me look over my shoulder one last time.

"Are you stupid, kiddo? I said, 'let's go!' We're gonna be late and there's a whole pile of paperwork waiting at the office." I see Reg give Dallas a satisfying, annoyed slap to the shoulders, so hard it almost sends him to the ground.

Dallas freezes. It's just a split second, but I see a rare anger in his eyes, a redness behind his patchy almost-beard like humiliation itself licking his face. "Dad –"

"Car. Now. Fuck's sake."

"Landon?"

"Coming," I tell Steve, but my feet aren't moving. For some messed up reason, I stand there watching the two Reeses.

A surly Dallas as he slips into the passenger seat of a sleek black Mercedes, his face hung low. Then Reg, taking the driver's seat. The car doesn't start for several long seconds while he points his finger at Dallas, too close to his face. The skin on the back of Reg's hand is mottled from a birth mark or scar or something.

An evil part of me wants to be glad I'm not the only one going to pieces since mom relayed the horrible, world-ending news about why dad didn't come home. But a fucked up part of me almost feels sorry for Dallas, who looks at the house one more time, as Reg backs onto the street and then floors it.

Maybe the kid I've never liked is right. My father's death has punched a hole in everybody's world, letting in a blackness that's souring everything.

Present Day

SONOMA IS A MISERABLE PLACE. Strange words, I know.

There's no good reason the bright, cool, sunny beating-heart-of-wine-country weather should make any sane human miserable, except for the company I'm in.

Maybe it's just that Milah Holly is a miserable person, and I'm regretting this job for more reasons than one.

It's not that I can't handle the gig. It's that I can't handle her type: pampered, constantly drunk, a complete hot mess falling all over herself and knowing she's doing it.

Always with her groupies behind, the reeling, sloppy-drunk worshipers she keeps around for an ego stroke known as the Siren Crew. Milah was wasted before she even went on stage for her first show at a private VIP event before her main concert venue.

Her Sirens were *worse.* High as fuck on lines of white dust snorted up before they were all over each other, chasing tongues and sometimes clawing at each other over stupid fights, while I had to do some rapid two-stepping to get those bags of coke out of their hands, out of the Green Room.

Anywhere else where they couldn't be traced back to me, Milah, or anyone on my crew. Only saving grace is my lead, Skylar, tracking down their local dealer and making sure he was banned from the premises.

It's been worse since the third small show at the private afterparty, more skin than clothing visible everywhere I look. A near constant contrast with amber whiskey bottles and freely flowing, very expensive local wine, most of which sloshes out on the floor and sends several Sirens toppling on their rears. Still giggling.

I can't believe these are *adults*.

Reb would never behave like this. I wish I could transplant her maturity into them.

It's weird for thoughts of Kenna to be a comfort during this clusterfuck, but when it comes to the lesser of two evils, I'd rather have that sexy little mess of emotional baggage than this fucking mess, period.

Their antics are wearing on everyone. I catch Skylar outside chugging coffee during a break, her pale blue eyes a quiet, tired fury.

"We having fun yet, Pixie, or what?" I growl. She gives me the evil eye whenever I use that nickname. Too bad it's stuck with the entire crew because it's fitting.

She's small, and usually a little scary.

"One more day," I tell her, brightening her mood. "Then this shitshow will finally be over."

"Thank God," she whispers. I can tell by the coy, but tense expression it's not just Milah that's got her counting down the seconds until her next day off.

"Any news? Don't tell me this crap up here is putting you off any important family business?"

She shakes her head furiously. As expected. Even if it were true, she knows I'd send her straight home if I ever caught wind of finding her missing niece.

"Nah. Nothing like that. The leads are cold as ever, boss. This is a shitty distraction, but I'll take it. Work works miracles."

I nod slowly. I decide not to press her, angrily digesting how impossible her case seems. The girl disappeared months ago. Snatched right under Skylar's nose while she was out with her sister, the mother. They think it's the asshole ex, the good-for-nothing sperm donor responsible for her, but nobody knows for sure.

Skylar's dead ends with the police and FBI are reason number one hundred why I took matters into my own hands, digging into Crown. You leave this kind of shit in the hands of the system, you might never get answers.

"Just be sure you're not running yourself ragged. I know what it's like, a fucked up personal situation, something with no clean end in sight." I stop short of dumping more advice. She's smart enough to know I'm not following my own rules for life, being as mired as I am in the bad blood my old man left behind.

"I know you do," she says quietly, sucking a few last dregs of coffee through the plastic lid loudly. "I also know you get it, boss. How a person can't let go. Even if it's one crappy thing after another, it keeps coming full circle, until there's an answer. Some closure. *Something.*"

I slap her shoulder, giving it a squeeze. "You'll have your something, Skylar. Soon as we're done with Miss Holly, let me put you down for some off time. Can't tell you not to spend your free days chasing every rabbit hole, trying to bring the kid home, but I hope you'll do something you actually enjoy for a few hours."

She shrugs, staring blankly at her empty cup. "There's always coffee. Great for multi-tasking."

It's so deadpan, so awkward, and so completely Skylar, I just laugh. "Let me get us both a new cup. Lord knows we could both fucking use it today."

By the time the last show and afterparty end late on Saturday, I'm ready for home.

I might have to face the music with Reb and I'm not looking forward to the estimate on repairing the guest house, but it's better than the stink of drunken, wet sex and stale champagne in the rooms under our watch.

I've just got to get Milah – *Miss Holly*, and just saying it makes me think of Dallas and makes my skin crawl – on her plane and then this is mercifully over.

Airport parking is a nightmare. Security, even worse with Milah throwing tantrums, alternating between bending over for the TSA agent with a slurring little giggle, and then demanding if these peasants know who she is.

It's hard to stand stoic and stone-faced while she makes a complete spectacle of herself, but sooner or later we get her through check-in and to the boarding area. She's missing her private jet this time. Can't stand first class. I hear something about her having a lien on the old plane thanks to her year in rehab, which clearly did no good, and she never paid for.

We only have to stay until she's on her flight, and they should be calling it any moment.

I'm ready to be gone and I'm about to tell my crew to pack up and get ready to head out, when I feel a hand on my arm.

I'm so keyed up and tired I flinch away instinctively, ducking out of reach. It's an old military habit ingrained in me.

Don't retaliate; just create defensive distance to assess the situation. And the situation I assess, right now, is a pair of wide blue eyes that perfectly fit the picture-perfect image Milah Holly projects to the media. The fake one where she's this innocent, leggy blonde Barbie with that whole sweetly-dirty schoolgirl thing going on.

And I'm not buying it for a second. Because by now I know everything that coy, mock-innocent smile hides.

I feel like a feral cat backed into a corner, and she hasn't even said anything. But I know she wants something, and from the way she catches her tongue between her teeth and the way her eyes dip over me, it's not hard to tell what it is.

"Listen, Landon." She's doing her baby-girl lisp, the same thing she peddles in front of the cameras. I've seen her practicing it in the mirror. It has no effect on me. "Since you're working my Bay Area gig next week, too, sweetie, why don't I stop by your place before we set up? I can't think of *any* place in the whole wide world safer than with you. Oh, and I'd so love to relax on the coast for a bit."

I stare at her flatly. I have to be professional, but for a

moment, it takes all my willpower to keep my face as neutral as possible.

"I don't know how safe my place is," I deflect. "Reese told you about the fire, didn't he?"

She lets out a fluttery, false little laugh. "Who cares? It'll be *fiiine.* Lightning never strikes the same place twice."

I choose not to correct her.

I also choose to keep my goddamn paycheck, even if it's starting to feel like it comes at the cost of my integrity. All of it. I grit my teeth, but force myself to nod. I'll let her interpret what that means.

I also remind myself this is part of the gig, and she can't possibly be serious.

She's probably still coked out of her mind. Or buzzed from her morning diet of mimosas and toaster waffles – go figure.

So much that she won't even remember this tomorrow.

I can only hope.

Hope, and signal my crew to get on the move so I can escape this hell and get home as soon as possible.

IX: HOMECOMING (KENNA)

*I*t hasn't been a half-bad day of writing.

Maybe all I really needed was a little fresh sea air. I've spent most of the day plotting story structure, but I think I've got a good framework for working out the basic pacing and character development.

More, though, I've got the framework and peace of mind to figure out how I'm going to deal with Landon when he comes back.

I've just got to stand my ground. I wouldn't be able to respect myself if I did anything else.

I'm perched at the kitchen island with a cat in my lap and another on the counter, chewing on the cap of my idle pen, when a rustling sound catches my attention from outside. It doesn't really penetrate at first.

Just the wind in the bushes lining the house in neatly trimmed lines, I think, until there's a sharp *crack!*

Like a twig snapping. I look up quickly.

A black silhouette straight out of a nightmare looks

back at me, standing at the kitchen window and staring in.

I nearly scream like a baby and fly out of my skin, while my bladder shimmies up inside me in a tight knot.

The cats take off like bats out of hell. I scramble off the barstool, stumbling back a step, desperate to remember where the nearest intercom is and how to work it, but when I look again that dark shape is gone.

Of course, it's gone.

It was a man. No mistaking it.

A man in a hoodie and dark glasses.

Had I imagined it? No, there's no way he could've moved that fast.

I skitter toward the door and yank it open, peering outside, first up one side of the house and then down the other.

Nothing. Nada. No one in sight.

I taste my own fear, bitter in the back of my throat. Maybe it was just a flasher on my eyes, imprinted after staring at the page for so long. I take another step out, turning slowly, looking toward the drive, then toward the back of the house, scanning one step at a time and –

– and nearly collide with the tall, looming shape suddenly there, hovering over me, large and menacing and silent.

This time, I do scream, stumbling backward, my heart a jackhammer that's about to make me pass out from the shock.

"Who are you?!" I demand, scrabbling for the kitchen door.

I've got to get inside, get to the security panel, hit the police button. He says nothing, only watching me in grim silence; I can barely see the shadow of his lips beneath his hood. "Answer me!"

He stays silent. Tall, imposing, and creepy as hell.

But then he takes a slow, purposeful step forward, startling me into scrambling back so quickly that suddenly the door is out of my reach. He's blocking my path, closing me off from safety.

Fuck. *Fuck fuck fuck.*

I rabbit back a little more, then trip and tumble down. Another step closer. I kick out with one foot.

"Stay back!" I shriek, flopping back on my butt, trying to get my feet under me. I hear a car coming up the drive, I realize.

Oh, thank God. Landon.

He's home just in time. I manage to grapple upright again and put a few more feet of distance between myself and this silent, staring man.

"Wh-what do you want?" I try to draw myself up, finding courage in the approaching engine grumble. "I'm not afraid of you!"

Ugh. Clearly a lie, and I also sound like I'm twelve.

Then the man stiffens, looking sharply over my shoulder as a car door slams, ready to take off.

I smile triumphantly, lifting my chin. *Yeah, jerk-face, you'd better run.*

"Really now," a strange voice says. "Is this appropriate behavior toward a lady?"

It belongs to another stranger. Not Landon.

All right.

I admit it.

I scream *again.* This time, bloody glass-breaking murder.

And it's like the sound repels the man in the hoodie. He's gone like a leaping gunshot; he turns and bolts, while I'm almost on his heels.

I've had enough of strange men sneaking up on me for one day. Something boils up in me, and I still don't know if I'm chasing him or just fleeing in the same direction.

I tumble against the side of the house, skittering away from the new voice, and catch a glimpse of a tall blond man in a perfectly pressed suit before I collapse against the wall and lean over my knees, practically hyperventilating.

"Oh God. Oh, God."

Threat number one disappears.

I need a minute before I can assess if this new man is threat two, or just the lucky break I needed today.

My chest hurts, my heart is racing so fast. I take several gulping breaths, trying to calm myself. The blond man leans in, trying to catch my eye.

He's tall, handsome, clean-cut, with a neatly trimmed beard and hazel eyes that darken with worry, his movements polite and restrained.

Not going to lie, he makes me feel a lot safer than that freak in a hoodie.

"Are you all right?" he asks gently. "I take it you didn't know that man."

"N-no, no idea, I..." Breathe.

Breathe, McKenna. I press my face against my palms, inhale, exhale, try again.

"He was skulking around in the bushes outside the kitchen window." I'm trying to get my scattered thoughts together, to think logically. "I should call the police."

"You should sit down and catch your breath, first.

Here." He opens the kitchen door like he has some odd familiarity with this house. As if he's been here before, often enough to seem casual and easy. "This way."

I balk, eyeing him. "Who are you?"

"Dallas Reese, an old friend of Landon's. Miss...?"

The familiar name instantly shocks me from my wary tension. I stare. "Wait. You're Dallas Reese?"

It's like a hammer hits me between the eyes.

Sweet Jesus. If there was anything Landon and I talked about more than the stars and my brother and high school, it was Dallas. The kid he grew up hating, before I probably took his place. All the dirty tricks the boys would play on each other when they were working with their fathers at the firm. Micah Strauss and Dallas' father, Reg, were business partners.

Dallas, in the flesh, blinks mildly. "You've heard of me?" There's a crinkle of amusement in his tone.

I'm not sure it's warranted just yet.

"I'm Kenna Burke," I venture, wondering if he's heard of me.

His expression clears. He smiles. It's warm, reassuring. He has the air of a quiet, sincere man, and I can't help thinking he and Dallas have both grown up in very different ways.

"Reb," he says, and that's how I know he's legit. No one who didn't know Landon would know that nickname. He laughs. "Landon would go on about you, yes."

"Oh. He did?" For some reason, my heart keeps pounding.

"I dare say the boy was smitten." He chuckles wryly. "Doubt he said such kind things about me."

I rub the back of my neck, wincing. "Um. Let's just say

you weren't his favorite person growing up. Hopefully it's better now."

"Boyhood rivalries," he says, his princely nose tilting up in the air with fond nostalgia. "With our fathers working together, we both wanted to be the crown prince of Crown Security. Pardon the pun. We were always striving to outdo each other for our fathers' approval." His amusement fades, regret coloring his eyes and darkening his brow. "Terrible shame, what happened to Micah."

"Yeah." I bite my lip, glancing at the door he's holding for me, then step inside and turn to walk backwards so I can watch him as he steps inside. I hate to say it, but I feel safer having someone Landon knows here, someone who's familiar at least by proxy, even if he's a stranger to me.

"Listen, Dallas, Landon's not back from Sonoma. Not yet. I'm just house-sitting for him." *And doing a crappy job of it,* I add to myself, without saying it.

"It's perfectly fine. No worries, Miss Burke." Dallas closes and securely locks the kitchen door, then taps the alarm code on the panel next to it – Christ, Landon let him have the alarm code? "He's expecting me, if you don't mind me waiting. Rather important business."

"Oh, um...no, of course that's fine." This isn't my house, I shouldn't be inviting people in...but right now, I don't want to be alone. I step deeper into the kitchen, and pull open the fridge. "Make yourself at home, and I'll grab you a drink. Any favorites?"

LANDON'S LATE, and I feel weird.

Maybe it was sharing a drink with Dallas like I have any right to play hostess here.

Maybe it was leaving him alone downstairs after he shooed me off and told me I didn't have to treat him like a guest, acting like it's okay for me to leave random people to fend for themselves in Landon's home. But I didn't know what to say to him, either, and he seemed totally happy snagging a book off the shelf and settling in.

Or, you know, maybe it's the whole creeper in a hood incident.

Yeah. Definitely the creeper in a hood.

Even if I almost feel a little silly for how much I freaked out. He hadn't tried to attack me, after all. Just stood there in broad daylight.

If I'd run at him, he'd probably have taken off. Just some asshole playing a prank, I'm sure, after Landon no doubt chased so many people off his property. I smile, my mind flashing back to our reunion, the pent up, turbo-sexy flash of fists and violent ink I saw on my doorstep that morning we met like strangers.

Except no stranger ever showed up to greet me with his haunting blue eyes, his muscles, his scowl, and that unwavering, mad thing between us we still don't say out loud.

Still. Back to tonight. I panicked and cut off my only avenue of safety, didn't I?

I let a freaking stranger *into the house.*

That could've been serious. Even if he's someone Landon knows.

He'll find out about Reese, sure, but maybe I won't tell Landon about Mr. Hoodie. Not unless Reese blabs first.

After calming myself down, washing off, changing,

and settling my nerves, I'm upstairs on the deck, Velvet and Mews nestled against my hip on the long patio swing, when I hear the grumbling roar of Landon's car coming down the lane.

I won't lie. I'm relieved.

Even with Dallas downstairs, entertaining himself in the living room, I don't quite feel safe until I know Landon's familiar presence will be here.

I can't believe he still has the old Impala. He used to be such a Jensen Ackles fanboy, even if you'll never get him to admit it out loud.

For a moment I can't help smiling with a fond pang of memory. The growl of the Impala suits the beast he is now, but it's the fact that he's kept it all this time that makes me think he's still got something of the old Landon in him.

The old Landon who used to talk to me about the stars, a long time ago.

While he hung out with Steve, I'd be sprawled out on the back porch writing fan fiction.

He'd always come out once he and Steve were done, tease me a little about my obsession with doing slasher fic based on a very popular boy wizard series, and then settle in one of the patio chairs.

He'd lean back with his sweet tiger body, and look up at the sky with this kind of quiet dreamy look that always fascinated me. Way more than figuring out how to get grown-up wizard boy to kiss his trusty sidekick, if I'm being honest.

He'd point out constellations. He had a gift. Just tracing stars from one to the next, and knowing them by name, showing me the patterns and pictures and dreams people have known for ages in the sky.

Once, he told me that no matter where he went in the world, he'd always try to find the stars that made him remember home.

I wonder if he still looks at the stars, now.

And I wonder why – seriously, *why?* – my heart leaps, at the sound of him coming home. Wonder if it's more than just sheer relief that he's back to keep the place safe because I'm apparently not that great at it.

It's not home, I remind myself, watching the Impala ease around the last turn and pull up to the house, my stomach sinking. *Not your home, anyway.*

I don't really know how to tell him about the prowler. Before that it had been an uneventful day, save for the occasional glimpse of Riker letting me know he was around – unfortunately out of reach at just the wrong time.

Besides that, it was just me, my notebook, and the first good writing day I've had in a long, long while. Maybe once I report in that I didn't destroy Landon's mini-McMansion, he'll be a little less hostile.

He looks haggard and harried, as he steps out of the Impala with a duffel bag slung over his shoulder and slams the car door shut, barely sparing a glance at the third car in the drive. I push myself up with one last scratch behind the cats' ears and head over to the edge of the balcony, folding my arms on the railing and leaning over.

"How'd it go?" I call down.

He stiffens like I've just slapped him, jerking and looking up. A peevish glare pins me in place.

There's something about it that just doesn't have the power to hurt this time. Not now. He looks more like a tired man at the end of his rope than that asshole who hates my guts. I almost want to laugh, but I don't think he'd give me a chance to explain that it's affection, not mockery.

He doesn't give me a chance for anything, really, when all he does is grunt, stalk up the front steps, and then inside, the door slamming in his wake.

I glance at the cats, who tense restlessly, ears perked, and grin. "Come on, boys. Let's go welcome Daddy home."

Yeah, I know. *I know.*

Don't leave me home alone for a day with a vivid imagination, two on-page sex scenes to write, and an old crush simmering in my veins.

With the cats trying to trip me every step of the way, I head inside and down the stairs. I catch him just as he's dumping his duffel bag on one of the kitchen barstools.

We always seem to meet in the kitchen, which feels weird. I think of kitchens as places where families come together, but it's not hard to tell he doesn't see me as family anymore.

I put on a smile anyway. While he was gone, I decided that no matter how much of an asshole he's being, I'm going to be as nice as I can.

Kill 'em with kindness.

That's what my mom always says, speaking from years of experience overseas, dealing with different people. Then again, my mom's feisty enough to kill 'em with a frying pan upside the head, too, but let's hope I don't have to resort to measures that drastic to get Landon to actually talk to me.

"So," I ask, lacing my hands together behind my back. "Rough time? You don't look happy."

He shoots me a dark look. His brows are thunderheads. "Why should I be?"

"Oh, I don't know. Big job, great paycheck, and it couldn't have been a disaster or I'd have seen it on TMZ."

"So you watch trash," he grunts sardonically. "Good to know."

Laconic asshole.

I grit my teeth, just knowing his parents didn't teach him manners this bad. I don't know where it comes from until I remember, *oh, wait, actually, I do.*

Okay. Whatever. So the Polly Pocket happy princess act isn't working on him. Guess I'll just have to level with him straight.

"Landon."

He doesn't answer me, pointedly looking down as he digs in his duffel bag. I sigh, hands on my hips.

"*Landon.*" This time, it comes out sharper.

His shoulders twitch. His jaw works, and then he grudgingly looks up at me. I stare at him, but staring him down is like trying to win a stare-off with a cat. Those flinty blue eyes give away nothing. I frown.

"How long are we going to do this?" I ask.

"Do what?"

"This. Freezing me out. Why can't we at least try to be friends? We're two adults. We're past age old childhood grudges. Don't we have it in us to start over? Aren't we *better* than this?"

I don't know the answer. Part of me wants to yell at him. Part of me wants to plead. Part of me wants to be blunt and say *I didn't tell. I didn't tell anyone about the jour-*

nal, no matter what you wrote – but I'm afraid if I do, he'll confirm it. He'll confirm murder. The blood on his hands, and I'm not sure I can stand to know without vomiting.

I sigh, long and slow. "Don't you remember the nights we used to stare at the sky together? Remember telling me about the stars?"

"I remember being a kid. And I'm not anymore. Some of us grew up." He glowers at me, cold and stern and authoritarian. Just a stupid, dangerously handsome dick. "Maybe you should try it, instead of still being that little girl who never should've gotten so attached."

To me, he means. That part, he leaves off, but it softens nothing.

I can't say anything. Every time I think he can't reach a new low, he proves me wrong.

Every time I think he can't still hate me, he proves that he does.

And every time I think I might get him to crack, he turns around and walks away from me – just like he's doing now.

Damn it all. I should probably warn him.

"Landon..."

He stops, back stiff, and stands there, ignoring the mewling cats around his ankles, his fists clenched. He's not going to say anything, I realize. *Just dandy.*

"Dallas is in the living room," I say, blurting it out.

"What?" He whirls on me, eyes blazing. "Fuck. Why wasn't that the first thing you told me?"

"Well you sure didn't seem that interested in having a conversation," I shoot back.

"The *hell* is he doing here?"

I don't know why I'm so surprised by the volcanic

reaction. I guess everyone's the enemy now, even polite, pleasant men who come running to the rescue.

I fold my arms over my chest. "He said you were expecting him for a meeting. And he chased off someone who'd been skulking around the house. He did us a favor."

"Favor? That man?" His eyelids flutter, the eyeballs behind them suddenly on fire. If it's possible for Landon to grow even more intense, he does. "Who? When?"

"This afternoon. I didn't get a chance to see who. They were just slinking around in the bushes. Some weirdo. When Dallas pulled up and got out of his car, they ran. All I saw was a hoodie. I thought I should talk to you before filing a police report."

"Fuck!" He drags a hand over his face, then points at me firmly. "Stay here, Kenna."

"Excuse you? I'm not one of the frigging cats, you know."

"Yeah?" he bites off. "My mistake. Because they don't listen, either."

Then he turns and stalks off.

Not even an *are you okay?* Or a *were you scared?* Or a *thank God Almighty you're fine.*

Just his stiff, tense back, rippling with wild muscle, disappearing into the living room.

Leaving me alone, wondering if maybe I never really did grow up.

And if Landon Strauss has grown *completely* out of my reach.

* * *

CONFESSION TIME: I'm eavesdropping.

Quiet and tucked against the kitchen wall, I listen to Landon and Dallas murmuring to each other in low, resigned voices as they face off in the living room. I risk stealing one quick glance, and it's like watching the sun face off against the moon.

A creature of darkness against a creature of light. Dallas is all gold and polish and smoothness and refinement, while Landon's black and bronze and surly. Radiating darkness from every rough edge.

Someone as kind and polite as Dallas should be every girl's dream.

So why am I *longing* for the nightmare of a man?

For all that Landon seems irritated about Dallas' presence, there's a familiarity between them that hints this is an old conversation, repeated many times. I can't quite make it out. Not completely. But I catch a few mentions of his father's name – Micah Strauss. Something about the police.

That's when I realize this isn't something I should be listening to at all.

Not if it has to do with *that.* Landon would lose it if he knew I was eavesdropping, and probably boot me out for good. Silent as a mouse, I creep away, gathering my notebook to find somewhere safer to be.

Somewhere that isn't haunted by secrets, desires, and dire promises I never should have known.

I EXILE myself back on the upstairs deck. Going to my room after basically being called a child – and then acting like one, tiptoeing around and playing spy girl – is a bit too much, and I need a little fresh air.

Fresh air, it turns out, is about all I need to fall asleep on the deck swing over a book. Thank goodness it's large, I'm small, and the seat is well-padded, or I'd be waking up in a lot of pain the next morning.

* * *

Six Years Ago

I'M OUTSIDE ON MY PARENTS' porch, trying to figure out how the hell I'm gonna get an elf princess out of a dragon's belly while she's *naked* with a human Prince, when I hear the tapping on the wood banister behind me.

I smell his ocean breeze cologne, the stuff he's started wearing the last year or two, before I even see him.

"Landon?" I whirl around, leaving my clumsy try at Tolkien fan fic with some really naughty parts behind.

"Nice night for a story, Reb. Clear one, too." He sits down on the step next to me, folding his hands neatly.

"Crap! I didn't realize you'd be home. Steve said you'd be gone for another week."

I don't want to stare too much, to let him know how hard it is to keep my eyes off him.

Of course, I can't control it.

He's only been gone in basic training for a few months. Maybe it's just having him back here. Or maybe it's because he already looks bigger, harder, a more chiseled, bestial strength sprawling over his old quarterback looks, but I like what I see.

I like it so much my blood turns strangely hot, and I'm clutching my notebook over my thighs too intently, hiding the burn intensifying between them, watching my knuckles turn white when I finally look away.

"Yeah, well, training wrapped up early and the flights were good. I haven't even told your bro I'm back and my folks are out. Still owe Steve like two hundred bucks for those fireworks last summer."

I laugh, grateful it sputters out to hide my blush, shaking my head. "He was *so* worried about that part of the fence you guys blew up before you left. Had to scramble all weekend to get it patched up before mom and dad got back from Japan."

"Great. So more like three hundred for labor and materials, then." Landon coughs into his hand and I giggle again.

"Mum's the word," I say, pressing a finger against my curling lips. "I won't let him know until you're ready to announce your grand entrance."

"Probably tomorrow," he says, nodding his thanks.

"So, why'd you come by anyway?" I ask, wondering why such a simple question takes so much freaking courage.

Then he gives me that blue-eyed stare, and I remember. The gaze that says *c'mon, darling,* in my dreams. The wild, crazy ones where I somehow think this man might ever consider me any kind of *darling* at all.

"Got a present for you," he says, pulling something from behind his back. Smirking, he pushes it into my hands.

It's heavy, cool to the touch, metal. It takes me a second to realize I'm holding a huge pair of army tan binoculars, their lenses slightly scratched.

"Wrong direction, Reb. Point them up. Here."

Suddenly, his hands are on mine, and it's way too hard to breathe. Landon Strauss helps me remember how to lift the lenses to my eyes, slowly eases my glasses off my nose, and then rotates the little wheel for focus on top.

"See anything yet?" he asks.

"I'm not *that* blind without my glasses."

He laughs, spinning the wheel just a little more.

Then it happens. I gasp.

The cool, crisp California sky comes alive with more lights than I've ever seen. Bigger, brighter, and bolder, like a magic trick happening in the yawning blackness above. "Holy –"

"I know. These things are military grade, about as good as it gets before you start getting into telescope territory. Shame about the damn light pollution."

"No shame. No, Landon, it's beautiful."

"You saying that to impress me, or because you know what you're actually looking at?"

My cheeks flush again, a heat like an invisible sun blossoming on my skin. I shrug. Landon laughs, that low, throaty chuckle so *so good* at making goosebumps on my skin.

"That's Perseus, Kenna," he says softly, shifting the binoculars very slightly, my face moving with them. "Little ways over there, we've got Aries the Ram, and below him, Pisces. Look a little lower. See that bright star on the horizon? Saturn. Can't see her rings with something this low powered, but –"

"Wow. Oh, *wow.*"

It's not just the majestic patterns named after ancient gods leaving me hot and bothered and totally speechless.

Every time I feel the rush in my blood, I know.

Every time he whispers a few more exotic sounding names in my ear, I know.

Every time his hands move, cradling mine, moving us so close to twining fingers it almost hurts while he helps guide my eyes to the sky, I know, I know, I *know.*

Wow is too weak a word for anything happening in front of me.

He didn't come here to lay out an abstract atlas in the sky for cold, distant stars no one will ever know up close for the next thousand years.

He came to show me the stars. The fireworks. The secret constellations that are there for us.

That's what I came to believe, anyway, that night he sat with me for over an hour. Just him and me and a lot of laughs and soft murmurs.

I knew if I ever fell for Landon Strauss, it'd be like soaring.

Just like I knew if we ever fell apart, the crash would be just as cataclysmic.

Present Day

I WAKE UP WITH A GROAN, rubbing at my eyes.

I drag myself out of sleep with my eyes crusty, my

mouth gummy, a crick in my neck, and a rather urgent pressure in my bladder. Probably because there's a furry lump curled up on my stomach.

Velvet, his weight pushing down in all the wrong places.

"Oof!" I shove at the cat blearily and uncramp myself with rickety, wooden motions. "Off you go."

Rubbing at my eyes, I stumble inside toward the bathroom. I'm just washing my hands, though, when a noise from downstairs – clattering, intrusive – makes me freeze.

Landon may be temperamental, but it's not like him to slam around his own house like that. It sounds like some kind of wild animal got into the kitchen and is trying to get out.

I take a shaky breath, eyes wide, and lean out the bathroom into the upstairs hallway. I can't even see the cats; the noise must have scared them away.

"Landon?" I call tentatively.

No answer. Just another crash.

Oh crap.

I really wish I had a baseball bat or a crowbar or something right about now. If Mr. Hoodie came back...

No. I nerve myself to head downstairs, creeping down the steps, trying to keep my bare feet silent.

My inner voice – my author muse – is shouting in the back of my mind, reminding me that this is the point in the plot where the stupid girl who goes snooping gets murdered when she should've run the other way, especially if there's a man in a black hoodie come back for round two to scare the crap out of me and possibly, you know, leave my insides all over my outsides.

My heart's running wild. I try to remember the security code and intercom locations Landon drilled into me.

Of course I'm coming up blank.

Downstairs, I edge toward the kitchen door, flattening myself against the wall, and peer around the open archway.

A heart-shaped ass in a leather micro-mini peers back at me, bent over just enough to make it very clear someone's pink panties are very, very crotchless.

What the hell?!

Said ass is currently about the only thing I can see of the person rummaging around in the refrigerator.

O-kay. So, Landon's got company. And that's totally not jealousy sitting sour and acid in my stomach. Never. Ever.

If crotchless panties and barely there skirts are his type to chase, no wonder he's never even looked at me.

Miss Nameless straightens, her dirty blonde hair swinging down her back in a long, bone-straight tail. As she turns to eye the contents of the fridge door sourly, that's when I recognize her. Her face has been all over TV, her voice all over the radio.

Milah Holly. Pop star. Singer. Celebrity. Multimillionaire.

Oh.

My.

God.

I must've made some kind of startled, strangled noise.

She stiffens, then turns to glance at me with a sort of wary suspicion, her surgically perfect nose turned up and slightly wrinkled. She gives me a once-over that makes me nearly squirm at the intensity of her scrutiny, as if she's comparing every aspect of my body to every factory-manufactured bit of hers. Then she flutters her lashes – and they *have* to be falsies, there's just no way – offering a smile so ingratiating it's just plain condescending.

"Ah, bitchin' timing. You're Landon's help, right? The cleaner?" She looks around with a cutesy little smile of feigned helplessness. "Do you know if Landon keeps any food in this house that doesn't belong in a man cave? I'm starved and it's all meat and eggs here."

There's something proprietary about her attitude that grates on me. As if she's not just sizing me up as a maid, but sizing up the entire house.

Like she's planning to move in. There's no way in hell Landon's with her. This isn't making sense.

She's the client, right? Not his date. So, I shouldn't feel jealous. I shouldn't feel this annoyance simmering and churning inside me.

And I shouldn't open my mouth and blurt, "Actually, I'm his girlfriend."

I curse myself before it's even fully out of my mouth, but there's no stopping it. *Crap.*

Crap, crap, crap why am I so impulsive? He's going to kill me. He's going to –

Milah laughs.

Holy hell.

I swear, I'll drag this woman out of here by her cheap blonde extensions.

I'm not a violent person, but the urge to knock that curling smirk off her lips is almost overpowering when she gives me another once-over and scoffs, "You? Hilarious! As *if* a man like Landon would ever settle for some mousy little C-cup. What are you even doing here?" She widens her eyes with a mock gasp, fluttering her fingers to her lips. "Wait. Did you wander in off the beach? Oh my God, you're a vagrant. One of those bums I've heard about prowling up and down the beaches. I should call the cops. Get you some help. He'll probably thank me!"

I'm suddenly aware of what I must look like. I'd caught myself in the bathroom mirror when I was washing my hands.

My hair is a messy, ratty cloud after sleeping in a ponytail in the outdoor humidity. My shirt's stretched all out of shape. I'm not wearing makeup, and I probably still have sleep marks on my face. So, yeah, I'm not exactly a tall, leggy knockout stunner with perfect French tips and boobs in a bag.

That *still* doesn't mean she gets to talk to me that way.

"Look, you little –"

"What the fuck are you doing?" Landon growls, cutting me off.

Milah and I both freeze. Landon fills the kitchen doorway, one arm braced over his head, shirtless in a pair of cotton sleep pants that fall sinfully down his narrow hips, a trail of dark hair leading from his navel. Dipping down, only to vanish past his waistband just short of fulfilling a *very* enticing promise.

This man is lethal. Even so early in the day.

His hair is a tousled, boyish mess, his fierce blue eyes drowsy and half-lidded, and despite his annoyance it's obvious he's not wholly awake yet.

Milah recovers before me, and puts on a coy little pink-sugar smirk before sauntering close to him with a little switch of her hips. "Landy," she purrs. "There you are. I *came.* Just like I promised." Her smirk blends with practiced ease into a little pout. "I'd hoped you'd come to meet me. Instead I get your hired girl insulting me and pretending to be your girlfriend. If she's into standup, she *really* needs to work on her act."

Landon's eyes widen, then narrow, darting to me. Almost accusing.

Crap again. *Crap crap crap.*

There's only one way to salvage this.

They say when your car loses control and goes into a swerve, you're supposed to lean into it to avoid a crash. Right now, I've got to lean into this, and hope Landon plays along.

I square my shoulders and stride forward as boldly as I can. My heart's beating as hard as my firm steps, but I walk right up to Landon, shoulder Milah aside – with a touch of satisfaction for her offended gasp – and plant my hands right on Landon's inked chest.

There's just a second to savor the feel of masculine heat under my palms, the sensation of soft, curling chest hair threading between my fingers, the sudden liquefaction that starts in the pit of my stomach but curls and pulls lower and tighter.

A second later, I stretch up on my toes and kiss him.

I'm scared.

Petrified in all the most wonderful, delicious, taboo ways, and it makes me a little wild.

Wild enough to kiss him harder. Wild enough that I tilt my head and lock my lips to his and dare, for just a second, to *demand* what I've been longing after all these years. What's been pent up since the second I made a huge mistake by showing up here.

One sweet breath. I just want him to kiss me back for

that, even if this explodes in my face later and he hates me for the rest of our lives.

I just want to feel him soften for me. Just once. Just today.

His chest is hard as a steel plate under my palms, rigid with tension. His mouth is firm. Unyielding.

Please, I beg, closing my eyes. *Please don't push me away. Please don't humiliate me in front of her. Please don't reject me.*

The next three seconds of nothingness, of my mouth on his and no response, last forever.

But the moment when his lips part against mine, when his hands clamp firmly on my hips, time stops.

Whatever control I'd had when I'd caught him off guard is gone. He drags me in close, pulling me into the heat of his body, enfolding me in that raw brute strength that makes me feel so small, that ignites me with the thrill of danger and the pure and utter certainty that he'd never, ever hurt me.

Not when his mouth is this hot on mine. Not when his tongue tangles and searches, exploring so deep. Definitely not when the low groan in the back of his throat is the only warning I have before he takes complete command of the kiss.

And of me.

I'm caught in a pure tempest, a thousand little impressions coming together into a single slow moving heat storm. The tingling scratch of his beard against my lips, my cheeks.

The points of his fingertips dig into my hips, just enough to make my body throb, my thighs aching and something deep starting to pulse low and fast in my flesh.

The impression of powerful sinew moving against me,

flexing under my palms like stroking a great beast. The hard ridges of his stomach and rib cage crushing against my breasts, making me painfully aware of their weight and fullness and sensitivity.

And the feeling of being possessed.

Of being taken.

Of being claimed.

He dominates my lips with languid, stroking caresses, his tongue flicking and teasing and tracing in sweet dizzy sparks, only to go deeper with shallower hot, wet dips. Just suggestive enough to feel almost too intimate, too knowing, as if that deviant tongue already knew every depth of my body, and just where to touch to light me up.

If this were one of my books, I'd say he's fucking my tongue with his, and God am I loving every second.

I'd only meant this to save face, but I've well and truly screwed myself. It's too late.

This kiss is everything I've ever wanted.

And it's not real.

He's not mine.

And I can't ever have this again.

MY EYES fly open after an eternity that lasts no more than sixty seconds.

If the sudden stab of pain in my chest hadn't stopped us, Milah would have. She clears her throat sulkily, a reminder that she's still there, and Landon and I jerk away from each other with mutual gasps.

I stare up at him, my breaths burning in and out of me,

my mouth aching and pulsing with the lingering pressure of his lips. His mouth is slightly red.

I can't help thinking *I did that.* I can't help being proud.

His eyes are dilated, full of the storms we'd kindled. He wasn't faking it, I think.

Maybe.

There's something there. Something building.

But Milah interrupts, grumbling and folding her arms over her chest, her voice small in that sort of staged little-girl way that fits her flimsy innocent public persona. "Well, shit. So, the two of you are really together?"

I'm half waiting for Landon to shove me away and say no. But he just nods, tight but not forced, and shifts his grip on me to hook his arm around my waist and pull me against him.

My face is so hot I must look like a tomato, my head reeling, but I can't say I mind the melting feeling when I mold myself against the warmth of his side.

"Over a year now," he says, looking at Milah pointedly.

She stares at him as if waiting for him to crack, to admit it's a lie, but when he doesn't move or change expression she sniffs, lower lip jutting out. "Whatever. Where's my room?"

He jerks his chin toward the kitchen doorway, arching a brow. "First door off the stairs."

Milah gives me a foul look. I have to hide a grin by turning my face away and burying it in Landon's side.

God, he's so warm – and he smells so good, like drift-wood and sun-warmed beach sand and this pure raw masculine smell. I try not to lose myself in it when I know he's going to thrust me away the second she's gone.

Even hiding my face, I can track her by her clacking,

stomping steps, heels rattling. Once I hear that sound pass through the kitchen archway, I save Landon the trouble of humiliating me by immediately detaching myself.

I clear my throat, patting over my clothing and smoothing my hair, then risk a glance at him from the corner of my eye.

But he's not looking at me.

His gaze trails after Milah, and only after she's out of earshot does he mutter sourly, "If the money wasn't so good, I'd toss her out on her ass. With pleasure."

I force a shaky smile. "Heh. Yeah."

Immediately, I wish I hadn't opened my mouth. His gaze snaps to me, trained like gun sights, penetrating and sharp. "Why did you do that?"

"Huh?" Like I don't know. My smile freezes in place. "Oh. I mean, I..."

Right. Crap. I clear my throat, then shrug, this nonchalant little thing feeling exaggerated and forced. "It's just, you know...I saw you were in trouble." I try for a breezy laugh. It comes out more like a hysterical giggle. I'm making this worse by the second. "I just wanted to help. Nothing else. We're roommates, right? And you seemed like you needed bailing out."

"I needed bailing out." Pointed. Deadpan.

I cock my head. "Don't tell me you *wanted* to deal with that this early in the morning?"

"Fair point."

But that's all he says. I don't know why I keep expecting a thanks.

There's an expectant silence between us, one in which I can hear the throb of my bloodstream filling the space, turning every sensitive point of my body into this pulsing tremor of need that remembers too well how he felt pressed close.

I can't stay here, with him looking at me like he knows exactly what's burning through me with enough heat to crumble my heart to ash.

"I gotta go." My smile feels like a rictus at this point. I point toward the stairs like he doesn't know his own house. "Duty calls. The novel. And. Yes. I need to write. Things."

"Right."

Still inscrutable. Still expectant.

Still making me want to run like hell.

So I do. Run, that is.

So much for letting him get to me. So much for telling myself I'm not afraid.

With a cheesy little wave, I turn tail and flee for the door.

Landon's gaze trails me the entire time, and even when he's out of sight I can feel his eyes drilling between my shoulder blades, touching me as intimately as those huge, earth-splitting hands that held me so tight.

X: IT'S SABOTAGE (LANDON)

*T*his is officially too fucking much to deal with after just waking up.

My cock hurts, my job is on the line, and I haven't even had a cup of pitch black coffee.

I don't think I'll ever quite shake the soldier in me, even if I was only on deployment in an active combat zone for a few years. Old habits die hard.

You learn to make your environment a part of your body. Learn to extend your senses into the area you've claimed as your home turf, until you feel an intruder, clear as if they'd just run their grubby fingers down your spine.

That's almost how having Kenna in my space felt – except, with her, it's someone constantly running soft, caressing fingers across my skin, melting every muscle in my body. Churning awake a deep, forbidden animal part of me that *needs* her flat against the nearest surface, legs spread, teeth sunk in my shoulder as she tries her damnedest not to scream.

Having Milah Holly here, that's more like scraping your teeth against unglazed porcelain. Intrusive, unwanted, and totally nasty.

And that feeling sure as hell woke me up when the sound of not one, but *two* women who shouldn't be in my home drifted up the stairs and dragged me out of bed.

Right into a fucking mess I don't know how to deal with.

Not when I want to tell Miss Holly to take her presumptuous ass out of here and chase after some easy dick that'd kill to be in her. There must be three billion men on the planet who'd love to fuck her spoiled ass.

I'm the odd man out.

Especially when I can't get the other woman in my house out of my skull. Not when I can't shake this vicious, biting need to throw little Reb over my shoulder, carry her up to my bedroom, and finish what that kiss in the kitchen started, what it promised, what it ignited hot and hard and heavy in my blood.

Everything I know I absolutely, positively *can't* do.

I'm torn. My brain, heart, and cock are all at war, and there's only one of them I should be listening to.

Brain first.

Deal with the problems as they crop up. Reb's upstairs, and Reb doesn't pay my bills, so Reb can wait.

Milah's still here. Looks like she skipped finding her room and detoured outside. I see her through the windows, out by the scorched beach house, stomping and picking around in this way that says she's trying to pretend to be curious about the burned-out wreck, but she's really just waiting for me to swoop in and show that I care she's upset.

God, I hate human beings sometimes.

Part of me is tempted to just ignore *all* of it and go for a swim. Lose myself in the coolness, the depths, forgetting time.

Forget everything.

I've got enough money to live on for a good long while. I don't need Enguard.

But it's something I built with my own two hands, and my pride – and Dallas Reese's voice taunting in the back of my mind – won't let me give up on this. I've got my people to look out for, too.

Good men like James and Riker. Talented women like Skylar. It's not just signing their checks. In Skylar's case, this job gives her fucking sanity. A chill runs up my back when I think of what that woman would be out doing with a missing niece she loved like hell, and nothing else in her life.

There's more, too. Some strange part of me that feels like if I just do this right, if I make Enguard Security what Crown Security was always meant to be, then somehow I can erase the past and undo my old man's sins.

I'm not scrambling. Or closing down. Or running.

Like hell.

I take the time to make a cup of coffee, even if I fall back on the Keurig instead of the drip brewer for the sake of speed. Not a huge K-Cup fan when they taste just a little plastic and artificial, but right now I care less about the nuances of pure Kona beans and more about lifting the caffeine content in my bloodstream to tolerable levels.

Once I'm fortified, I pull on a shirt, jeans, and shoes, and then head out to deal with my little problem princess. When she hears me coming, she stiffens her shoulders up and lifts her chin in the air, tossing a pouty look over her shoulder at me before turning her nose up. Part of me wants to remind her that I'm not her boyfriend, I'm just her employee, but…

Professional. Right.

So, I stop a *professional* distance away and wait, hands in my pockets. She says nothing for a long while, this tense silence where I know I'm supposed to speak first, to beg, to grovel, but it's not happening.

She's the one upset, so I'll wait until she's said her peace, then remind her she has no right to be upset about what I do in my life beyond professional boundaries.

Especially when she barged into my house unannounced and – technically – uninvited by anyone but herself.

Finally, Milah makes an offended sound in the back of her throat. "Give me one good reason why I shouldn't just fire you right now."

She's trying for icy, bitchy, and superior. It comes across as fake as her on-camera little-girl lisp. "Dallas Reese and Crown Security would never treat me so rudely, you know. Dallas is a *gentleman*."

Then go try to fuck Dallas, I snarl inside my head, but restrain myself fiercely.

Even if Milah's a brat, my knee-jerk reaction to the mention of that asshole isn't her fault.

I take a slow, deep breath. "Because I know what you don't. My old man founded Crown. It was supposed to be mine. I left because they're just that bad at what they do under Dallas' management." It's not the only reason, but it's the only one she needs to know.

"Think for a minute, Milah. Think *hard*. And then

think about the fact that I know what I'm doing. So much that you don't even know what my crew saved you from this weekend." I pause, waiting for her to bat her eyes. "We blocked three psychos trying to break past security. One of them had a knife. Rambling about how you were Marilyn Monroe's second coming and how you killed Kennedy. They never even got close enough for you to know what was happening."

Her eyes widen. It's not fake shock, or even indignation.

It's real surprise. Real fear.

It shows how young she really is, and how damn clueless, too. It's part of why I haven't kicked her to the curb yet even though she's a royal pain in my ass. Nobody, no matter how spoiled, deserves to be threatened or made to feel that kind of terror.

I can't stand her ass, but I'm not going to let anything happen to it, either.

Of course, she doesn't need to know that.

She just needs to know I can do the job, and she needs to stay on her side of the line.

She hasn't said anything. I've got the advantage here, now. Knowing the real danger she's in and the possibility that Dallas can't protect her? Has her off-kilter. That's what happens when reality slaps people in the face when they've been in denial.

Heh. I'm a fucking hypocrite, aren't I?

Kenna-driven thoughts try to shove their way in. My father, too.

My old man and that question that's remained unanswered for five years, a promise I made and haven't yet fulfilled. My focus right now is on Milah, and making sure she knows I can keep her safe, and second, I don't have to if she really wants someone like Dallas.

"You've made a lot of enemies," I say into the silence, speaking slowly, firmly. "Honestly, after the way you've been acting, you're lucky I'll even do the job. But I don't want to see you hurt in Dallas' incompetent hands. That's the *real* reason I'm willing to stay on. No pile of money in the world could make working for your entitled ass worth it." This time, her widened eyes are definitely offended, but I don't give her time to snap back. "Think about it and make your damn decision," I bite off.

Then walk away and leave her fuming, sulking, little sputtering sounds chasing after me.

I'm past caring. She can make the right choice that'll leave her alive, or go for the pretty boy who feeds her ego, but I can't force it on her.

Besides, I have bigger things to worry about, right now.

Like why, with every word I'd said, I could still taste Kenna Burke on my lips.

AFTER SHE'S BEEN TRYING to talk to me for days, it's almost laughable that now I can't fucking find her.

I've got two cats trying to wrap around my ankles like leg warmers, but no Reb. She's not in the kitchen, not in her room. I prowl through a few of the common rooms and find nothing.

Shit.

Maybe I did finally scare her away.

Why does that twist a knife through the pit of my stomach?

As I pass the open French doors leading out to the upstairs deck, though, the fluttering sigh of wind against paper catches my attention. I pause, glancing out. That black book she'd been writing in sits open on the deck table, the pages fanning in the sea breeze.

My eyes narrow. When I'd caught her writing in it, she'd looked almost guilty.

I shouldn't look, should I?

But if she can pry on me, ripping my damn soul out in the process, turnabout is fair play.

Even if it's not. Deep down, I know it's not. I know it's not fair. I know it isn't justified.

But I'm also painfully curious, and I'm only fucking human.

Human enough to want to know what's in those pages, that she might feel so guilty about. It's just a book, right? Fiction?

Oh, fuck yes, it's hers. I find that out when I drop myself in a chair and flick the pages open.

It's her book, her story, her make believe...but it's also an ode to my body, and I don't know whether to be confused or hard.

SOME MEN WEREN'T MEANT to be men. They were born beasts, powerful and primal. Every time they move, thick muscles bunching and slinking, you know them for what they are: the wild, chafing against their human skin, ready to break out any moment with flashing eyes and bared teeth and hackles raised. All growls and sensuality, raw feral power.

THAT'S Logan Kane in a nutshell, the asshole next door in his cabin, secluded from the world. It's why he's so unpredictable. So frightening. So frustrating.

AND SO DESIRABLE.

I SHOULDN'T BE WATCHING him like this. I was supposed to get the laundry in off the line when I heard a splash in the river behind our house, bigger than the sounds usually made by fish or small animals. We've had park ranger warnings about bears getting too close to people's houses lately, so I was worried there might be one on our property.

I'D PEEKED out past the fence just to be sure, in case we needed to call animal services.

INSTEAD, I found Logan Kane. Stripping down on the shore, boldly and gloriously naked, erasing any questions about what he was even doing on our property, when he's been sneaking away from his awful family to swim in our river since we were children.

BUT HE'S DEFINITELY no child now.

SOMEHOW, *Logan grew up when I wasn't looking. He's hardened, bronzed, his body a litany of battle scars telling a tale I don't know how to comprehend.*

THOSE SCARS BLEND SEAMLESSLY *into the stories written across his body in raging ink, darkly spiraling and swirling designs like spells cast in flesh. They cast a spell on me, winding down his arms and over his chest, darkening his already bronzed skin to a point of sin. There's a bruise on his shoulder, as if he'd been in some kind of brawl recently, but it only adds to the raw, primitive edge of his feral beauty. He's breathtaking, with his dark hair falling across his lightning blue eyes, and that pensive blue gaze staring across the water.*

BREATHTAKING, *magnificent, and someone I...*

I CAN NEVER HAVE.

LOGAN? *Logan.* Like that's really such a stretch from Landon.

Fuck my life, McKenna Burke is writing a romance novel about me.

Those are my tattoos she's talking about. Black hair. Blue eyes. Even the bruise that even now makes my shoulder hurt like a motherfucker even though it's starting to fade into tinges of green and yellow.

It's me. Obviously.

And the girl in this story, the one I flip through, reading about the trademark frames on her face and the day she found this Logan asshole's diary...

I don't even realize my mouth has been hanging open half the time I've been reading until I realize how dry my tongue is. Or how my heart has gone straight to my cock, beating like it's ready to tear through my pants.

I swallow, closing my lips forcefully. My face feels like I just stuck my head in a damn oven, my chest is tight, and my balls burn molten.

I don't know if I'm so fucking turned on I'm furious about it, or so fucking furious the raw adrenaline of it is getting me up. I don't know *how* to feel. Maybe five years ago I'd have found this sweet and funny, but now? *After everything?*

It's insane. Confounding. Frustrating. Sexually and mentally.

And, yeah, hot as hell.

How could it ever be anything else? It's this weird kind of high, not quite an ego rush, but more like this powerful fucking hit of being desired, and it's just tangling my feelings about that gorgeous human train wreck up even more.

I flip through a few more pages. Her writing gets rougher, and there's a few scrunched, angry lines on the blank side of a page, most of them half-scribbled out. Barely legible.

My eyes drift over it, taking in character names, places, and then a name I finally recognize.

LANDON, *you're an ass. A lie. A memory. A sin. A yesterday I shouldn't want so badly becoming tomorrow.*

YOU'RE CRUEL. *You're gorgeous. You're beautiful. If you could pull your head out of your own ass for two seconds, you'd even realize you could still have the world. And the painful truth, the one I'll never tell you to your stuck-up jerk-face, is you could have me.*

BECAUSE YOU NEVER LOST ME *with your words. Or your looks – the ones that leave me confused whether you want to fuck me or stab me to death. You lost me because you shut down, closed off, and because you ran. All the things I want so, so badly to do, and never can.*

BECAUSE HERE'S THE TRUTH, *you prick. It's not over. It never was. And maybe it never will be.*

YOU'VE MOVED ON. *Still snarly and handsome as ever in your screw-the-whole-world attitude. You're still something, at least. Still a man. Still living.*

AND ME? *I'm still this battered, messed up wreck you left behind. Still a girl-shaped ruin, trying to reassemble in a world that ended the day you cursed me to my face. I'm still not over you, you fucking prick, but someday, God willing, I will be.*

THERE ARE NO WORDS.

None, whatsoever, for these piercing angst bomb words. Or for their author.

That gorgeous human train wreck who is, right now, standing over me with her soft eyes wide and her face so brilliantly red she looks like a cherry tomato.

I'm ripped from my absorbed reading by Kenna's spluttering sound, only for the journal to fly out of my hands a second later. She slams it closed and then hugs it protectively against her chest. "You...you read my book?" she demands. "What the hell?! I never said you could!"

Never said you could read mine either, I almost snap back, but don't.

Once in a blue moon, I *can* be a damn adult.

"It's not bad," I can't help mocking, though. "You've come a long way from fan fic."

She scowls at me, and somehow manages to go even redder. I'm almost worried she's about to pop a vein. "It's just ideas for the book."

"Ideas based on me."

She makes a gargling, bizarre sound that almost makes me laugh. "It's *not* based on you!"

"Uh-huh."

I curl my knuckles against my temple and lean on my elbow, just watching her. Even red down to her collarbone, she's adorable. Delectable.

She's coming apart in all the best ways a woman can.

Her green eyes wide, her luscious little pink mouth open, her chestnut hair pulled down and wafting around her face in wild, witchy tangles that catch on her glasses and tease at her lips and make me want to brush those teasing tendrils from her face and kiss her and do *some-*

thing about this fucking hard-on that's getting worse the more she stammers and fumbles and acts exactly like the nerdy little monster I used to adore.

And now hate more than anyone in this world save for one.

I let her dangle for a few moments longer, then say, "It's fine. Consider us even for that fake girlfriend thing. You bailed me out there, so I'll let you license my breathtaking, magnificent body in your story." I can't help the smirk. "Good thing we're not fucking for real. I'd get pretty pissed if you called me *Logan* in bed."

It's like the day goes still, a blanket of silence falling over us, while this wavelength yawns between us. This connection made by those words, that possibility I've put between us. The idea of us, in bed together.

And I can see it, too – how her flush changes into something breathless and delicate, deep in denial, in how her lashes tremble around her gaping eyes, in how her breath picks up in subtle, shallow puffs past her parted lips, making her throat move in flutters and her chest lift and fall against her loose tank top. Her instinct is an invitation to take those sweet tits in my palms and suck them raw.

She's thinking it, too.

In her vivid little imagination, she's seeing *exactly* what I am.

How she'd look in my bed. Pale against my dark sheets, her shoulders dotted with the little golden freckles she's started to pick up after just a few days on the beach.

Her glasses tossed aside to leave those clear, vulnerable, sweetly questioning eyes looking up at me with so much trepidation and such complete trust.

That way she has of telling me with a single glance that she sees who I used to be, and not who I really am. Sees someone I can never be again.

But when I think of her naked skin soft and yielding under my palms, when I think of her back arching and her breasts thrusting against my chest as I touch and tease her, kiss and taste her, exploring every inch of her until she's tossing against her wild mane of chestnut hair, clutching at me...

Fuck. It's so real I can almost taste her, wet on my tongue.

Drenching herself with the heat and hunger I know I can coax past that shyness...

Yeah.

When I think of that, when I think of what could have been if we'd had normal lives and grown into ourselves side by side, realizing what we'd been ignoring for years...

I almost want to be that man again.

That man I can never be, when if I touch her, if I take her, if I discover for myself just how sweet and tight the depths of her body could be, I know what happens next.

Not think. Not imagine.

Know.

I'll defile her.

I'll ruin her.

I'll leash her heart and her mind and her sweet, sweet cunt to every piece of me, and I'm a maniac who won't let go.

It's not like she could ever look at me with that kind of trust for real, anyway, no matter how many little longing glances she throws my way, glances that tell me she expects better from me.

It's not hard to tell she still fears me as much as she wants me.

She should.

I've given her plenty of reason.

Still, it's hard to remember that when the blood throbs lightning in my temples and my cock, and I'm five seconds away from dragging her into my lap and finding out what it's like when we kiss for real.

This time without any damn spectators.

I regret that last thought a split second later. An imperious little rap interrupts us, knocking against the doorframe leading out to the deck. Reb jumps from the surprise, and I'm almost right behind her.

Milah.

She's standing there, looking smug, her little pouting petulant fit apparently forgotten. In fact, she almost looks triumphant as she tosses Kenna a sour look, then shoulders past her.

Ducking her head, Kenna retreats a step, hugging that journal to her chest like a shield. I push to my feet.

More interested in positioning myself as a shield between them when Kenna looks like a kicked puppy, but Milah doesn't give me the chance. She inserts herself in my path, raking me with a once-over that feels so possessive it makes my skin crawl, turning a saccharine smile up at me with her lips pursed, as if inviting a kiss.

I don't even get to ask her if she's made up her mind yet before she's already baby-lisping at me.

"Good news, Landy. I've decided," she purrs, "that you can still be my good boy."

My eyebrows fly into my hairline. A growl rises up the back of my throat.

There's a *fuck that* stalled on my lips, but she keeps talking, tossing another of those victorious, cruel looks over her shoulder at Reb.

"I heard everything," Milah says. "Girlfriend? I *knew* it couldn't be true." She smirks. "Did you think I'm stupid? Like those ratty, shit-flinging tabloids all say? Fun fact: nobody lies to Milah Holly."

Then her slender hand – with nails that feel like claws that could easily dig hard where they don't belong – cups over my erection. It immediately withers, my gorge rising, but she doesn't even seem to notice, her smirk widening. "This will be mine by next week, Landy, and there's nothing your fake girlfriend can do about it. I'll suck it, jack it, whack it, ride it, and love it *allll* I want – and you'll damn well enjoy every splendid second."

My eyes flash to Kenna. There's a raging, almost violent look in her eyes I've never seen before. I'm expecting her to physically assault my very crazy, disgusting, self-absorbed client, and I'm almost ready to let it happen. Deal with the fallout.

I'm under half a breath away from shoving back from Milah as violently as I can – doing the damage so Kenna doesn't have to – when she pulls back herself, freeing me from that nauseating hand.

I'm fucking furious. Lungs heaving black smoke. It couldn't be more obvious, but she's completely blind to it. Another proprietary look that I guess is supposed to be sultry, seductive, and then she's sauntering away, leaving me alone.

Alone, because Kenna's gone.

And it's suddenly important that I tell her I'm not into Milah.

I could *never* be into Milah, because Milah Holly's the most entitled asshole I've ever seen. A universe apart from a shy, pretty girl trying so hard to pretend to be grown-up, just so I'll finally see her as the woman she is and not my best friend's bratty little sis.

So fucked. That's what this is. Don't even know where to start untangling it.

I only know that I can't do this.

No Kenna, no Milah, none of it.

I've got to step back, reassess, get my head on straight. This sideshow is messing up everything, especially after the talk I had with Dallas.

I fling myself through the deck doors and toward the stairs, already digging out my phone and thumbing through my address book for Milah's agent's number.

This job is off.

Getting grabby with me like that goes too far. Not in the contract. You don't fucking do that to *anyone* when they've made it crystal clear their skin's crawling.

But before I can hit the Call button, my phone vibrates in my hand.

Skylar again – holding things down at the office today while I'm not there. I pause on the stairs, sighing, then take the call and lift the phone to my ear.

"Yeah?"

"Hey, boss." Skylar sounds out of breath, and I can hear something that sounds like boxes being shoved around. Probably dragging crates of surveillance gear. We've got a few new toys recently, and Milah's next show was supposed to be their trial run. "Everything's set. Thought you'd want to know. We've done the leg work and tactical assessment at the arena, but we've got a problem."

I drag my free hand over my face. "We always have problems. What is it this time?"

"Crown Security." She pauses tactfully. "Don't shoot the messenger."

Fair disclaimer.

My gut feels like a rock. "What the fuck is Crown doing? Skylar?"

"Working with us, apparently." Skylar's soft voice has a rare wry rumor. "An arena this big is way too huge for us, Landon. Milah's team made that call, not us, but it's not wrong. They over-sold her show. So, we're handling the VIP area and the stage with Milah herself, but Dallas and Crown are going to handle out-perimeter security."

Fuck. My. Life.

If I could somehow stop my fists from wanting to slam into the nearest surface, I'd admit it's smart. Sensible.

It also pisses me off, and leaves me in a bind. I have to stay on the job now, just to save face in front of that asshole.

If I'm honest with myself, though, I'd have stayed on anyway. I'm not the only one affected by this job. I might have enough money to keep myself square for a while, but I'd be stiffing my crew out more than half their pay on this job if I had to compensate it out of my own pocket instead of Milah's fees.

I can't do that to them.

Doing the right thing, right now, means dealing with goddamn Dallas.

I close my eyes, taking in a deep breath, then continue down the stairs. *Where did Kenna go, anyway?*

"We'll make do. It's just one job. Play nice with the guys from Crown. Their shitty boss isn't their fault."

"You're taking this well. I'm glad." Skylar actually laughs, which makes me blink. Then she grunts. "Crap, yeah, gotta go. Sorry. Riker needs a hand, heavy lifting."

"Don't do anything to get me reported to OSHA, Pixie." She's anything but a soft little fairy, hence the name.

I hang up after another of her laughs, which brings a smile to my face, knowing everything she's been through the past few months.

Then I stop at the foot of the stairs and glance around, raking a hand through my hair. My house suddenly feels too large. I feel too helpless in it.

Feels empty, too.

Like I'm the only one here.

My old military sense tingles. Just like I have an uncanny sense for intruders, I also know when there's no one else around.

Kenna wasn't in her room when I passed. She's not in the kitchen or anywhere else on the first floor, either.

How does she do that? She's practically a green-eyed little cat, disappearing without a sound.

Maybe she's out at the beach house again, digging for more of her stuff in the wreckage.

For some screwed up reason, I hope that's where I'll find her.

I head outside. It takes a second to register that her Prius isn't in the driveway anymore, but I don't think much until I see the note tucked under my Impala's windshield wiper.

Blue paper. I already know it's from her, because those blue Post-It notepads were always her thing in high school, books and notebooks bristling with them tucked inside and full of random scribbles.

Any hint of nostalgia from that memory is gone when I see what the note says, tugging it out and unfolding it between my fingers.

I'M SORRY. *I can't do this. Goodbye, Landon.*

I WON'T SAY ANYTHING. *I promise.*

AND I PROMISE *I never told anyone. Believe me, or don't. Your choice.*

YOU'LL ALWAYS BE *safe with me.*

-REB

EVERY INCH of my body prickles with a cold sweat.

Safe. That's what she said.

More than the gut-punch at knowing she's gone, it's that single word that hits so hard. I know what she saw in my journal.

The darkest part of me, a part of myself I still haven't reckoned with, a part I'll never unload until the day I can find and confront my father's killer, and find out if I have the strength to take another man's life when he's not an enemy combatant determined to kill me if I don't end him first.

And Reb, little Reb...

Has been fucking protecting me all these years.

She isn't lying. I'm not sure if she's ever told a serious lie in her whole damn life.

I've hated that she saw that part of me. Hated that she knows what I'm capable of. Hated like I didn't know I could, knowing she's been protecting me.

It's like I'm underwater. Lungs heavy. This crushing feeling bleeding inside me.

I can't let her leave like this.

I have forty-eight hours.

Forty-eight hours till the end of next weekend, and my life belongs to Milah Holly and Dallas Reese.

Forty-eight hours to find that little cat of a woman, drag her back here, and set things right between us.

I rush through the next half hour. Put out extra food for the cats, make sure Milah hasn't overdosed in some weird corner of my property, and lock up the house before I toss an overnight bag in my car and peel out.

L.A. isn't a long drive, but she's got a head start on me. I'm going to find Kenna.

We're going to talk about this.

About what she saw in my journal.

About that kiss.

About everything.

And then, willing or not, I'm bringing my little Reb home.

XI: SEEING STARS (KENNA)

*T*he great thing about having a big brother is that he's always willing to be a big brother, oversized puppy that he is.

And when I showed up at his doorstep all wet-eyed and sniffly, he didn't even ask questions. He just hugged me tight, took my bag, and settled me down in the guest room with a pint of Rocky Road and his Netflix password.

His wife, Melanie, is just as kind and doting, inviting me out for a spa day and just hugging me cheerfully when I say maybe not today.

Today, I just want to be alone, and try to lose myself in the story I'm failing to write.

I don't want to be me, right now.

I'd rather live in someone else's head.

That's why, stomach full of Rocky Road, I'm perched at the red-painted picnic table in Steve's back yard. It's quiet out here under the dappled shade of the trees, save for the distant shouts of someone's kids at the playground down the street.

Steve's settled so quietly into suburban life, with his sprawling house and fenced-in, manicured yard. He's such a good guy, and the kind of hero I'd never write about. Or maybe I'm just not that into the Prince Charming type.

Maybe I should try to be.

Because staring at this freaking Landon stand-in jumping out from my pages, larger than life, has chased me right back to the hellish dungeon of shitty, awful writer's block.

So much for not living inside my own head, when he's everywhere. On my mind. On the page. Burned into my body, when I still remember the look on his face – devouring, blue eyes pure wildfire – when he smirked his devil's smirk and talked so casually about *fucking*. Me.

I could feel it. I could feel it like the word fuck was a sick, sweet dirty violation sliding inside me.

This thickness. This heat, parting my flesh and filling up inside me until we locked together and I couldn't feel anything but the deep hungry thrust of his cock inside me.

My face is burning, and it's not the summer heat. Oh, God.

Maybe I should take a dip in Steve's pool to cool myself off. I close my eyes and thunk my head against the blank pages of my journal.

I'm not like this. Not usually.

Sure, I have dirty fantasies about imaginary men and then put them on the page. I share what gets me off with the whole world, bestselling romance author that I am.

But it's not *like* me to get this hung up on a real guy and sit here numb, suffering in my clothing with my nipples aching against my bra and my panties clinging to me in a sopping wet mess. Just thinking about that moment when, for just a second, I'd have sworn Landon was ready to pull me onto his lap with those big, coarse hands on my hips while I tore my clothing off and rode him.

It's never been like this. Not even when my hormones were exploding in puberty and he was the closest thing I had to a boy idol. But back then, I was young, and sex was just a nebulous idea in dirty books or on TV after my parents went to bed.

Now?

Now I know exactly what I want, and just the thought makes me throb.

Why can't it be as easy as it is in my books?

Smoldering chemistry. Undeniable desire. That beautiful moment when they can't resist each other. No words, no mess, just sudden perfect need.

Everything crashing together. Knowing what they want without saying a single thing.

If only real life were so magical.

I shrug, lost in my head. Maybe falling back on that trope is why my books have been falling flat lately.

I just plotz away there for hours. Hours where the misery and frustration of failure and no income do dark wonders to calm my reckless libido.

I'm watching a ladybug trundle its way across the picnic table in the waning twilight, the sun sinking just enough for the automatic sensors to trigger the flickering string lights Steve's strung up all around his backyard like little bits of floating embers. I can't help but smile, as I lift my head and look up at the tiny motes of light in the trees.

Steve is such a human cinnamon roll, I swear. All goodness, comfort, sweetness. Too pure for this world.

And being around him makes me feel so much better, even when he's not here, away at his engineering job most days.

It isn't perfect. But at least I feel...home.

At least until motion catches my attention near the fence. I jerk, tensing.

When you're home alone in a home that isn't your own, it only takes a millisecond to ramp from peaceful solitude to *masked stalker here to kill me.*

Yet when I turn, it's not a serial killer in a creepy hockey mask climbing over Steve's fence. It's not Mr. Hoodie, the stranger who ambushed me at Landon's place, returning for a bad re-run.

It's someone much better and worse.

Landon.

Cold jolts through me with surprise, followed by heat roaring through with the force of seismic waves so heavy they take my legs out from under me when I try to stand. I manage to rise about half an inch before I thump numbly back down on the picnic table's bench. He looks like everything that's been running through my head since I left: wild, primitive, this dark leviathan god full of so much primal energy it practically vibrates off him.

He also looks like every heartbreak I've ever known.

And I *can't* have him here while I'm still breaking over watching Milah crawl on him this morning, after he found those words I'd never wanted him to read, every wayward thought I've refused to acknowledge since I was a teenager committed to incriminating paper.

He drops down lithely from the top of the fence, then just stands there, breathing heavily, his hands curling and uncurling at his sides. There's something dangerous about him right now, something volatile, this vibrant dynamite that could go off anytime if I just light the match – yet he's different, too.

The dark shadow, that haunted and cruel air that's hovered over him for years, isn't there when I look into his eyes.

We hold for long, breathless moments. My chest tightens. The silence hurts. Beyond painful.

"I..." I, nothing. I swallow, licking my lips. "There are doors, you know?" I offer weakly, my voice nearly drowned in the soundless thing building between us.

"Didn't want to deal with Steve. Didn't need him knowing." Low. Growling. Steady. Whatever he's here for, he's certain of it. He steps closer to me on prowling movements. "I came for you, Reb."

My heart does a suicide run against my rib cage and smashes into it hard, nearly compressing itself flat. "I...what? But you –"

"Don't want you around? Can't stand you? Won't ever forgive you?" Every word is a bullet fired from the cruel gun of his mouth.

Every one is punctuated by another step closer, while those penetrating eyes hold me in place until I can't even run from the pain. "Except you're wrong. I've been running away, and I won't do it anymore. And I won't let you, either."

I shake my head. My pulse going so fast I'm almost

dizzy, and I curl a hand against my throat as if I can force it to calm. "I don't understand. I'm *not* running."

"Bull. You ran from me today." He's so quiet, so calm, but that charged energy is everywhere, latent and bursting. "You've been running from confronting this thing between us."

"I've been running because you chased me away!" I flare hotly, then tense, bracing for the blowback of his temper.

Instead he only sits down on the bench next to me, leans forward, and rests his elbows on his knees, a heavy sigh drifting off him.

He's not quite close enough to touch, but he smells like sea salt and male musk and I don't think it's just my pulse making me dizzy. He laces his hands together – so coarse, the ridges between his knuckles rivet me, my brain everywhere, bouncing around trying to find something stable to latch on to.

But I'm left free-floating, and completely unprepared for this conversation that's been five years in the making.

"I did chase you," he admits quietly. "Because you saw me for what I really am, and I couldn't *stand* disappointing you."

My mouth works incoherently. *How?* I want to ask. That word, and so many more. Questions like, *What are you saying? That I mattered that much to you...that you cared that much what I thought of you?*

And Jesus, if you cared so much, how could you be so cruel?

"Landon..."

He exhales heavily, lowering his eyes, his jaw tightening as he stares at his hands. "I know. I'm not starting this the right way. I'm coming at it sideways. But if you'll just let me talk, let me get my thoughts out...then I'll answer anything you want to know."

I nod feebly. That, I can do. Maybe by the time he's done talking I can figure out my thoughts and feelings and form words more coherent than "Okay."

Still, he says nothing for what feels like forever.

I just see him gathering himself, and part of me wants to reach out to touch him, to say it's okay, but I can't. I'm afraid if I touch him I'll break whatever this fragile moment is, this bubble in time when suddenly we're teenagers again, sitting out under these stringy bright glitter-bulb stars, and he doesn't hate me.

And he'll actually talk to me. And look at me. And instead of forcing me away with the pure vibrant force of his anger, we'll find an understanding.

Finally, with a deep exhale that lifts his shoulders heavily, he says, "You shouldn't have read my journal. But I shouldn't have reacted the way I did, either. That day years ago, Reb..." His brows draw into a thunderhead. He lifts his clasped hands to press his thumbs against the insides of his eye sockets. "It was too fucking much. I'd just found out what my father was really up to with Crown. Bad shit. Dirty, underhanded black market deals. I don't know if he was actually involved in the drugs and trafficking, or if he just looked the other way, but it was bad. It cost him everything in the end. His family. His life. His honor."

My blood chills. I remember Micah Strauss. He'd always had an easy smile on his big square shoulders. He was always kind to me, Steve, and my parents. Never someone I'd label evil.

My jaw hangs open. "Mr. Strauss? Dirty? You're *sure?*"

Stupid question, but it still falls out. Of course I already know if there was any doubt, Landon wouldn't be the tortured man he's become.

"Yeah. And I was so fucking angry. Angry with him for betraying us. Pissed with myself for not seeing it sooner, and finding some way to save him. There's part of me that *wants* to believe he was just a good man who fell in with the wrong people so he'd keep making money for his family. Another part of me curses his fucking name for ever being so vile. I don't know if I love him or hate him, I just know he's not here for me to figure it out, and I'm still fucking livid over it – and pissed at myself for not finding out who pulled the trigger." He lifts haunted, haggard eyes to me.

"I wrote that the same day you read it. And my emotions were a fucking wreck, and you got the brunt of it. But it wasn't your fault, Reb. Nothing was your fault, really, from then till now."

I swallow the knot in my throat. This hurts to hear, but I need it. I need it so much. "Then why...? Why did it take you so long to say...?"

"You know why," he responds grimly. "My father was murdered. Killed. And you're the only person who knows what I intend to do about it. What was I supposed to say to you after that? You always followed me around with stars in your eyes. Didn't want to see them go out when you saw me for the monster I am."

I suck in a breath, focused on one heavy word among many.

Intend, Landon said. *Not intended.*

So, he hasn't done it. Not yet. He hasn't murdered anyone.

But he might.

I shake my head quickly. "You're not a monster," I manage to choke out.

God, why is this breaking my heart? Why do I want to cry, pull him close, kiss him until he sees that he's still the same Landon, and I *still* see that boy with bright blue brilliant stars he gave me reflected in my eyes?

"I ran today because you wanted me to go, Landon. Not because I didn't want to stay."

He looks at me with such a desperate, dark-eyed stare that it seems he might say something else – something I painfully need to hear – but instead he continues flatly, "You don't think I'm a monster? What if I told you the only reason I'm still on this job with Milah is for a chance to sniff out what's going on at Crown Security and with Dallas? That I don't give a damn for her and I just want to destroy that fucked up company from the inside-out? Because it ruined my father..."

He's incandescent, hushed and rough-edged words, leaning in closer to me. Nearly overwhelming me with his presence. "What if I told you, when I find the man who killed my father, I'm going to *snap* his neck with my own two hands?"

I'm trembling.

Trembling, again, but I lift my chin. Desperately trying to make my shaking, rioting body calm when every last part of me rebels. There's a small, frightened, animal part of me that's screaming to run before the predator eviscerates me – but there's a dark needy twisted part of me wanting to be eviscerated.

One thing you learn writing romance is that part of the appeal in dangerous men is the thrill of flirting with that sharp edge. Knowing he wants you, needs you, *loves you* too much to ever cut you, but the danger's there none-theless.

There's a reason attraction is terrifying, and fear can be arousing.

The very same reason I made Landon into Logan, and put way too much of myself into those passion stained pages.

It's like a chemistry experiment. Landon ticking every box. Right here. Right now.

I'm scared of him in delicious ways, but hurting for him, too. Aching like I didn't know I could.

"I'm still not afraid of you," I whisper, and manage a wry smile. "Sorry. Still a starry-eyed idiot, I guess. I don't see a monster. I see a man faced with complex choices and a lot of pain, and I don't think you have murder in you."

"And if I do?" he demands. His eyes crackle, cold and demanding, mysteries and intent and just enough fierce-ness to steal the breath from my lungs for the hundredth time today.

"Then you do," I answer, wondering what it means. That if he killed the man who killed his father...I'd see it as a righteous act of vengeance, distasteful as it might be. Not sheer monstrosity.

And I'd see the dark potential consequences, too. Landon winding up in prison, or worse. Ruining his life, or losing it in the process.

My smile strengthens, and I shake my head. "Sorry. You're gonna have to try harder than that to scare me."

"I don't want to," he spits. "That's just the thing. I don't *want* to scare you away anymore." He makes a frustrated sound. "I want you to come back, Reb. With me."

That's when it hits me.

He didn't just come here to clear the air so we didn't part with bad blood.

What is he here for then? When it hits, I'm gone.

No apology can clear years of self-doubt. I can't let myself hope or assume too much.

Can't let myself do anything.

Because even if I understand him better now it doesn't change the stone cold fact that the two of us together are a volatile mess. More pain than pleasure, guaranteed.

"Landon, I can't," I say. "God. I've wanted to hear you say you forgive me for years, but I...we don't work. We're a fucking mess, all claws and teeth and misunderstandings. It took five years to talk out one conflict. What happens when I leave the milk out on the counter and it goes sour? We don't talk for five more years while we build up more tension? More hate?"

"Wouldn't happen," he says firmly.

I want so bad to believe it.

"How can you be so sure?"

"Because Velvet and Mews would chew the carton open and drink the milk way before it went sour."

It knocks me for a loop so fast I can't help the sharp burst of laughter, easing some of the tension between us, even if that tight prickling is still behind my eyes.

"You know what I mean, jerk."

"I know." He's smiling, though, and I haven't seen that in forever. One-sided, easy, confident, with just a touch of arrogance. Softness, too. The heart-stopping kind. "But are you so sure we don't work? Because I'm not. There's something between us, Reb. And I'm done running from it. I just need you to stop running from me."

My heart remembers to beat hard enough to punch me. I hesitate, then ask, "What are you asking?"

He falters, then glances away, looking out across the deepening twilight of the yard.

Then he looks up, at the trees full of string lights overhead. For a moment, with them shining down on his swarthy skin in little dots of gold, he's that boy again, looking up at the sky and counting stars.

"I could still use your help with Milah," he says, reluctance catching in his throat. "I could use a fake girlfriend."

I bark out a hurt laugh. It feels like swallowing glass. "Seriously? She already overheard us. What good will pretending to be your girlfriend do, Landon?"

"By telling her it's real *now*, and not only am I off limits, but she can keep her shitty little comments about you to herself."

"But it's not real now." I smile weakly. "And to be fair, I looked like crap this morning."

His modesty fades, leaving only a thoughtful, stripping sidelong look that flicks over me. He's assessing me, taking me in, consuming until there's nothing in my world but brilliant blue and the frantic rush of my heart.

"No, you didn't," he murmurs. "You always look damn good, Reb."

Those words are arrows, but they don't strike my heart until he touches me.

Not until he reaches out, traces his fingertips along my cheek, their bluntness and coarseness so hot against my skin.

A shiver flutters over every inch of me as he tucks my hair back, his gaze riveted on his fingers as they trace backward, then curl against the back of my neck, his hand so heavy. So possessive.

I swear, I can't help licking my lips, outlining my tingling mouth. It's like waving a red flag in front of a bull. His gaze snaps to my mouth, locks there, lingers with a touch I can feel.

Before he leans in and kisses me.

There's a scratch of beard and a burst of fire. Then I'm spinning and lost and seeing the fire's red, drunk on the passion, lost in my heart's deafening throb.

Landon kisses like he's intent on conquest, and I'm already claimed in one sweeping blow.

He takes control of my mouth, surges into me, teasing with such bold and hungry strokes. Every time his tongue slides hotly, obscenely deep, I feel it clenching and wet deep inside me.

His kiss makes me full to bursting with a tingling need. Achingly, painfully empty with a desire to be filled, hyper-aware of every inch of my body. Every part of me he isn't touching.

Until he is.

Until his hands are on me, dragging me across the bench as if I weigh nothing, pulling me into his lap.

Until my ass is against his thighs and there's something hard and hungry and oh-so-thick pressing up against me, hot even through the denim of his jeans, burning against the naked backs of my thighs.

Until his arm is hard around my waist, caging me against the steel of his body, giving me everything I need with the pleasure of his touch crushing against me.

Until *everywhere* he touches me, pressed chest to chest,

stomach to stomach, makes me aware of my senses in the way no Cabernet-swigging douchebag ever could.

It's like when Landon touches me, when he kisses me, I come alive.

I'm all bright lights, and he's the yawning darkness that makes them glow so sweetly.

He bites at my mouth, stinging and bruising and all delicious heat.

I bite right back. Fighting him, giving back need for need, kiss for kiss, lick for lick, nip for nip until we're a tangled mess of rushed breaths and grasping hands.

Tangling my fingers in his hair, I stroke back through his thick black nest. He lets out a thrumming, feral growl against my lips before burying his face against my throat.

He sensitizes my skin with the rasp of his beard, then ignites me again with kisses and gentle, slow bites trailing at my throat, following my pulse.

My gasps come low, at first, turning into startled cries as he lifts me, shifts me, his possessive, rough hands on my thighs.

Making them shake as he pulls them apart, repositions me, settles me down on his lap again until I'm straddling him.

Suddenly, this is so much more intimate.

I'm wide open, my panties drenched and pushing up against sensitive, needy, wet-slicked flesh. His hands dig into my ass, making that empty clutch in me, that need to be filled, pulse ten times harder.

He grabs at my shorts, handfuls of my flesh, and brings me down against him.

The pressure of his cock against his jeans is almost fucking me, sliding and rubbing between my thighs, scorching my own wetness into me with heat and friction, and there's no escaping it when his body is *so large* between my legs that my inner thighs ache. It's the effort to span him, to straddle him, bared in all but name.

The thin fabric between us can't keep him from ripping my senses to shreds.

I'm spinning, struggling to breathe, clutching at him, struggling to keep the sounds rising in the back of my throat from leaving the back of my throat. It's too much, too intimate, too dirty, and everything in me craves it with the addiction of a heady drug with a high more intense than any other.

And we're out in the open, in my brother's backyard. Steve might wake up from the exhausted nap he and Melanie both crashed into after their evening yoga class after work.

Perish the thought. All I *need* right now is my brother walking out here and finding me straddling his best friend with those dark heavy hands all over me, and my body so tight-strung and wet I'm probably soaked through my shorts.

Please. Just give us time.

I just got Landon back, after all.

I can't let him lose Steve over something like this, too.

"Landon," I protest weakly, digging at his hair, tugging gently. "Landon, we can't. Not here. S-steve....Steve will never forgive you – *mnh!*"

His answer cuts off my startled cry, burying his face against the low neckline of my tank top, dragging the delicious friction of his stubble over the upper curves of my breasts. He only pauses to dip his head, captures my nipple in his mouth, sucking and nibbling and teasing through my top and bra.

It's molten, the fabric trapping the wetness and heat of his mouth, slicking it against my skin.

His tongue lashes fire against me in jolts that leave me writhing against him, rocking my hips, grinding myself against him greedily until I'm all wildness and pulsing, desperate need, completely stripped of my senses.

He makes a deep, satisfying sound with one last little lick, then lets go, looking up at me with those blue eyes smoldering.

"You were saying?" he growls.

I can't talk. Can't move. I'm a wreck, completely shattered inside, and if I don't give in to this wanting I'm going to lose my mind.

But I'm trying to think straight, still trying to be an adult. "I can't let you ruin your friendship with Steve," I whisper. "It's –"

"If me wanting you ruins our friendship, then it wasn't a friendship at all." But he relaxes his tight, clutching, entirely distracting grip on my ass, and strokes his hands up my back.

There's a gentleness at the contrast with the demanding fire in his eyes. "Be with me, Reb. Right here under the stars. We'll spend the night like we used to." That darkly arrogant smirk flashes a glimpse of teeth. "Only this time, you won't have to write the sex. You're talented, yeah. Good luck ever finding the words for the shit I'm gonna do to you."

I can't help a shaky laugh. I lean in, resting my brow to his, breathing him in. Breathing in the scent of raw desire between us. "You're out of your mind."

"Must be. Feels like I've gone crazy." He kisses me again – softer this time, a gentle thing that ends in a taunting nip, a promise. "Feel like being crazy with me? Breaking a few rules?"

If I say no, I'll be lying to myself, and him.

But if I say yes...holy hell.

If I say that, with another kiss, then I'm tumbling from one heartbreak to another when this man is so volatile and wild he can destroy me with a single touch.

Too bad, right now, I *want* to be destroyed.

Completely shattered inside and out, if only to know what it's like to have him this one time.

I bite my lip, tasting him on it, then curl my fingers against his shirt, gripping at the hem and tugging upward. "Let me touch," I whisper – and that's the closest to a yes he's going to get, when my common sense is screaming Danger, Will Robinson, danger! at the top of its lungs.

His eyes brighten, then darken, and he leans back from me enough to grasp his shirt and pull it up over his head.

Muscle flexes powerfully, writhing like licking tongues of steel coiling and sliding over each other in pure filthy suggestion. *He's* filthy.

Made for sex and secret things in the dark, for those little twisted whispers you never speak in the light of day. I can't decide where I want to touch him first.

I start with the tattoo curling over his shoulder, a primal pattern that makes me think of deep tribal drumbeats and the rhythm of the ocean answering a tidal moon's call.

Sea and stone. Harshness. Smoothness. Fire.

That's his entire body, this titan masterwork crafted from the elements themselves, and I lose myself tracing over his beauty. Every time my fingertips skim his shoulders, his chest, the ripples of his abdomen, a shudder rolls tensely over taut hide.

He's barely holding himself in check, breathing harder and harder, while every part of him I take in makes my body ache deeper and deeper.

Until my fingers stray down to his navel, that trail of tempting dark hair, and lower.

Landon's control snaps.

Suddenly, I'm tumbling on my back, spilled across the grass, fresh green blades licking cool against my overheated skin while he hovers over me. There's a dark god pushing between my legs, taking up my world, framing it in the light from the twinkling stars overhead.

In the darkness he's this looming, menacing shape. A silhouette cut in hard edges, pinned by the glow of blue – but it's the warmth and need and softness in those vivid blue eyes that turn him from the monster in the dark into the silent secret lover.

Consumed and all consuming in his intensity. He takes me in with a lethal gaze, an eye-fuck that strips me naked. His splayed fingers skim up my body, pushing the hem of my shirt up, taunting me with the sensuous scrape of calluses against my skin. Every touch comes like a spark kissing, burning out, melting into my flesh.

I suck in a breath as his hands rove higher, as he lifts the tank top over my breasts, baring me save for the barely-there bra cups that are no protection at all.

Not from his gaze. And not from the heavy, heavy touch of a possessive hand curling against my breast, cupping and kneading my flesh against him, until I feel like putty in his hands.

A whimper slips out of me. I can't help but writhe, lifting myself up, digging my fingers into the ground, eyes slipping half-closed as I bite my tongue on pleasure.

His knee braces against the grass between my thighs. Every time I move, I'm grinding myself against the hardness of his thigh.

Struggling not to completely lose myself in these deep, drawing feelings he pulls out of me with every touch, every kiss, every beastly glance.

I'm so weak for him. A level of undone I thought only existed in my books.

So shamefully weak, he strips what last strength I have as he lowers his body over me, licks his way up my stomach in sizzling trails, catches my bra cup in his teeth, and drags the lace down to bare me to the kiss of night air. And to the kiss of his lips, as his mouth teases me once again with no buffering layer between us, pulling my hardened, tightening, tingling nipple into his mouth.

Desire shoots through me in hot bolts, every last one arrowing straight down. And his huge hand follows them, like he's guided by the invisible arrows of my pulsing need.

I'm so lost, such a mess, digging my dirt-stained fingers into his back, feeling like a little animal myself as I squirm against him...holy hell.

I don't even realize what he's doing until my shorts are open and suddenly there's the heat of hard, thick knuckles against tender skin, slipping down, exploring and brushing over my folds.

I can't stop my cry this time.

It rips out of me, a sweet hot tremor as everything inside me clenches. His fingers belong to the devil himself. They glide down slow, knowing to find where I'm already wet. *So wet.*

He had me in the palm of his hand before he even jumped the fence, as if my body sensed him coming and was ready.

He traces every dripping soft bit of me like he's known even this secret part of me his whole life, a feeling more exposed than any I've ever known. I'm going to burn up inside. Going to die of this fever.

Just gasping every time pleasure crashes over me in rushes so raw they're almost painful.

He knows how to make me writhe. Knows how to make me spread my straining thighs and lift myself desperately toward his stroking fingers. Knows how to make me lose my breath when he teases one greedy point and then the next.

And he knows how to *completely* break any last resistance I had when he lets go of my sore, throbbing nipple with one last loving lick, swirls his fingers through my dripping wetness, and growls huskily against my ear, "...so you did miss me, Reb."

Oh, God. I want to call him an asshole.

Want to tell him to fuck off. Want to tell him to fuck *me,* because he's driving me crazy with this slow foreplay, this languid exploration that seems to strip away the civilized woman bit by bit to make me just as wild as him.

But whatever rises to my lips is silenced, choked off, as those devil's fingers search deeper. Just two fingertips, sliding inside me, slow and testing – but they're enough to set me off.

"Landon!" I gasp, arching hard against the grass.

Only the thick, pinning bulk of his body holds me in

place. His fingers respond, surging slowly deeper, anchoring me with a rough confidence and certainty that twists me up inside and leaves me feeling so deliciously helpless.

No one else I've ever been with has made me so entirely, immensely aware of every sensation. I feel him down to the ridges of his knuckles, caressing inside me.

He conquers my whole world, in this moment; there's nothing but the heavy rasp of his breaths in my ear, the heat and pressure of his body, the unyielding planes of hard muscle beneath my digging fingers, the sweet violation of his fingers coming deeper and deeper.

Twisting. Pumping. Taking. Pushing.

Thrusting me higher and higher each time he strokes, quickening his delicious pressure against the trigger points on my inner walls.

I can't take it. My pussy can't.

He's too damn much. He's *always* been too much, but I never thought I'd find myself like this, wrapped around him and pleading with soft, needy keens in the back of my throat.

He'll destroy me if he doesn't end this soon. If he doesn't bring me off...

I turn my head, lips against his ear. "Landon," I whisper.

I want to say *please, please stop teasing. Please be with me. Please let me feel you.*

But there are no more words. I'm hollowed out, and there's nothing but this twisty-aching-wonderful-awful-beautiful-terrible feeling inside that has to have him. And it won't go anywhere until he's had his fill of *me*.

It's like the wavelength stretching between us speaks

for me. It's as though he understands me, understands me the way the old Landon used to, the boy who called me Reb and told me I was better than all the people who hurt me. He stops, gently slipping his fingers from my body. That dark, commanding voice murmurs against my ear, my jaw, my throat.

"You want me?"

I nod, struggling to catch my breath as my entire body throbs with the after-impression of his touch. "Please."

He's already dragging my shorts, my panties away – peeling them down my legs, stroking over my thighs with his fingertips in the process, until they quiver.

Then I'm bared before him, the last scraps of cloth clinging to me, and his zipper drops with a heavy rasp. I bury my face against his shoulder, feeling hard heat pressing against me, the tip slick and dripping and burning against my flesh, thick and teasing against me until my stomach clenches and my breaths hitch.

"Landon."

"Say it," he demands in a low, broken growl. "Say you want me."

It only feels like torture because it's true.

I feel small inside, when he asks. Vulnerable and frag-ile, as if he's asking me not just to bare my body to him, but to open my soul and trust him enough to let him inside after all these years of hurt and pain. As if he's asking if I truly do see him as someone other than a monster.

As if he's asking if I could *ever* see redemption, enough to give him my naked heart.

It's only a breath of hesitation, before I know. Before I

find my voice, even if it's just a shaky whisper. "I want you," I whisper. "I've always wanted you, Landon."

He lets out a low, almost tortured groan, but doesn't move.

For half a broken second I'm afraid I said the wrong thing.

Then I hear a condom wrapper crinkling and the brush of his hand between us in practiced movements before that heat is against me again, barely dimmed by the shield of latex, and he's capturing my lips.

Capturing my body.

Capturing my heart.

"Kenna," he whispers against my mouth. "Reb. *Fuck.*"

That last word is a warning. All I get before the full force of his primal, animalistic power hits.

He rolls his hips against mine, a hard surge of muscle bunching under my fingertips, plunging his cock into my trembling, clenching depths.

It's slow – so slow.

A sweet, delirious eternity I've wanted forever.

I can't escape the feeling of every inch of him gliding inside me, moving with such perfectly controlled strength and giving me that feeling of fullness I've been craving one heavy, gasping moment at a time.

I can't help rocking toward him, needy and hungry, but he gives no quarter.

One rough hand pins me to the ground with brute force, his fingers digging tight into my hip, forcing me to take him only at his pace. Forcing me to wait for every new burst of fire until I'm a whimpering mess just craving more.

My pussy hurts in the best way it can. Physically aches

to take this man so deep, engulfing every inch of him, drawing his thickness halfway to my soul.

And then I feel it.

That fiery moment when our hips crash together, when we lock so perfectly, when he fits inside me *just right.*

That moment when he's touching *all* those places that turn me into fireworks and stars. My clit seethes, buried under his pubic bone, gently grinding against me each time we collide.

I'm gone. Bonelessly limp with pleasure, melted underneath him while he kisses me fiercely, delving into me until there's no part of me he hasn't touched. I feel the whirling stars overhead in my bones, the grass and earth underneath me, the dark god of primal things inside, this animalistic thing that's less human and more a force of nature.

It's sex incarnate, and so are we, two old souls locked together in mindless ecstasy. His hips crash harder. Faster. His fucks come insanely deep, driving into parts of me no man has ever touched, a feral growl pouring out his lips every time he makes me gasp a little louder.

Then Landon clutches me to him, wraps my thighs around him, and moves...

And all else falls away.

I remember him as Poseidon in the waves, and he moves me like the tide.

Slow and subtle yet no less cataclysmic, with the strength to change the landscape inside me.

Every thrust hits hard, a barely-caged brute force, restrained just enough to keep me teetering between pleasure and pain.

He draws out one slow fraction at a time, teasing and tormenting me, only to surge in harder and give me everything I need in the sensation of his big cock stretching me, burying me, touching me deeper, deeper, oh sweet hell, *deeper*.

I'm overflowing with heat. It steams out every pore. I'm tangling my body with his and riding his rhythm until I'm in constant flux, my entire body a heartbeat of pleasure and fire and screaming, mad sensation.

His name on my lips, kissed between us again and again.

His body inside mine.

His weight everywhere, trapping me and keeping me safe. His hands on me, shaping me, molding me, memorizing me as if he'd brand me into his palms.

Then wildness between us, riding higher and higher, until I can't take it anymore.

I turn my face from his, bite down on his throat like the little animal he's made me, tasting the salt of his sweat.

Then I'm gone in throbbing white heat.

Sharp convulsions roll through me, seismic and hot, centered on that thick brand of fire moving between my thighs, dragging me under into a drowning sea of sweet darkness, of delicious friction, of shuddering, dick-riding release.

I'm sinking, spinning, barely aware of him shuddering atop me, a faint whisper becoming a snarl in my ear. "Reb, fuck. Look. Give me those eyes, baby. Right here."

I listen, losing myself in his blue gaze, fierce air storming from my lungs. His own eyes narrow, more like a tiger's than a man's anymore.

Then he says what I've been waiting for. "Want to see

159

your green when I lose it, Reb. Want your eyes on mine when I give it the fuck up, spill every screaming drop I've got into you, woman."

Holy hell.

My hips start pounding into his, a shrill sound coming in the back of my throat. I just came, but my clit can barely stand how hard he starts to fuck. Landon pushes his forehead against mine, and we're eye-to-eye when our O comes together and the universe spins apart.

So gone.

Just a few sharp jerks of his hips. That moment when his whole body goes rigid and he growls my name. His dick swelling while my pussy pulls at every inch, and then a magma heat I swear I feel, even through the condom.

I scream one long spasm, losing myself in the storm of his body slamming into mine.

All I can do is cling to him, adrift, my heart fluttering loudly and strangely, and my body forever branded with his mark.

* * *

I THINK I actually passed out.

I think Landon Strauss honest-to-God fucked me into blacking out.

That's a first.

I'm only gone for a few seconds. I think.

Enough to miss him separating our bodies, which I probably couldn't have handled anyway when I'm sensitive inside and out, a live wire waiting for a spark.

I come dimly awake as he lifts me into his arms. Through my half-closed eyes I think I see the spent condom falling forgotten under the picnic table bench, before I drift off again.

When my eyes open a second time, struggling, I can't really see the used rubber anymore and think it must've been a dream.

Everything does, no surprise.

"Landon?" I mumble drowsily.

"Shhh," he murmurs. Okay, and I'm definitely dreaming because that's tenderness in his voice. "I'm just getting us settled. Sleep, Reb."

"But...outside..."

He chuckles, a quiet thing that rolls through me, shaking his shoulders and my whole body where he holds me against his chest. It's a warm sound, a comforting sound, and without even opening my eyes I snuggle against it, pillowing my head to his shoulder.

"Newsflash: people have been sleeping outside since caveman days," he says gently. "We'll be fine. It's beautiful out here tonight."

He's moving, then, and I manage to pry one tired eye open long enough to see he's settling us down on one of the lounge chairs by the pool. Then warmth drapes over me as he snags a beach blanket from a stack folded on the patio table and wraps it around us both.

We settle into this dreamy warmth, comfortable against the reclining lounger. I should probably protest being curled up in his lap this way, but my sore, sated, deliciously tired body doesn't want to move.

Spent is the word I always use after my fictional ladies get fucked into the next universe. Whatever I am right now, it doesn't seem powerful enough to describe how utterly drained I am.

"'Night, Landon." I manage to slur, already sinking away again, fighting an expansive yawn.

Another chuckle. A kiss to the top of my head. "Sweet dreams, little Reb."

I want to say something else, ask him what this means, but my head is heavy and my tongue is thick and his arms feel far too good.

Forget it. I don't want to ask. Not now.

I just want to enjoy this strange, miraculous thing, and drift off to sleep in his arms.

I guess it really is as easy as it is in my books. I should have seen it coming.

Except I'd be lying.

Because there's *nothing* easy or predictable about Landon Strauss at all.

XII: CATCHUP (LANDON)

*C*learly, impulse control isn't my strong point.

If it was, I wouldn't be waking up under the blistering SoCal mid-morning sun with the only things saving me from a sunburn being an overhanging tree, a beach blanket, and Reb's near-naked body.

Shit!

Is this real life? Did I really get in my car, chase McKenna Burke down, and fuck her on the grass in her brother's backyard?

Yeah. Yeah, I guess I did, and considering how good she felt wrapped around me and how good she feels against me right now, I can't really say I've got too many regrets.

Even though I know it's a massive mistake.

It's a life changing fuck-up, even, but the only thing on my mind is how hard I am against her thigh. And how fucking good I bet her pussy would taste on my tongue as a wake-up call.

Then cold reality hits me between the eyes.

Right now, I've got enough drama in my life that I don't need more. While I don't regret sex with Kenna, I'm gonna regret the fistfight if her brother walks out here and finds us like this.

Guessing by the sunlight, it's about ten or so, and it's a miracle Steve hasn't already come outside to water the ficus or something, and wake me up with a ferocious smack across the back of my head.

"Kenna." I nudge her gently. "Wake up."

"Mmph."

That little fucking kitten of a woman just burrows into me deeper. And it's really not helping things, considering her shirt is still rucked up and her bra is still mangled down. Her pale, soft breasts and those strawberry-pink nipples rub against my naked chest, and if I wasn't wearing jeans, having her bare skin against me would probably just end up with us doing it all over again instead of me struggling to ignore my growing hard-on.

"Kenna," I repeat, louder, shifting my body to jostle her a bit more firmly. "Wake the fuck up. We're half naked and your brother's home. You want Steve to see us like this?"

She jolts upright at Steve's name like someone flicked a switch on the Energizer Bunny.

"What? Steve?" It comes out in a breathy little screech, only for her voice to trail into a squeak as the blanket falls down around her waist. She lets out the most adorably chirpy little "Fuck!" I've ever heard, clutches at the blanket, pulls at her tank top, freezes for a moment, then rapidly sets her bra and tank to rights before clutching the blanket around her waist.

She shoots me a nervous, wide-eyed look. "Oh. Uh. Crap. Morning."

I grin. I can't help feeling like the cat that got the cream. "Morning, beautiful. Let me get our clothes so you can stop wearing that blanket as a shawl."

Her cheeks burst with color. It just makes me want to taste her tongue again.

She glowers at me, but it doesn't have much effect when her glasses are falling off her nose – and you can bet it was hot as fuck last night, seeing her arching under me, eyes wide and wet behind those sexy librarian glasses – and her hair's a wreck and she's clutching a blanket for decency.

"Pants, Mister," she says firmly. "I want my pants before we talk about this."

I smile, quirking an eyebrow. "Yes, ma'am."

Lifting her off me gently, I keep the blanket wrapped around her so I don't get kicked in the junk, and shift to stand while simultaneously twisting to deposit her in the seat. I lean down to kiss the top of her head. She plants a hand on my face and shoves me away.

I just kiss the center of her palm, then grin and saunter away to fetch my shirt, her shorts, and her panties.

I shouldn't feel so light about this.

Too bad I've been an arrow strung tight to a bow for the past five years, and the tension's finally released, shooting straight home.

Yeah. Sometimes, it feels like Reb is the last bit of home I have left. The rest has been a mess of death, dad, Dallas, and bad fucking memories.

I push them out of my head for now, plucking my dew-damp t-shirt out of the grass and pull it on, settling it over my chest. Then I drape her shorts and panties over my arm and return to the poolside lounge chair. She's made herself a kind of blanket nest, burrowed down in it. She's looking out over the pool with that dreamy look in her eyes, her brows knit together.

I sink down on the edge of the chair and offer her clothes.

"Here."

She darts me another one of those nervous glances, then snatches her panties and shorts. They disappear underneath the blanket. There's a little wriggling, a little cursing, a lot of blushing, and then I guess she's dressed because she's no longer clutching at the blanket like it's her last line of defense.

She bites her lip, pulling her knees up to her chest, watching me over the little round hillocks they make.

"Hi," she says in a small voice.

I smile again, this time wider. "Why do you look like I'm about to tell you to go fuck yourself?"

"Because that's been the pattern for the past five years, hasn't it?" she retorts dryly. "Though, I guess I don't really need to fuck myself since you did a pretty thorough job."

"Thorough, huh?" I grin wolfishly, and she scowls. "I'll take that as a compliment."

"I – you *know* what I mean!"

"Do I? C'mon, Reb. You write romance books. You start making clever sex puns, you gotta own them."

"I *write* romance novels. I don't live them, Landon." She groans, dragging a hand across her face. "Oh, hell. I'm living a romance novel...aren't I?"

"Doesn't have to be that complicated. Or that much drama. We're both grown-ups here, babe." I lean over and nudge her with my shoulder, then toss my head. "Come on. Let's get your shit and sneak out before Steve sees us. We'll talk it out back at my place."

She stills. "You were serious about...about me coming back?"

"As a heart attack."

"Just to be your fake girlfriend...with benefits?"

Shit-fire, she's got me there.

I clear my throat. "Well, it might be a little more complicated than that, but yeah...that's the gist of it." I hesitate.

I don't want to give her an ultimatum, tell her that we'll only talk it out if she agrees to come back with me, but her brother's back yard is seriously *not* the place for this conversation.

She seems to pick up on what I'm thinking, as she casts a nervous glance over her shoulder toward the house, then unfolds herself and rises. "Okay. I'll come. Most of my stuff is still in my car. Let me get my bag from the house."

"You want to drive, or ride with me?"

"I..." She pauses, blinks, remembering her car is here. There's a touch of that shyness I remember. "Well, it'll be easier if I ride with you, won't it?"

"You know it." And I'm not thinking of her straddling my lap, crushed between the wheel of the Impala and my body. "Saves on gas."

Lame excuse. Doesn't mean she doesn't beam like the sun after it's out of my mouth.

She clears her throat, rolling her eyes playfully, hiding the genuine happiness seeping through her. "Okay, fine. I'll ride with you."

"Good answer. Move, Reb. We've got five minutes."

That just earns me a snort, a light slug on my arm, and a blush before she ducks her head and runs inside quickly.

I feel like a teenager again with us creeping through the back door, peeking around, listening for Steve, before scurrying through the empty halls to the guest room. She stuffs her things in her bag quickly and skitters for the door, then jumps with a half-yelp, half-giggle, when I slap a hand against her tempting little ass as she passes.

"Don't," she hisses, pushing my arm. "What if he's still in the house?"

He's not still in the house.

He's five steps ahead of us and just getting into his car as we come tumbling out the front door and head for my car.

Steve freezes. His wife freezes. I freeze.

Kenna might as well be a block of petrified wood.

We just stand there in icy, confused silence, staring at each other. Then Steve suddenly breaks into the widest, happiest grin.

"Landon!" He's already coming for me, and I know already I'm about to get hit with a hug. Steve is the huggiest damned man I've ever seen.

It's like being smothered by the Stay Puft Marshmallow Man half the time, when he wraps around me in this big bear hug and thumps at me like he's trying to crack my ribs. "Holy shit, how's it going? I haven't seen you in way too long."

"Because you don't answer my phone calls," I growl, but I can't help hugging him back, giving his back a brotherly slap.

Steve, too, is part of that feeling. Everything I'm not supposed to have. *Home.*

And maybe if he's busy hugging me, he won't think too hard. Won't remember to ask why Kenna's blushing up to her ears.

Steve pulls back from me, though, giving me a puzzled look. I know I'm fucked.

"Say, what're you doing down here, anyway? Aren't you supposed to be working a gig?"

"Last-minute trip." I glance at Kenna, then take Steve's arm and pull him aside. Kenna did me a solid by covering for me, so I guess now it's my turn to do that for her.

I lean in close, muttering. "Look, man, Kenna hit a major slump. I had to do something to help her clear her head. She was talking about walking away from her book, and left before I could talk to her."

Steve frowns, glancing past me at Kenna. "Jesus. It's going that poorly? She sounded happier on the phone the other day..."

"I don't know. She said something about not having the inspiration. The muse, or whatever. I thought, maybe if I could talk her into coming back and giving it time, she wouldn't give it up."

"Huh." Steve folds his arms over his chest. He looks at me, questions brimming in his big eyes.

Shit. It's not hard to tell something's not sitting right about my story, but if I'm fucking honest, I'm not an amazing liar – especially not on the spot like this.

We both know Kenna's wanted to be an author since she was barely tall enough to walk, and the idea of her just flouncing on her whole career like that is totally out of character. But it was the best I could do at the time, and after a moment Steve seems to accept it, if only to keep from making a fuss with an impatient Kenna only a few feet away.

"Well, hell, I'm glad you got it sorted. Thanks for looking out for her, Landon. I owe you one." He pitches his voice toward Kenna. "So, you're heading back up to Landon's place?"

Kenna smiles weakly, shakily, and hefts her bag. "Already packed! Mind if I leave my car here for a few days?"

"No problem. I was going to invite you out to brunch with us, but maybe next time. We're taking Gam-Gam out for her belated birthday waffles – she loved the card I picked out for us both!"

Kenna gives a strained smile. "Ugh. I really need to see her soon. I'm sorry again, Steve, for being so AWOL lately."

"Sis, don't apologize. Just finish your book." He steps up, tugs her close, and kisses her forehead. "Be good, baby sister. You'll tell our grandma all about it when you hit the NY Times' list again."

She leans into him, then hugs Melanie, before giving me a secret, pleading look. "Let's go. I'd rather not be on the road all day."

So bossy.

It's cute.

We say our last goodbyes, retrieve the rest of her stuff from the back of her car, and then climb into mine. As she fastens her seatbelt and I start the engine, she gives me a dry look.

"Really? The *book?* You told him I had a complete emo

flail and gave up on my writing career? You're bad at whispering and lying, by the way."

I don't say anything. Just give her a quirk of my lips and back the Impala down the drive. "Look, I needed something. He caught me off guard."

"You know he didn't believe you."

"I know." I sigh. "That's what worries me. But at least I bought us some time."

For what, though?

That question lingers on my mind as I push the Impala into Drive and head off down the road, toward the highway.

"It's just as well," she whispers. "I'm kind of a screw-up lately. Can't even stay in one place long enough to give my grandma a real birthday present."

"You'll get her back sooner or later. And if this is screwing up, you'll fix it. Don't lose sleep over it." That's all I say, going no further with my own problems.

Kenna's silent in the passenger's seat, looking out over the road with her fingers curled against her lips. She's disheveled and still has grass in her hair, just another reminder of her body clinging to mine, clutching against me, wrapped around me and drawing me deeper.

What did I buy time for, really, when I have no idea what the fuck just happened between us?

IT'S A QUIET DRIVE BACK. Not necessarily tense, but definitely pensive.

We pull into my place just as another ripping red California sunset blazes over the water. Kenna's all smiles as she grabs a few of her bags and I grab the rest. The awkward moment comes when we're taking her things upstairs, and I make a beeline for my bedroom, while she heads for the guest room.

There's a frozen moment. A long look.

Does she belong in my bed now? We're both asking it with our eyes, but fuck if either of us say it out loud.

And by mutual truce, we leave her things in the hall for now, heading down to make dinner.

Two cats come crashing into our legs, one at a time, purr-butting their heads against us. We both reach down, having something crazy with Velvet and Mews. Something that feels way too much like a family moment.

Later, I'm fixing our supper while she settles on a barstool with her little black book, biting her lip and scribbling away. I'm busy tossing seared strips of beef, baby snow peas, chili peppers, onions, and paprika in a sizzling pan, but I can't stop watching her from the corner of my eye.

She's not really writing. Her pen scratches now and then, but for the most part she's just chewing on it, wrapping those delectable lips around the cap, sucking on it in ways that give my twitching cock some evil ideas.

Fuck me.

One taste, and I'm already *addicted*.

I'm also worried. Last night may have been a major fuck-up, and not just because of lying to Steve.

It's not hard to tell she's questioning, too, dwelling on doubts, wondering where we stand. I'm kind of glad she's not asking, because right now I'm not sure I'd have any answers that would satisfy either of us. I don't know what I'm doing here.

Don't know how I went from *get the fuck out of my life* to *can't get you out of my head.*

Maybe if she hadn't kissed me in front of Milah, none of this would've ever happened.

If she hadn't offered me an out, a fake girlfriend story that quickly fell apart. If I hadn't taken it, and used it as an excuse to bring her back.

I'm just setting dinner on the kitchen island, slinging piles of my version of stir fry onto plates piled high with steaming beds of rice, when Kenna makes an exasperated sound and slams her little black book closed hard enough to make me jump.

"Okay," she says. "Fine. I'll be the one to say it."

I arch a brow over cracking a couple of beers and setting them out next to our plates. "Do what?"

"Start the conversation. We. Uh." She's blushing again. I don't know how she stays conscious with all the blood rushing to her head. "We weren't exactly in a position to talk last night."

I dip my gaze downward. She's still wearing what she had on last night, grass stains subtly darkening her deep tan tank top. "I remember. I was there last night, too."

"Stop that!" She folds her arms across her chest, but that only plumps her breasts up more, keeping my attention on them. I'm listening to what she's saying, I swear. "Landon, what *was* last night?"

"Reb, c'mon. I know you're not so innocent you don't recognize a good fuck?"

She scowls. "Don't be coy, Mr. Strauss."

"Perish the thought." I settle on a barstool across from her and rest my elbow on the table. "We had sex, Kenna. I put you under me in the grass and we fucked. You came on my dick twice. And that can mean something, or it can mean nothing at all, but I'd like it if it meant something. I'd also like it if you're in my bed tonight, legs spread, moaning real sweet for my tongue while I burn the taste of your clit into my memory. Whatever we've got, it's more than casual, so let's stop pretending."

She smiles weakly, trying to disguise a blush. "I think that's supposed to be *my* line."

That pathetic little smile actually makes my heart ache. I reach across the countertop and brush my thumb under her chin. "Is it really so surprising I'd say it first?"

Her lashes lower. "A little. You've been pretty clear you hate me for years."

"Fair. And I've been pretty damn confused over hating you for years." I trace my touch up to her cheek. "Maybe what happened last night was meant to clear a lot of shit up. Like five years ago. When I was young and immature and stupid. And somehow, that incident between us with the black book got codified into the norm. Rejecting you before you could reject me for showing you the monster inside. The dirty fucking secret nobody else was ever meant to see."

"I don't see you like that. You're *not* a monster." No matter how many times she says it, my gut twitches like it's been punched.

I want to believe her, but I can't.

Still, there's some relief when she presses her delicate cheek into my palm. "Some kind of wild beast? Maybe. But you expect animals to act like animals. That doesn't make them evil."

I laugh. "I'm no animal." At her skeptical look, my laugh deepens. "Not *that* much of an animal."

"You pulled my bra down with your teeth last night."

I grin broadly. "And I'd do it again."

"But...should we?" Her touch of amusement fades to a worried look. "Not gonna lie – I almost died of a heart attack when Steve and Melanie caught us. I thought they'd see right through it. Did we just screw ourselves?"

"Technically we screwed each oth–"

"Landon."

"All right, all right." I'm taking the conversation seriously. I promise. Just can't help having a little fun after finally having things easy between us again, even if we've made a million other problems. "Look. Does this feel like a mistake to you? Because it doesn't to me."

"I don't know," she admits with a frankness that's so very Reb. "It feels good. It feels like I'm in the middle of some weird teenage daydream. But that doesn't change the fact that things could go south really fast."

"Okay. What ways are you worried about?"

"Well, one, we get in another fight."

"And then we talk it out like adults instead of the teenagers we've been acting like," I point out. "Next."

"Milah." She wrinkles her nose.

I snort. "Fuck Milah. Her private life is my business. A job. My private life isn't hers."

That coaxes a laugh from her, eyes glittering, a touch of the tension leaving her shoulders. "Fine. Last obstacle. Steve."

"He's your brother. He loves you. He's my best friend. He won't murder me, just potentially take off a limb or two. But sooner or later, he'll accept that we're adults, and it's our choice." I smirk. "You worry too much, Reb."

But I'm the one with pensive thoughts on my mind, as I realize I'd said sooner or later.

As if this could be something long-term.

As if one night of hot sex has already got her embedded way too deep in me.

But she's smiling again, letting out a sigh of relief. "You're right. I probably do. And I mean...last night was nice. I wouldn't mind doing it again."

"Yeah?" God, she's got such a strong pull on me.

I can't help pushing myself up, leaning across the island, catching her lips. I taste her deep and slow, just enough to feel her go soft against me, then draw back with one last caress of my thumb over her lower lip. This raw, primal thing inside me wants to claim her all over again.

Her eyes are smoky, dazed, dilated, and I love it. "Sounds like a deal. Now, eat, before it gets cold."

I sink back in my seat. She settles in hers as well, picking up her fork and pushing at the stir-fry, then peeking at me shyly. "So, you're telling Milah I'm your real girlfriend now?"

Am I? Is that what Kenna is, now?

Fuck. I don't know. Don't know what she is.

Don't know how to define this, other than a ceasefire and some really hot fucking.

And I'm afraid to admit it, but I really don't know what I'll do if Reb gets under my skin and then winds up hating me after she sees I really am a monster, and I'm capable of things she can't imagine.

No matter how many times we fuck, or how deep the feelings go, they won't change the past or future. I still have a killer to find, and a lot of bad blood to drain with Crown.

"I'm not telling Milah anything. It's not Milah's business," I deflect, picking up my own fork. "And I don't care about Milah, either. I've missed five years of your life. Catch me up on your writing, Reb. Catch me up on everything."

That's all I want over dinner. Just her and me and a dying sunset through the glass, two dark sleepy cats flopped out near our feet.

I need tamer, innocent words.

Something to keep me warm, when the day comes that she knows me for the monster I am.

XIII: NOT QUITE PARADISE (KENNA)

*V*elvet and Mews shouldn't make me wonder just how good Landon might be with children.

I'm not going there. Not yet.

Not when it's only the morning after and I'm still sore inside and sex shouldn't be making me wonder what life could be like with him. Yet, it's hard not to, when right now this moment feels so good. Bright and new, comfortable and sweet, me perched in one of Landon's oversized shirts on a barstool while he makes breakfast shirtless – and feeds more of the ingredients to the circling, mewling cats than he does into the sizzling skillet.

I prop my chin on my hand, watching him fondly. "Hey, Landon, will there be anything left for *us* by the time you're done?"

He glances over his shoulder with a grin. Mews hops up on the counter and yowls, demanding more, only to purr as Landon feeds him another diced bit of smoked ham that's supposed to go in our omelets. "Now you know why they're so fat."

"Are they? I couldn't tell under all that fur."

"It's pretty dense, isn't it?" He strokes a palm over Mews' ears, burying his fingers in short but thick gray fur. "They're British blues. Shorthairs."

I arch both brows. "Wow. Big words for someone I didn't even know was a cat person."

"I wasn't, I just..." He glances back at me again. Something like chagrin darkens his eyes. "You asked me about them before. And I shut you down."

I offer a smile. I get it now, I really do. "If you want to tell me, I'm all ears."

He hesitates, then laughs and ducks his head, almost boyishly. "It's my Mom's fault, really. My aunt passed away, and left these two behind. My mother was supposed to take them, but her condo association doesn't allow pets, other than those yappy purse dogs." A rueful smile bends his lips up. "Never doubt a mother's power of persuasion."

Never doubt a man's power of persuasion, either, when he looks at you with soft blue eyes and lets his gaze drift over your naked body with only a thin layer of cotton in the way.

My face goes hot. Sweat beads on my brow. I can't resist the magnetism in his stare, and I slip off the stool, padding barefoot across the floor to tuck myself against his side, picking up a bit of ham to feed to Mews.

"I think it's sweet," I murmur, resting my head on his shoulder as his arm slides around my waist. "And I like these little guys. I think they like me, too."

"*Mew!*" Mews looks at me, giving the definitive answer.

Seriously. Is it really this easy?

It can't be.

We'll be fighting again by noon.

* * *

ALL RIGHT, so maybe it is this easy. Some days.

I can't believe how I'm just falling into things with Landon. We click.

We got lucky, too. Milah's latest show was delayed due to technical issues, which meant no snotty little Barbie prancing around, offended that Landon's not drooling all over her. We don't know where she's gone since leaving his place, and thankfully, we don't need to care.

It's nice without Landon rushing off to put out figurative and literal fires. Just two weeks of quiet, sun, sand, some heavy wordcounts, and the most amazing sex ever.

Well, there was *one* fire.

Down on the beach, a few drunken kids started a bonfire. It spread to an old abandoned fishing shack. We got one hell of a scare when we were sound asleep, naked and tangled in each other, and heard the familiar wail of sirens.

After that, though, Landon seemed to relax more.

If those kids caused one fire, then they were probably behind others – including the one in the beach house that had him so worried about his mystery arsonist. I try to convince myself, too, slip into a convenient explanation for my strange hoodie prowler.

I like Landon relaxed. His eyes go soft in a certain way, and I remember him dreaming of stars.

Only, now he looks at me the way he looked at those stars.

I want to say I can't fall in love with Landon Strauss.

But I'm not sure I ever fell *out* in the first place.

Especially when, in the early morning light, I can't take my eyes off him. I'm awake before him, for once.

We're both early risers, but he's usually out for his morning swim before I'm awake. I'm downstairs making coffee before he comes in.

Last night was a little rough. As we get closer and closer to Milah's rescheduled gig, he's been more and more tense, and his crew has called with more problems. Last night he'd almost called the whole thing off.

And when he was shaking with anger, when he was furious and drawn taut with every line of his body hard and angry...

I'd touched his arm.

And he'd responded, wrapping me up and holding me tight. Just breathing hard and fast, until he went lax against me.

It felt strangely like sheltering him. Keeping him safe.

But he'd been so exhausted by the time he climbed into bed that he didn't even want to touch me. Just hold me, tangled close, skin to skin, quiet in the dark.

I tell myself this isn't a relationship. Not formally. We've dodged defining it for the past two weeks.

Still, it's something. Something magic as I trace the beautiful, brooding lines of his sleeping face, following the path the sunlight makes over his storming brow.

He stirs under my touch. This man doesn't wake up like most people, snuffling and groaning and yawning.

The way he wakes up is just another part of what makes him an animal: one moment he's still and quiet, the next he's stone-tense and flooded with this vibrant energy. It's like switching on the lights in a darkened room.

Instant alertness. Predatory and oh-so-ready to strike at any danger.

Like now. One blue eye snaps open, assesses me, before softening.

He catches my hand and turns his head to kiss my palm, stubble rasping over my skin.

"Morning," he rumbles. "You're actually awake."

"You overslept today." I can't hide my smile.

"Bull," he growls, though there's a touch of drowsy laughter in it. He rubs his cheek against my wrist, raising those little shivers I love. Goose-bump prickles every-where. "Guess I'll be skipping my morning swim."

"You still have time. You don't have to deal with Milah for a few more days."

"Mm. But if I go swimming..."

Suddenly, he's got a better idea for his wake-up ritual.

He's tumbling me onto my back, his naked body shifting gloriously over mine, taut-stretched and tawny and hard. His weight is hot as a furnace, burning into me.

Holy hell. There's nothing to protect me from him; nothing to shield me from how every inch of my body electrifies just being near him.

He pins me with his bulk, barely holding himself up on braced arms that strain to hold the heaviness of packed muscle, forearms drawn tight and veins ridging against his skin, his tattoos.

And when he presses against me, his rousing cock slides against my belly, slipping lower. Teasing me until I can't think of anything but wanting that feeling when he slides deep, takes me over, makes me wild.

"If I go swimming, Reb, I can't do this," he finishes, and leans down to capture my mouth, enveloping me fully in his stone-fire warmth. "We both know that'd be a damn shame. You're so fucking wet for me."

He strokes between my legs, winning a sharp moan from my mouth. His fingers are already dangerously familiar with my body. I whimper against him, bucking my clit into his hands, which pull back to a comfortable, teasing distance.

Good morning can't even cover this. My naked breasts crushed against his chest, my entire body vulnerable, twined, until I feel like a rabbit caught in the wolf's grasp.

And he consumes me – touching every inch of me, finding every place on my body that turns me from a woman into a lava flow of pure desire.

He's the only one who's ever known how to do this to me; how to possess me so utterly I just lose myself and can only cling to him for some kind of safe mooring. Always gasping for more as he traces me with his fingers, his tongue.

Sweet Jesus, his *tongue.*

If I thought he had a magic ability to light me up all kinds of ways with just the words bouncing off it, I've learned it isn't half of what he can do when it's against my skin.

Landon's mouth owns me. Leaves burning hot kisses

and angry little bite marks over my chest, my stomach, my hips, my thighs, then delves between my legs.

There, lost in my folds, is where he pulls me apart. Sharp, clutching pleasure comes as his tongue circles my clit, traces my labia, dips inside, drinks from me like every last drop he coaxes from my flesh will leave him intoxicated.

His mouth works my pussy to the brink. Expert teeth pull me apart with a growl, make my clit a willing prisoner for his tongue, all while his stubble leaves delicious burn marks on my thighs. I ride his face for all I'm worth, before I'm whimpering his name.

"Landon!" Oh, hell. "Landon, fuck!"

I can't.

I need to come on his face, if only he'd let me. But this man knows my own flesh better than me.

By the time he lifts me up, wraps my thighs around his waist, slides his cock deep inside my body, I'm ready to fly right off the edge. He takes me in slick, deep, rhythmic strokes that make my heart race and my blood burn like napalm, turning me into someone I don't know.

I'm not one of my heroines, wanton and sure of her sexuality.

I'm not this crazy, wild girl who becomes a complete sex addict for anyone – much less this beast shaped like a man who's swung my heart wild like a kettlebell for the past ten years.

I'm totally *not* surrendering every fiber of my being to Landon Strauss and all he's been: lover, hater, destroyer, protector, friend, foe, best and worst and final word.

But actually, when I'm stripped completely bare, shaking on his naked body, I can't deny the truth.

I am.

With him, I feel so much I can't escape it, can't deny it, can't control it – and I writhe with pure and utter abandon as he plunges deeper, harder, faster, pushing closer and closer to his end.

I watch that lost, tortured, beautiful expression taking over his face while he's holding me. I don't even know what pushes me over – his touch, his manic strokes, or the way he looks at me – all his human wilds tethered to me.

For me.

I just know that when my body goes tight around him, when he hits the perfect spot inside that makes my vision go white and my breaths turn ragged...

He's ruined me.

He's ruining me right now as he locks his arm tight, fisting my hair, growling his pleasure as he drives deep one more time and unloads his pleasure into mine.

He's ruined me forever.

He's ruined me for anyone else, and I'm gladly letting myself be torn apart.

* * *

HE'S ALSO MADE WALKING in a straight line difficult.

I should be used to this, after the last two weeks, but when I get up and try to follow him into the shower my legs are pure jelly and my spine feels like cooked spaghetti.

He knows it, too, judging from the smug look he keeps giving me. *Ass.*

But he's my *jerk-ass.*

185

Sort of.

I totter into the bathroom, and twenty minutes later, he's got to lift me out of the shower after pinning me against the wall. The man's libido is relentless. I can't show a flash of skin anymore if I don't want to be absolutely ravaged – and, of course, I do.

I'm trapped face-first against cool tile while hot spray pours down over us both and my voice rings off the shower walls. He's busy making these low, animalistic sounds against my back while he ruts against me, skin to slick skin, turning my depths into a swollen-soft mass of silk that thrills at every touch, every stroke, every vicious thrust.

I stand on the tips of my toes, rocking into him, enjoying the loud slap of his balls on my skin.

I don't last long. He fucks straight through my first orgasm and keeps on going, a tattooed train of a man. "Legs apart, Reb. Take it fucking deep for me," he whispers, thunder in his voice as he shifts my thighs open.

He holds me tighter as he pulls his pleasure from my body. My breasts sway, pendulums shaken by everything quintessentially Landon Strauss. I'm on the ledge in no time at all again, and this time, he falls with me.

The heat of his release burns into mine. I'm making sounds in the back of my throat I didn't know I could, milking his cock with everything I have. It blurs in the sweet delirium of him growling my name, his balls heaving everything into me.

Mercy.

I'm a wreck after, gasping and dizzy. He's gentle and tender and considerate. Wiping me off with a washcloth, letting me lean against him, wrapping me up in a cozy towel and carrying me from the shower into the bedroom.

I kind of hate him for *still* being able to stand after doing *that* to me.

Twice in a row.

Jerk-ass, again. I wish I could decide if it's an insult or a show of affection. Maybe both.

He's just setting me down on the bed when a rattle comes from downstairs, clattering and loud and a little too familiar.

Landon goes tense, eyes flashing as he stiffens with a growl.

"If that brat just came waltzing into my house again, I swear to Christ, Buddha, and Krishna..."

I groan, flopping back on the bed in a tangle of wet hair and damp towel. "I'm glad you're invoking all the major powers. Because, I don't exactly have the patience to deal with her right now."

"Too bad. Remember, you're my shield." He winks, setting me a little at ease, even if there's a tight edge to it. "Get dressed, Reb. Time to greet the company."

I give him a sour look and kick one foot out to push at him. Not that it does any good, landing on his rock-hard stomach and not even making him tilt.

He catches my foot, lifts it up in a way that spreads me pretty embarrassingly, and then he kisses my ankle – but his eyes aren't on my foot.

There's no doubting where he's looking, eyes glinting, that grin turning devilish. I squeak, yanking my foot back and drag the towel over me. His gaze leaves a delicious burn between my legs.

"Don't you even start!" I mutter, cut off by another clatter from downstairs. My heart jumps into my throat, remembering the intruder. "Ugh. I don't want her to hear us."

"So, you're possessive now? I'm liking the new you, Reb." He winks again, then sidesteps, dodging the pillow I throw at him, laughing.

It's like that the entire time we get dressed. Completely detached from the serious situation.

Teasing, stealing kisses, trying to be quick but fumbling over each other when we can't seem to keep our hands off each other or stop laughing.

But I manage to get my jellied legs into a pair of tight-fitting jeans and a button-up sleeveless shirt that shows off my C-cups more than I normally would, the top button undone. I keep my hair loose and shower-tumbled, spilling in wild waves all around me. I skip the glasses for now, tucking them into my pocket, even if it means a bit of a blur more than five feet in front of me.

Look, I'm not preening. Or showing off.

I just want Milah freaking Holly to get a really good look at what she thinks Landon *shouldn't* want.

And maybe I feel a little buzz in my veins when Landon slips his hand in mine before we head downstairs. He's already steeling himself, his expression blanking, shoulders and jaw tight.

His hand grips mine a little too hard, but it doesn't really hurt, and I don't want to pull him out of what's clearly a preparation for war. I just squeeze his fingers tighter, reminding him that I'm here, and square my own shoulders as we round the wall into the kitchen.

There's another shock waiting.

A tall, regal, graying woman stands at one of the open

cabinets, murmuring under her breath in a softly cultured accent while she meticulously organizes Landon's scattered dishware by color.

It's been years since I've seen her, but I recognize her air immediately.

Shirley Strauss.

Landon's mother.

My face blooms hot, and I let out a mortified squeak, letting go of Landon's hand and hastily buttoning the top button of my shirt over the small glimpse of my bra I'd let out.

Oh my God. Oh my God.

Of course, I try to play the vixen and the femme fatale and the smug not-quite-fake girlfriend, and so, *of course* I walk in boobs out on Landon's *mother.*

Wicked sense of humor doesn't describe what this universe has in store.

That squeak must've tipped her off, because she glances over her shoulder, brows lifting mildly. Her eyes are as blue as Landon's, but where his are all electric charge hers are more a still calm sea. She blinks at me, then smiles, warm and pleasant.

"McKenna?"

She's always used my full name. She comes toward me with her hands outstretched, moving fluidly despite the curious cats twining around her ankles like she's soaked her stockings in catnip.

Still blushing, I let her pull me into a hug, exchanging wide-eyed, half-amused, and half-horrified looks with Landon over her shoulder.

"Great to see you again, Mrs. Strauss," I murmur,

giving her a squeeze and then stepping back, edging to the side.

I feel like I'm in the way of a weird family reunion, but her entire attention stays on me.

"All I get is a hello and one awkward hug, young lady? I haven't seen you since you were still all knees and elbows, and I left the old neighborhood. You've grown up so lovely." She laughs, turning her gaze on Landon, one slim hand laying on his arm with a mother's gentle possessiveness. "Why didn't you tell me McKenna moved in for the summer, dear?"

Landon makes an embarrassed noise and shrugs. He's trying to look casual, but he just looks flustered, and I bite my lip on a smile. *Adorable.*

"It wasn't a big deal," he says, every bit the little boy in front of his mother.

"Oh, is *that* what you think?" Mrs. Strauss gives me a knowing look, her eyes glittering. "Some men wouldn't know what a big deal was if it landed right in their lap."

My blush turns volcanic. Are we so obvious?

Does she think we're a serious couple?

I glance at Landon, but he's gone kind of glassy with an easy, careful smile that says I'll get nothing out of him.

Of course not.

Because I'm still his pretend-girlfriend, and we're just playing house.

I don't even know what the expiration date on this is. *When he doesn't need someone to watch the house anymore? When I'm done with my novel?*

What are we even doing, other than screwing around and avoiding actually looking at ourselves head-on?

I don't get a chance to dwell on it any longer, though.

If Landon is a hurricane, then Mrs. Strauss is a gentle breeze, but she still moves things when she blows through.

And she manages to get us moving, fussing and fluttering around us the entire time with her graceful airs, to make breakfast. It's almost like old times.

Almost.

* * *

I WONDERED if Landon's mother would stay a few days, but no – she apparently has a habit now of surprising him for breakfast because he never calls home, too busy with Enguard.

Today was just another in a series of typically Shirley Strauss surprises.

She wheeled in for breakfast, charmed us entirely over omelets, and then wheeled out to get back to her life organizing charity work. I've never met anyone more gracious than Mrs. Strauss, and even with the awkwardness between me and Landon, there's still a kind of ease left in Mrs. Strauss's wake even after her departure.

But I can't get one thing off my mind.

I was loading the dishes in the dishwasher while Mrs. Strauss and Landon picked up out on the patio, and I'd caught wind of a conversation I probably shouldn't have heard. Turns out all these open spaces and white marble carry sound way too well.

"Now, Landon," Mrs. Strauss had said. "I've always known you needed a decent woman, but Kenna's a darling. Listen, son. It's easy to see how you've blossomed with her around. I've been so worried for you, with everything you've been through. But do be a dear and don't make a mess of this, *hm?*"

Landon mumbled something that sounded like he was back in little-boy mode, being chastised, which just set Shirley off laughing.

It left me flustered, nearly dropping the dishes, and brooding for long hours after.

Including now, as Landon and I linger on the upstairs deck, looking out across the water and drinking wine. It's too hot for anything else. Heavier liquor would just feel sickly in this sweltering heat, though I almost wish I was drunk enough for the courage to ask the things I *really* want to know.

We're leaning together on the deck swing, quiet and comfortable and taking in the silence.

I don't want to break it, but so many things are boiling up inside me.

If I won't ask him the serious questions, I can at least satisfy my curiosity. "Hey, Landon?"

He glances up from a distant contemplation of the waves, his gaze pensive, but clearing as he looks at me. "Yeah?"

"This morning..." I trail off, looking down, tracing my finger around the rim of my wine glass. "Your dad didn't come up. At all. I mean, not even the smallest mention. Do you not talk about him with your mom?"

He lets out a fierce grunt, and for a moment, I'm afraid he's about to lock up on me again.

Then he sighs. "She doesn't know," he rumbles. "Ma doesn't know a damn thing. I never told her about what Dad was up to. I couldn't. She'd already lost her husband. I couldn't let her lose her faith in him, too. But I don't like talking about him, either. I'm not polishing a dead man's corpse. Not when it's a lie. Even if I'll throw her a word or two about missing him once in a blue moon."

"Oh." I bite my lip, leaning harder into him. My heart sinks, hurting for him. "I'm sorry. I didn't mean –"

"Don't be." He shifts, draping his arm across my shoulders, gathering me against his side. "It's complicated, babe. Took me *years* to put together what my old man did. Sifted through a billion cold leads. Wherever drugs were mentioned in the media, close to where Crown ran security for warehouses and trade shows. Sniffed out his accomplices, too. His old partner, Reg, was in on all of it. And that's Reg's son running Crown Security, Dallas fucking Reese." He grinds his teeth.

I suppress a shiver. There's hatred in his voice, but it trails into resignation.

"Fuck, Kenna. It was easier to just bury everything. For myself, and for Mom. I wanted to just live my life, be a better man than he was. I was still struggling with that, the day you read my journal, after I'd vomited those thoughts down on paper."

But you think you're a monster with the strength to kill someone for vengeance, I think. *Even if I know that's not all you are.*

I settle into him, tucking my legs up and making myself small against his side. My hand curls against his chest. "I know what burying the hard stuff is like."

He smiles faintly, eyes softening. God, does he know I'm talking about the crush that never died?

Of course he knows.

It's like he's inside my head all the time.

Inside my heart.

Inside every beating chamber. And he captures my hand, then, lifts it from his chest to kiss my knuckles, before letting go to cup my cheek.

"No more," he says. "Life's too fucking short for hide and seek. Or for digging holes."

"No more," I repeat, nodding.

But I'm a liar.

Because I'm hiding right now, and refusing to face the enormity of this ten thousand ton feeling crouched over me like a demon waiting to strike.

XIV: HE AIN'T HEAVY, HE'S MY BROTHER (LANDON)

*B*eing with Kenna shouldn't be this comfortable. It's like there's a time bubble that exists around us. Long as I'm with her, I'm back in the days before I knew how terrible the world could be.

Before I knew what a piece of shit my father was. Before I knew how horrifying war was. Before I had to pull the trigger on ending lives with my own two hands in Iraq, killing for my country, my men, and sometimes just raw fucking survival.

Before I knew what I'm capable of, when so much blood is already steeped in my skin.

Being with Kenna lets me avoid facing that. It brings an eerie calm, this peace that says maybe, deep down, I could still be the man she thinks I am.

Maybe Old Landon isn't dead.

Maybe I could be someone who won't disappoint her, won't blow her heart to smithereens all over again.

But I know that's a lie.

I know what I am.

I know what I have to do.

These stolen moments are just a brief reprieve from the harshness of reality.

Nothing more.

I'm languishing in one such stolen moment, now. I only have a day left before I'm heading down to the Bay Area again to deal with Milah. I'm soaking up as much sun and as much Kenna as I can.

We'd dozed off on the patio last night, sprawled out under the clear bright sky on the outdoor lounger, and now I'm half-asleep, drowsing and lingering on how insanely good she feels in my arms.

I don't really want to wake up. I don't want to leave this woman. I don't want to push her away because all the bad shit puts me on my knees.

But the feeling of someone watching us puts me on high alert.

I hold completely still. Trained combat reflexes, everything I learned by fire not to let a potential enemy combatant know I'm awake and aware of their presence.

Carefully, I crack one eye open.

And then release an explosive, pent up sigh, opening both my eyes fully for the hell that's in front of me.

Steve. Sitting there on one of the patio chairs, watching us with a hangdog look.

"Jesus, Steve," I mutter.

Oh fuck. It's sinking in.

Steve. Here. Watching. Us.

And I'm here with Kenna in my arms.

I start scrambling up, but there's no use denying it now.

Shit! I sink back down in the lounger, while Kenna

stirs sleepily, burrowing into me in that kittenish way she has. I bump her with my elbow.

"Wake up, Reb."

"Nah...no...five more minutes..."

This is *not* the time for her to be this cute. "...you really want to wake up. We've got company. And he doesn't look too happy."

"Understatement of the year," Steve growls, his voice tight.

I haven't seen him look this pissed since we lost our last game of football Senior year.

His voice doesn't match. Mostly, it sounds dejected. Worse than pissed off.

At the sound of his voice, Kenna stiffens. Her eyes go wide, and she turns a slow, dread-filled look over her shoulder – only to scramble upright, prying away from me, skittering to the other side of the lounger.

That shouldn't sting, but it does. The truth is out.

It's too late.

Rejecting me now won't really help.

She stares, frozen, between me and Steve, then stammers, "I-it's not what you think..."

"Don't. Please, Kenna," Steve interjects quietly. "You already lied to me once. Can't stand it again."

That stark, heavy look in his eyes – fuck. I'd expected anger.

I hadn't expected the open, naked betrayal on his face, or how deep it cuts me as he continues, "Melanie found the condom. You should've been more careful." His jaw clenches. "Or, hey, maybe you both could've just told me the fucking truth instead of sneaking around behind my back, screwing around on my property.."

I close my eyes, dragging a heavy palm over my face.

Getting caught before breaking the news to my best friend was always a risk. I hadn't expected to feel this fucking guilty.

I don't want to feel this guilty, and it makes me snarly, though I try to rein it in. "I thought you'd be angry, and you should be," I mutter. "Don't be mad at Kenna. I lied to you, Steve. She just went along with it. We haven't talked about it since."

"Yeah. Communication isn't your strong point," Steve whispers flatly. "So, you're telling me you'd rather I never trusted you again than deal with me being annoyed?"

"I didn't know it'd stop at annoyed!"

"Of course you didn't," Steve bites off. "Because apparently you don't know me, and I don't know you anymore, Landon. I love you like a brother. I love Kenna. Why the fuck would I be upset with you for being together? Why couldn't you trust me?" That hurt in his eyes hardens. He's hitting me like bullets, peeling me open in the way only screwing over my oldest friend can. "That's not why I'm up in your face," he growls, coming closer.

I never thought this man had an intimidating bone in his body, but here he is: up close, eyes wide, drilling my betrayal into me. He pauses, shaking his head. "I'm not pissed off because you're with my sister. I'm *livid* because you couldn't come clean with me, when I'm practically the only real friend you've got."

Fucking ouch. It stings because it isn't wrong. At Enguard, I have co-workers. Associates. Employees. Steve's the only one who's stayed with me through thick and thin. Only one local, too. I keep in touch with a few of my hardass military buddies like Gabe, but they just knew me under the stress of battle. Steve knows who I was, and what I've become.

He's talking again. "Because you can't trust anyone, right? Not since Micah died. So you just treat everyone like they're the enemy."

"That's not fair," Kenna cuts in. "You don't know what Landon's been going through –"

"You're right," Steve answers. "I don't. Because Landon never trusted me enough to tell me. I've put my faith in him all these years only to find out he can't even trust me enough to tell me how he feels about my sister." His fists clench and unclench. "How *do* you feel about my sister? Do you at least trust her, or are you just using her, too?"

Too much.

I know I've been a prick these past few years and Steve doesn't really have any reason to believe in my character, but I can't sit here while he cuts holes into me with the reminders of all the ways I've fucked up – until even the people I love the most can't trust a single word I say, because I'm too damaged and broken to ever trust them.

I thrust to my feet, fists clenched tight enough that my nails dig into my palms. "Fuck this. Ask her, why don't you. Rather than talking about her like she's not here. I'm out."

Steve never moves. Kenna stands, pushing herself between us. Her hand rests on my arm, a reminder of that soft warmth that's been broken, dashed to pieces at my feet.

"Landon, don't go," she pleads, then turns to her brother, stepping toward Steve. "Please, just...just...I'm sorry. I know we should've told you the truth, but it happened on impulse. We were caught off guard. We meant to tell you everything, we just didn't have enough —"

"Time?" Steve cuts in. "Two weeks isn't impulse, Kenna. You had plenty of time to tell me."

Steve looks like we've broken something in him.

Fuck, this is so wrong.

This is all my fault. I didn't mean to fix the rift between me and Kenna only to create one between her and her brother.

If I have to lose Steve, I'll deal with the consequences, but I can't be the reason for a break between brother and sister.

But before I can say anything, Kenna says, "We did. But we were...we were..." She shakes her head, losing the words. "I can't say what we were, really. But it was selfish. Just give us a chance to explain. Please."

"Not now," Steve says, his voice cracking. "I can't even look at you. It's bad enough you lied to me, Kenna. But you." His gaze transfers to me. "I kept giving you chance after chance, Landon. All these years of you thrusting me away. Of you lashing out. And I kept saying you just needed time. You'd be okay. You'd sort your crap out. You just needed us to be here for you." He swallows hard. "And you just shat all over that because you couldn't tell me the truth." He shakes his head, stepping back. "I can't be here right now. I just can't."

And then he's walking away. Kenna makes a forlorn sound and starts after him, then stops.

She stares helplessly between us. I should go to her, comfort her, but right now I feel like if I do I'll just poison this more. Poison her because I'm fucking toxic.

And if Steve can't be here right now, then neither can I.

I turn and walk away. I need to prep for the job, need to pack my car, need to do anything but keep standing here, wallowing in the guilt that's eating me inside like black fire.

The fuck do I have to feel guilty for? It's my fucking private life. Not Steve's. It's not his business who I'm sleeping with, or who Kenna is either.

But I know I'm making excuses. No matter how hard I stomp, how rough I try to shove it out of my head, I can't get that look of his out of my brain.

I storm into the garage, practically seeing red. There's a twinge inside me telling me I'm just using anger to hide, but fuck it, it's worked for me before.

I start throwing my gear together, stuffing it into cases and duffel bags. A few moments later, soft footsteps trail after me. Kenna stands in the door of the garage, a dark shape backlit by outdoor sunlight, her eyes nearly glowing in shadow, shining wet.

"Landon?"

I say nothing. Just rip the trunk of the car open and shove one of my kits inside. If I talk to her right now I don't know what'll come out of me, but it won't be good.

Everything's all fucked up.

I'm fucked up, if I ever thought anything like this could be for me.

I'm a bastard. An exile. Alienated from everyone who ever tried to care.

A monster who can't trust, and who can't be trusted.

Reb, she's better off without me.

And I have no time left to fix this fucking mess, not with this goddamned job breathing down my neck.

"Landon, please talk to me!"

No. I've got the words stitched up inside me to keep their ugliness from spilling all over her. I shake my head tightly, throw another bag in the trunk, and slam it shut.

I have to go.

Have to take myself away before I do something explosive, something that could hurt her the way I hurt her years ago.

She makes a frustrated sound, as I move around the garage gathering the last of my shit. Then she snaps, "So, what? This is it? You're just gonna shut me out and run *again?*"

That's exactly what I'll do. The only scenario that doesn't end with me destroying her a second time.

When I don't answer, she forges on, her voice growing thick. I don't have to look at her to know she's close to crying. That's the kind of asshole I am. Even my love hurts, damages, destroys.

Melodramatic? It's fucking true. And the evidence is right in front of me, a gorgeous green-eyed girl who worked magic on my body, mind, and soul, coming apart because I didn't have the balls to come clean with Steve.

"Landon...I'm not going to let you do this again. Not after the last two weeks. Go ahead, you asshole. Try it. You can turn right back into that hollow, numb shell of a man again, but I won't believe it for a second. Won't believe you're a monster, even if you try to convince me. I'm not going anywhere, and I'm not running from you. Not anymore."

I jerk the door to the Impala open. I let myself look at

her one last time, standing silhouetted with her hair a wild mess of beautiful tangles and her face still lit with every bit of passion and fury welling inside her.

She's beautiful. She's perfect. She's kind. She's wonderful.

And she's not for me.

No one who believes in someone else this much should ever have to deal with someone as fucked up as me.

"The cats will appreciate the company," I bite off. I know it's cruel. I know it's harsh. But I need her to let me go.

Just like how I tell myself I have to let her go, when I shove myself into the car and only give her a second to skitter out of the way before I'm backing out, peeling down the drive, refusing to look at the hurt, angry look on her face in the rear-view mirror.

But as I tear down the highway, fingers gouging lines in the steering wheel, I wonder.

What the fuck is wrong with me, that the only way I can think of to save her is to hurt her – and to ruin myself?

XV: HATE TO LOVE YOU (KENNA)

*I*f life were a book I was hate-writing, this would be the point where the intrepid, bespectacled heroine realizes her hero is actually the villain, and suddenly realizes she'd be better off in a monastery.

Yes, I do that sometimes. When I get frustrated with story dead ends, I have my characters hang it up and do the craziest things, before they come back to their senses.

Seriously, I'm about to hang up my hat, become a nun, and give up on Landon Strauss, because I'd bet you the advance on my next book that the ascetic life would treat me nicer than that asshole hypocrite I've fallen far too deeply for.

Too bad I'm not super religious.

I sprawl on the patio alone, stretched out on a wicker sofa with Mews perched on the sofa's arm above me, tail flicking down over my nose. Velvet snuggles up against my thighs in the nook made by my bent legs. My notebook is closed, propped on my stomach after a morning of hate-writing some of the best conflict I've ever penned.

Probably because it's coming from a place of very real, very personal fury.

I never thought Landon would end up being my muse in all the best and worst ways, but at least I'm getting this book done.

I blow out heavily, making a rude sound with my lips and ruffling the fur of Mews' tail. He makes a disgruntled noise, until I poke at his tail with the capped tip of my pen. Narrowing his eyes, he twists to bat at it, while I feint it in and out. Watching the cat play mighty hunter without ever uncurling from his perch is the first time I've smiled since Landon went storming away yesterday morning.

"Why's your Daddy such an asshole, baby?" I ask, and gently boop Mews' nose with the pen. His little eyes cross and I chuckle. "At least you're as nice as you look."

Yep. I'm gonna be a stereotype.

The writer with ten cats, no boyfriend, but one hell of an active fantasy sex life in my books.

If I'm honest, the cats are the only reason I'm still here – and not just because of that nasty parting shot Landon made.

I can't leave Velvet and Mews to fend for themselves, even if it aches to haunt this house where we spent two solid weeks making fire, making rain, making storms of the elements until we were thunder and earthquakes, wind and trembling flames, and the heartbeat of everything wild.

I've exiled myself back to the guest bedroom, and tend to either stay there or out here on the patio.

They're the only two places we hadn't fucked yet. The only places where I can't remember the taste of him and feel his rough hands on my body. He made me feel special, for a little while. Made me feel loved.

And then he thrust me out into the cold again, cutting me off and destroying everything between us once more.

At least the bastard is consistent.

Even if this time, he's the one who ran away.

I think I'm going to be gone, the day he's scheduled to come back. Make sure the boys are fed and taken care of, then make myself scarce. I can't stand to see Landon again. I feel numb, right now.

Numb I can handle.

I can't handle the stab of pain that's going to hit me when he walks in this house and looks right through me like he doesn't even know my name.

My eyes well sharply, flinching at the vision. *Fuck.*

So much for numbness. I can't do this. I've already messed up the new pages I'm writing, blurring ink with big wet splotches soaking through the paper.

"You don't look so good," a voice interrupts, jolting my heart into a startled little leap.

I scream.

The cats bolt.

Mr. Hoodie flashes in my head before I even look up.

Velvet catches the back of my thigh with a hind paw as he launches off the sofa, raking a burning scratch down my skin. I yelp, clutching at my thigh, sit up sharply, and crash my forehead right into my brother's.

Pain hits me like I'm a ringing bell, my brain rattling inside my skull. I drop back down to the sofa, crashing against the cushions.

Steve had been leaning over the back of the sofa, but now he reels backward, swearing, clutching at his reddened forehead. I'm not much better, hissing under my breath and rubbing at my brow.

"Jesus, Kenna," he mutters, squinting one eye open. "I *know* you're mad, but that's no reason for assault and battery."

"You startled me!" Wincing, I push myself up on one arm. "Why'd you sneak up on me like that?"

He looks sheepish. "Guess I thought if you saw me coming, you'd lock yourself in the house and refuse to talk to me."

"Why would I do that?"

"You don't remember how we fought after I broke your Etch-A-Sketch?" He tries a smile, though it's tired and strained. "Mom made me apologize, but when I tried, you ran away. Locked yourself in your room and wouldn't talk to me."

I scowl. "I was *eight.*"

"I'm just saying, people have patterns. Sometimes set in stone."

"You're not cute." With a grimace, I shift to sit upright. My head is throbbing and my thigh burns, and I twist to peer at the underside, where Velvet left a deep, bleeding scratch from the back of my knee to the hem of my shorts from being startled. "Actually, every time you show up, I get hurt."

Steve's silence says that stung hard, and drove deep. Low blow, maybe.

I close my eyes, cursing at myself. I must be taking lessons from Landon: how to hurt the people you love in twelve easy words.

Except I'm pretty sure Landon never loved me, and never will.

I'm not hanging my star on him anymore. Or hoping for the impossible.

Opening my eyes, I make myself look at Steve's hurt, kicked-puppy face, sighing. "I didn't mean that," I say, pushing my feet into my sandals before standing and tossing my head toward the house. "Let me get some alcohol on this so it won't get infected, and get us both some Advil. Then we'll talk."

Right now, it feels weird for me to be the one leading the situation, with Steve.

All our lives, he's always been the first out of the gate with everything. Not exactly a natural leader type, more like he's just so effusive he goes charging in with total enthusiasm and tends to take the lead in situations without even meaning to. Having him trailing in my wake, subdued and quiet, while I dig some alcohol out of the bathroom cabinet and wipe myself down before passing a bottle of Advil between us?

It's weird, and makes me feel like I really did kick a puppy, and it's afraid I'll do it all over again.

I know that's the guilt talking.

The sour realization I lied to my brother, that I made him feel so shut out and betrayed because I was so wrapped up in Landon. I wasn't thinking about anything but us, and what *I* wanted.

I think the term, when a heroine ignores everyone she cares about for a man, is *dickmatized.*

God, writing my books is so much more fun than living them.

* * *

AFTER I'M DONE PATCHING us up, I settle us in the kitchen with tea.

It's tense, quiet. I'm upset with him. He's upset with me.

Suddenly, that innate sibling understanding we've always had is a curse rather than a blessing. It's so easy for us to read all the simmering emotions between us – easy enough to know neither of us wants to touch them and possibly kick off an explosion.

But finally, I exhale into my tea, blowing a cloud of steam, and mutter, "You first."

He cracks a smile. "I was gonna wait you out."

"I don't like meaningful silences, or soggy middles."

"Sis, I'm never going to completely get your weird literary references." He groans, propping his elbows on the kitchen island, looking at me frankly. "So. Landon."

I shrug tightly. "No Landon anymore."

A wince wrinkles his brow. "That bad?"

"I don't want to talk about it."

"You sure?" Steve shakes his head. "Look, I don't think you should be here if he's hurting you, Kenna."

"He's not –" I break off. I can't get the lie out.

Because Landon *did* hurt me, but it wasn't hard to see that under his vicious counterattack, he was hurting, too. Lashing out.

Damn it, why am I defending him when he broke my heart *again?*

I divert, pressing my lips together. "Is that what you came here to tell me? That I should leave?"

"Something like that."

"I don't understand. Landon's your best friend."

"And I've been around him a lot more than you have

over the past few years. I've seen things you haven't, Kenna." Steve reaches across the island, offering his hand. "Just hear me out, sis. You owe me that much."

I wince.

I owe him an apology for lying, but I'm not ready to get it out past my pride just yet when part of me still blames him for bursting the idyllic bubble Landon and I were living in. It's not wholly Steve's fault, of course. Something would've stepped between us sooner or later, and brought out just how wrong we were.

Wrong for each other.

I have to tell myself that until I believe it, or I'll never tape the pieces of my heart back together.

But Steve is still waiting with that outstretched hand, and after a moment, I sag and slip my fingers into his. Even if I'm this tangle of anger and guilt inside, I can never quite turn him down when he's offering the comfort of a large, warm, steady hand wrapped around mine.

"Okay," I say. "I'm listening. Go."

He hesitates, then starts, "Don't get me wrong. I love Landon like a brother. Never thought that'd be so close to almost literal, but it's true." He squeezes my hand, stroking his thumb reassuringly over my knuckles, but it's hard to take comfort when he continues, "There's something different in him now. Something dangerous. It's like this dark seed was planted when his old man died, and it's been growing and spreading its roots through him for years ever since. I thought he'd come back. Kept hoping he'd find his way free from it...but it feels like it's the only thing holding him together now. And while I want to believe that the man I love like my brother is in there, that darkness will always come first. You have to know that, sis. And I'll be damned if I want to see you get hurt while Landon's busy destroying himself."

I swallow thickly, my throat tight. There's too much truth in his words. So much I try to deny, to deflect. "That's a cruel thing to say about someone you care about."

"But I care about you, too. I can care about *both* of you enough to see you'll only destroy each other. For Landon, you're too tangled up in that darkness riding him." He sighs. "I just don't want to see you hurt. Him, either. And I don't want you to get dragged down with him."

I yank my hand back. I don't know why this is upsetting me. Maybe because he's right, but I don't want to believe it. I can't.

"I know him," I say. "I do. Maybe better than you, if all you can see is this 'dark seed' and not who he really is. He's more than his demons, Steve." I wrap my arms around myself, squeezing tight. "I know he's dealing with things poorly. You're right. But I know why, too. And I think if we give him a chance, he'll fight his way through. I have faith in him, even if you don't."

The look Steve gives me is almost pitying. "Enough faith to stay? Even when he doesn't want you to?"

I feel like a balloon that's been punctured, sagging. I press my trembling lips together. "We had a fight. We'll talk it out when he gets back. If I run..."

If I run, then what?

I'll be proving Steve right.

Even worse, I'll be proving *Landon* right.

That he's beyond redemption. Not worth someone

willing to wait for him, fight with him, fight for him, believe in him.

No, I can't save Landon from himself.

But I can be loyal enough to be there for him while he finds his way to the light.

I can remind him who he really is, and what he isn't. That he's not a man who would murder someone in cold blood.

But I can't tell Steve that. I can't tell him what I read in Landon's journal that day, or what Landon confessed to me.

He'd go into full-on protective mode, from Labrador to Rottweiler, and try to drag me away from the cold-blooded murderer. Maybe he'd be right to, but I can't believe that. I can't give up on Landon just yet.

"I can't run," I finish. "Steve, I know you're upset with me. I'm sorry we lied. We were seriously just riding on this high of a new thing and not thinking. It wasn't that we didn't trust you, we were just drunk on ourselves. Being young and stupid and wrapped up in each other. I know you're looking out for me. I know what Landon is, and how hard it is dealing with him. But you've got to let me decide this for myself."

Steve just watches me in silence, his brows knit together, his eyes dark with worry. I feel like he's still seeing the girl I used to be, awkward and nerdy and always hiding behind his status as that popular football player everyone loved for his easy nature. He's always been my buffer, deflecting so much of the cruelty people hurled my way.

But I can't hide behind him anymore.

I need to handle Landon Strauss myself.

And it's then I realize I can't be gone when he comes home.

No matter how much I want to run away. I told him he couldn't chase me off, and I'd meant that as a promise. Now, I have to fulfill it.

I won't be yet another person who lets Landon down, when so many have before.

Especially when he feels like he's let himself down plenty.

Steve watches me with his eyes dark and haunted and sorrowful, a low sigh escaping his lungs. "Damn. Guess I can't change your mind, then?"

I shake my head. "No. I..." I bite my lip. "Maybe you should go. I've said enough. Agree to disagree, and I don't want to fight anymore. I'm sorry we lied, but you had no right to come barging in like that, either. We're adults. What happens between us is between us, you know."

I know it's cold. But I need to shut this conversation down or I'm going to break and lose my resolve.

And if I break in front of Steve, he'll never let up. He'll try to convince me to leave with him, get out, while the going is good.

He just stares at me, his gaze oddly flat, though it's not hard to see he's still hurt. It's not hard to see that he can tell, too, that I hurt him on purpose to push him back to the other side of the invisible boundary of thorns around me.

What the hell am I doing?

Maybe Landon and I really are right for each other.

Sometimes, I'm more like him than I want to admit.

Steve shrugs, slipping off the barstool, moving slowly, like he's nursing an injury. "Whatever," he says, voice quiet and empty. "I'll go, sis. It's your life. If that's how you want to be about it, fine. But be careful, Kenna. You can't trust Landon."

"*You* can't trust Landon. Maybe I can." I shake my head. "I don't understand how you can have so little faith in him. How would you feel if it was our father killed?"

"Look, I loved the hell out of Micah Strauss like a second dad myself. You don't see me acting like Landon."

"You have no freaking reason to beat yourself up!" I flare. "Landon does. He's been carrying that inside him for so long. I saw Micah right before he was killed. So did Landon. When those men rushed him and his crew into their cars and –"

"What?" Steve stills, his blank expression turning bewildered. "What're you talking about, Kenna? Micah was alone when he died. It was in all the papers. Police report confirmed it, I remember."

I blink. "But I *remember.* All those black cars. It was his whole team, a bunch of men in suits. They went rushing out. I watched them through the window as they pulled out of the driveway, and I remember seeing Landon standing in the door of their house. And then...and then no one saw Micah again. Not until they found his body."

Steve blinks. "You're sure you aren't mixing that up with one of your stories?"

"That's cold, Steve." My ears burn; my jaw sets tight. "Screw you. I know what I saw."

"If you say so." He holds his hands up. "Jesus, I'm not starting a new fight with you when we're still not done with the old one. Can't change what happened years ago, anyway."

"Maybe we're not done with the fight, but I think I'm done talking to you right now."

He sighs, shoulders sagging. "Yeah. Sure. Just…"

"Just *what?*"

But Steve only shakes his head mournfully. "I'll talk to you later, Kenna. Maybe when we're both ready to forgive each other for being jackasses."

I don't say anything. I feel too messy right now, and he's right.

We're both being jackasses. Both too spiky, too defensive, just now.

But I have to look away, because I can't stand to watch my brother walk away the same way Landon did.

For the longest time, I stay there. Curled up on the barstool, propping my feet against the edge and hugging my legs to my chest.

I can't shake the last bit of our conversation.

Digging through my memories feels like trying to remember the plot of a book I read years ago.

I *know* what I saw, don't I? My memory's pretty good, and I can still see it.

The strained, urgent look on Micah's face. The grim men in suits around him, many of them in sunglasses that turned them all nearly identical, so that in my memory they're all just copies of the same man.

Except one. I remember a scar on the back of his hand, that hand curled just a little too tight against Micah Strauss' shoulder, guiding him into the back of a large black Escalade.

And Landon. Standing in the door helplessly, this darkness and confusion hovering over his brow, the first shadow of that dark seed waiting to take root. His father yelled something back at him. It had to be something like "stay!"

I hadn't realized it then, but I was looking into the future then. Head-on at the man Landon would become.

I don't feel right.

Something sticks with me, and it's making me sick. Just like something else, the story about the fire at the beach house doesn't add up.

This mysterious pile of brush that shouldn't have been there...but it's somehow just an accidental fire.

The men who were with Micah Strauss, but who mysteriously were never mentioned anywhere.

Something vile chews away inside me, and I'm trying to find just the right place to click the edges together and make this little logic puzzle make sense.

I'm not sure what I'm thinking, but it's ugly. Scary. Suspicious.

And I'm not sure what drives me outside into the fading sunlight, but I want to have another look at the beach house.

Obviously, I'm no forensics investigator. I don't even write crime fiction.

But I'm learning to trust my instincts, and my instincts say we missed *something* about that fire.

My heart drums too loudly in my chest as I cross the grass to the beach house. My palms are tingling and sweaty. I think some part of me expects another shadowy figure to come crashing out of the trees, and this time there'll be no Dallas here to sweep out of nowhere and save me.

My entire body hums, adrenaline drunk, on high alert.

The beach house is the same, with large tarps strung over the burned-out areas of the roof. I circle the house slowly, taking in the scorch marks up the sides, the bubbled and blistered paint. Where the worst of the damage is, an entire black-edged section of the house has been chewed away.

There's a pile of ash near the wall, the remnants of a few twigs in it. Obviously poked and raked through by the firefighters.

It looks almost like the remnants of a bonfire, almost too perfectly placed.

Like it was set intentionally.

I can't breathe. Every time I try, it kind of bounces off my lungs. My chest is tight, my pulse frantic, and I rub at my chest as I lift my head, looking around, wide-eyed and throwing sharp looks everywhere.

The beach house is almost fully surrounded by open space. So, how could someone get up here to set a fire without being seen? There's only a small wall of bushes leading out into the trees and –

Wait. *The bushes.*

The bushes with their branches broken out in one place, as if someone had forced through them on a path from the trees to the house.

Don't go back there, a voice screams in the back of my head.

This isn't a horror novel. I already tempted fate by being That Heroine once, and got a face full of Milah Holly's crotch for my troubles. I won't be so 'lucky' a second time.

I push forward into the bushes.

Don't. Go. Back. There.

Branches scratch at my arms. Cool, waxy leaves slide against my skin.

I squeeze through the bushes. The shadows of the trees fall over me. When I break out of the hedge, my feet sink into soft, squelching mud. I freeze, looking down.

The earth under the shade of the trees looks damp and muddy, without the sun to dry away the dew and occasional light summer shower. I'm in up to the soles of my feet, the flats of my sandals disappearing into the mud, cold slickness clinging to my skin. It feels just like the dread-film clinging to my heart.

Because my footprints aren't the only ones here.

Clear prints mark a path through the mud, leading across a clearing half encircled by trees, the rest by the hedge, except for a break that leads across a little slope of scrub brush down to the service road near the house.

Even as I stare, wide-eyed and frozen, a truck goes trundling along the dusty road, its low engine whine reaching up to me. It's only maybe a hundred feet down the slope from the break in the trees to the road.

And there's a cigarette stub stuck in the mud, half-crushed in one of those footsteps.

Holy shit. *Holy shit.*

My brain's on panic overdrive, stumbling over itself wildly.

I finally see it.

I can see it in my mind's eye, a car parked on the edge of the unlit service road, probably black to blend into the shadows. There'd be no one to notice so late at night.

It's almost too easy. Just creep up the slope, gathering scrub and twigs along the way, dry sere grass and fallen branches perfect to start a fire in this heat. Slip through the hedges. Light the blaze.

Then vanish, no one the wiser.

It's so clear it's almost real.

Gasping, I stumble forward, slogging through the mud, then breaking free onto the grass, ducking through the trees, tumbling down the slope. I don't know what I'm thinking I'm going to find. Tire tracks, maybe, peeling out at high speed and leaving a stain of black rubber. A dropped wallet, like it would be that easy.

What I find, instead, is a discarded gas can, tossed to one side behind the guard rail on the road.

I stop, staring down at it. It's new. Not dusty or faded or old, so it can't have been out here for long. A little battered, but that's it.

I nudge it carefully with my toe, not wanting to contaminate evidence with my fingerprints, and something sloshes inside. A few last drops of gasoline.

Oh. My. God.

Landon was right. Someone's out to get him. Someone tried to.

Maybe someone who knows he's looking for his father's killer. Maybe someone tied into all the bad things Micah Strauss was tangled up in from the past.

Maybe someone who wants to take Landon out next.

I don't know what to do. Call the police?

No. They'll just ignore me because it's not my house, and think I'm just some weirdo making up conspiracies. I've got to tell Landon.

And Landon won't pick up his fucking phone.

Even as I stumble back through the brush toward the main house, snapping photos on my phone the whole way, I'm dialing his number between shots, calling again and again and getting his voicemail over and over. Fuck my life.

I can't believe he's being a stubborn asshole. Even if he's planning to ignore me, he can't ignore this.

"Landon, pick up," I snap to his voicemail. "This is *important*. Not about us. It's about the fire."

Then I hang up and stop outside the house, breathing hard.

Dammit. I left my car at Steve's place. But there's another car in the garage, a big black SUV, a lot like the one I saw Micah Strauss getting into. Despite being a newer model, it gives me an awful sense of foreboding.

I don't care. I don't have the time.

I guess I'm stealing Landon's backup. I find the keys on the hook, scrape the mud off my shoes, and only take a moment to leave food and water for the cats, lock up the house, and grab my wallet before I'm scrambling behind the wheel of a vehicle that's much too big for me.

I go lurching out of the garage. Don't know why I can't wait for Landon to get home. But I can't. It's too important.

Call it a woman's built-in intuition, instinct, or a sign from above, but I just know I've got to go to him.

Even if he won't talk to me, I'll make him listen.

Because a sick, scared feeling in the pit of my stomach tells me that fire was just the beginning.

XVI: EVER SHIFTING GROUND
(LANDON)

I don't think I've ever hated my life as much as I do this exact moment.

I've walked away from Kenna.

Forcibly shoved her away from me, to the point where I've been refusing to pick up her calls all night. Ruined my relationship with the last friend who ever had any faith in me. Plus, I'm stuck working with fucking Dallas on the worst job of my career.

And the poison cherry on top is that I currently have a very naked, very insistent, probably extremely high Milah Holly pressed against me, backing me against the wall of her private backstage dressing room.

Even if my dick wasn't still leashed to that maddening little kitten I left behind, I wouldn't have touched Milah with a ten-foot pole. She's my anti-type.

She's snotty. She's entitled. She's a professional liability. And she apparently missed the "no means no" sexual harassment seminar in high school, because the only thing keeping her from unzipping my pants and hopping

221

on my dick is my hands around her wrists, pushing her away to arm's reach.

My phone's ringing in my back pocket for the fiftieth time tonight, vibrating against my ass, but I'm too busy right now to go for it.

"Cut it the fuck out," I snarl. "I'm not playing, Miss Holly. I'm here to do my job, the one you hired me for. That's it. Don't make this hard for both of us."

She smirks in this weird, sloppy way. If she's not high, she's definitely drunk. "I bet it's already hard, Landy. C'mon, why're you still pretending you don't like me?"

"Not pretending," I grunt firmly. "I'm your employee. Not your fuck toy."

She tries to sway closer, angling between the tangle of our arms, but I persistently push back out of her reach, keeping a tight but careful grip on her wrists.

Like fuck I'm going to accidentally mark her up just to defend myself, if she thinks she's touching me, I swear to Christ...

She lets out a soft little whine, jiggling her body purposefully as she strains against my grasp, like she thinks this is some kind of cute little game.

I just wait, refusing to let her closer, until she gives up and relaxes after a last frenzied minute of straining pulls and slumps.

"C'mon, Landon. This isn't cute."

"I'm not trying to be cute. I'm trying to keep you off me."

She sucks in a soft, offended breath, then gives me a flutter-lashed, sulky look. "You really don't want me?"

"No."

For a split second she actually looks hurt. I hate to be

cruel, but I'm hoping it's finally sinking in. Even if there's part of me screaming in the back of my mind – *so you can give a shit for Milah's feelings, but you're gonna hurt Kenna?*

Sure. Milah signs my paychecks.

Kenna needs to stay away from me for her own good.

She's so wrong.

I'm not just a monster, I'm a shitty person.

Milah grimaces at me. This time her sulking is real, her look wounded but oddly vulnerable. "Shit. You're serious, aren't you? You're, like, serious about that plain little girl pretending to be your girlfriend. You actually love someone like *her.*"

The fact that I bristle at the implied insult to Kenna before I bristle at that fucking question tells me an answer I don't want to face.

It hits like a slug to the gut, and I can't speak. *I won't.*

I'm not going to bare myself to this wretched little brat when I can't even face those things myself. But it says a lot that even with a naked woman millions would give their left nut to fuck trying to rub herself against me, all I can think about is Kenna.

So much that I'm imagining her voice.

"Landon?"

Not my imagination.

Kenna's actually here.

Why the fuck is Kenna *here?*

My head whips up, heart booming like a cannon, just in time to see her stumbling through the door with one of the guards reaching for her arm. She's a mess – her arms and legs scratched, her sandals caked in mud, her feet filthy. She's sweaty, disheveled, her hair a tangled mess falling half out of its tail.

She's never looked more beautiful.

And I've never looked like a bigger ass than I do with a naked Milah practically in my arms.

Kenna staggers to a halt, staring between us, her eyes wide and wounded, like shattered green glass threatening to let her hurt seep through the cracks.

Fuck! I know exactly how this looks.

I open my mouth to protest, but my boy, James, leans around the door, reaching for her arm again.

"Miss –"

"Let her go," I snarl, then follow my own advice and drop Milah's wrists like I've been burned. Kenna snaps that recriminating gaze to me, her mouth trembling, but before I can say anything else Milah lets out a huffy, annoyed sound.

"Don't even start," Milah snaps. She stands there brazenly naked, cocking her weight on one hip, and folds her arms over her burgeoning plastic chest. "Look, the last thing I need to deal with is a tantrum from the C-cup he just ditched me for."

Kenna trains her glare at Milah. "Excuse the fuck out of you?"

"I mean get over it, Plain Jane." Milah scowls. "God, you're dense. He doesn't want me. So don't start no shit, won't be no shit. You're lucky, okay? Really fuckin' lucky! The only thing he's been thinking about is you, you, and – oh yeah – *you*. He turned *me* down. For you. Can you believe it? Because I still can't."

Kenna just stands there, a sort of dumbstruck, blank expression on her face.

I know just how she feels. Hell, I'm frozen, too, my tongue swollen thick in my mouth, my gut in knots and my hands itching to reach for her, shake her, hold her, touch her, shove her away. All my conflicted feelings rammed together simultaneously.

Meanwhile, here's Milah Holly, baring my goddamned soul for me like it's hers to give.

Milah gives us both almost pitying looks.

There's something weird in her expression. Her eyes are wet, her face crestfallen, and suddenly instead of the little-girl act there's just a little girl someone broke a long time ago, who's been trying to find someone to tell her she's worth something ever since.

Suddenly, I can see Milah for who she really is, and deep down I'm glad I made the choice to protect her even if she's still an ungrateful little shit.

Fuck. These thoughts aren't like me.

I blame Kenna. For showing up and turning my world upside down.

But we're both just standing there, wordless, and Milah lets out an exasperated sigh, a watery smile trembling her lips. "You're both so stupid," she says, then reaches out and pokes Kenna in the forehead. "Don't let him go, okay? This stuff, with him...it's special, C-cup. Fucking annoying, but special. You can't buy real these days."

Kenna stands frozen a moment longer, eyes crossing on Milah's manicured finger, before a grit-toothed smile crosses her lips. She snaps her hand around Milah's wrist and pries her back.

"Touch me again," Kenna says through her teeth, "and I end you."

Then she lets go of Milah's wrist, her fixed expression gentling. "But thanks, lady."

It's Milah's turn to blink, disbelieving, before she goes red through her makeup and looks away with a flustered "*Hmph.* Whatever, Plain Jane."

She turns in a toss of her hair, blonde tail nearly lashing Kenna in the face, and saunters off to snag a robe and pull it on, finally covering her naked body.

"Work your shit out," she tosses over her shoulder, settling at her vanity. "You can thank me later."

"Even when she's being sweet, she's cocky," Kenna grumbles under her breath, finally snapping the confused spell of silence.

"Part of her charm," I growl, then shake my head. "What are you doing here, Reb?"

I can't even be angry. I'm too confused. This doesn't make a lick of sense.

I should be shouting at her, chasing her off again, but I still can't shake the trembling feeling when that question of do I love her hits me right in the face like an uppercut.

My feet are unsteady. My vision blurred. Like my emotions are about to burst out of me and betray me before I can push her away again for her own good.

But all thoughts of how I feel about her vanish when she fixes me with a grave look, considering, then says, "I found something at the beach house. Related to the fire. Also remembered something you may want to know about the day Micah died."

I feel like all the blood's drained from my body. I'm pure ice, granite, a block of cold, rigid stone.

"What? What're you talking about?"

She glances over her shoulder at Milah, then steps closer to me, lowering her voice. "Is there somewhere we can talk? Alone?"

I want to tell her that Milah doesn't give a damn about my personal life, but I can't find words. My lips are numb. I just nod slowly, touch her arm, then jerk back when the contact sparks between us like static. With a grunt, I jerk my head toward the door and lead her outside, then growl at James.

"No one in, no one out. Not until I come back. Radio Skylar. Get her over here and have her watch Miss Holly. She'll be sure our client behaves."

James nods, hiding a grin. We both know Milah is more than a little afraid of my lead, and Skylar might be the only woman on the planet who can make our pop star listen and keep her out of trouble. Or maybe my boy's just happy he doesn't have to deal with Milah himself.

Under James' watchful eye, I lead Kenna around the corner of the hallway, past a jumble of rigging for stage lights and into a dead-end storage cubby. She trails after me in almost furtive silence, as if expecting someone to jump out at us at any moment. I don't blame her.

It's like those words roused the ghosts, conjured the dead, and now they're trailing after us with invisible, grasping fingers.

Once we're alone, I turn to face Kenna, taking in her nervous, slightly too-wide eyes. Everything in me wants to comfort her, but I can't even let myself touch her, knowing I'll break her again. "Talk."

She wraps her arms around herself. "Your father first, or the beach house?"

"My old man."

"Okay." She takes a deep breath and tucks her mussed hair back. "I know this sounds nuts, but just stay with me...remember the last time we saw him? You were standing in the doorway while he left with his crew that day?"

"Yeah."

"Did you recognize those men?"

I frown, searching back through years of memories. "I'm not sure. It was all so fast. Maybe one or two of them. Dad came out pretty fast, brushed past me, told me to stay put."

"But not the rest."

"No."

"Okay. I didn't think so." She exhales shakily. "Back then...I think he was being forced into the car, Landon. I think maybe you couldn't see it past the car door, but I remember a man with a scar on the back of his hand holding his arm tight enough to bunch up his suit, and practically shoving him into that SUV."

A man with a scar on the back of his hand? I ransack my memory.

"I don't – fuck, no, I don't remember anyone like that. But you're saying you think my old man was kidnapped? That he was a *victim?*"

She looks up at me with those trusting, liquid eyes that seem to see the best in everyone, even me. "Don't you think it's possible? He had a partner, didn't he? What if he was oblivious to everything until he stumbled on the wrong thing and had to be eliminated?"

"That's fairy tale bullshit," I snarl. "Too clean. Convenient. The real world doesn't work that way, Reb. In reality, it turns out your father's a piece of shit and there's nothing you can do to fix it."

"What hurts your pride more?" Kenna asks softly?

"That your father was weak enough to be dirty, or unfortunate enough to be a victim?"

"Enough!" I can't face this right now.

Can't face the fact that five years of anger burrowing deep troughs in my heart, my flesh, my bones might've been for nothing. That all this confused hatred and loss and grief and vengeful fury might have gotten all twisted around, snarled on the wrong things.

It's too much to sort, and I don't have much time before I have to go back to Milah. Her show starts soon. "Tell me about the beach house."

"I found tracks," she blurts out. "The branches were broken in the hedge bordering the trees. I went through and found a man's tracks in the mud, and a burnt cigarette. There's a clear path through the trees to the service road...and I found a fresh gas can dumped behind the guard rail. Still had gas in it."

"Bullshit! That's too convenient, too."

Her eyes flare with a spark of anger, red spots of furious color appearing in her cheeks. "You were the one who said it could've been more than an accident," she bites off. "Don't believe me? Look."

She fumbles in her pocket and fishes out her phone, then swipes to the photo album and shoves it at me. I take the little phone and thumb through quickly, frowning. Fuck.

Fuck. Muddy footprints, left by what looks like a man's dress shoe. A cigarette.

And I know the area she's talking about. I could see it, right down to the getaway down the slope and into the waiting car. An arsonist could be in and out in less than ten minutes, fire set and the culprit already miles down the road before it ever took hold.

Somebody burned down my goddamned guest house.

Somebody from Crown Security.

I don't want to think Dallas would be fucking insane enough to have authorized it, even if he might not have been the one to light the match.

But I don't want to believe he's not, either.

There's a hideous hum in my ears. Like reality coming unglued, heaven and hell both laughing in my face, at my ignorance as everything I thought I knew shatters.

I drag a hand over my face, thinking, letting my brain just run wild.

Dallas is here. Where I can keep an eye on him. That's good.

Can't prove that it was him. Not yet. I gotta get home, get that cigarette, maybe see if I can get the police to test it for DNA or something.

The gas can, too. Check for prints, unless he was smart enough to wear gloves. I can't let him know that I suspect anything's up, not while we're here. He might just slip off and head back to clean up the evidence he was too over-confident to leave in the first place.

"Landon?"

Kenna's voice yanks me from my thoughts. She's watching me, worry drawing her brows together. I frown, shaking my head and reaching for the radio clipped to my belt. "Sorry. Planning. Listen, I've got to get with my guys and find Dallas. If you run into him, do *not* let yourself be alone with him if you can help it."

"Dallas Reese? Why not?"

"I think he's the one who set the fire."

She gasps. "What?! Why would he do that? Why would he set the fire and then rescue me?"

"That's a damn good question."

Things are ticking together in my head, falling into place.

A man with a scar on his hand. An old story my dad and Reg Reese used to tell about a camping accident when they were teenagers hits me. How Reg burned his hands, leaving him wearing gloves or hiding them in his pockets most of the time.

I'd never paid attention to his hands before.

My memory of that day is hazy through the fury of a fight I'd had with my old man, something stupid, and I only vaguely remember familiar shapes. Can't place Reg. Back then it wouldn't have pinged as out of the ordinary for my father to be leaving with Reg when they were part-ners. Emergencies and on call bullshit came up all the time.

But if Reg was forcing my father into the car? And Kenna says that's what she remembers...

Do I trust her?

I have to trust someone for once, don't I?

But if what she said was right...

Then Reg Reese killed my father.

And his son, Dallas, probably knows it, and he's busy carrying on his father's dirty, underhanded ways. He was willing to set the beach house on fire without even knowing if Kenna was in it, for fuck's sake.

Meaning he'd probably kill Kenna without a second thought.

White-hot fury burns through me, scouring me hard enough that there's no doubt about how I feel about her.

No doubt that whatever I fuck up, whatever I ruin, I'll *always* come back to her.

She's a riptide, constantly pulling me under, and I'll sink away and drown before I come up for air.

But we'll sort that out later. I have to get through tonight. Especially when my senses are tingling, and I suddenly think Dallas had ulterior motives for maneuvering his way onto perimeter security for this job.

How far would he go to eliminate the competition?

Shit. *Far enough to eliminate the client altogether?*

Shit. Shit, shit, shit.

I want to stay with Kenna, but right now, Milah's probably in bigger danger. I capture Kenna's arm, steering her gently back toward the dressing room.

"I want you to stay in here," I say as I push the door open, ignoring James' curious look and Skylar's deadpan stare and Milah's offended hiss. "James will keep an eye on you. No one in, no one out."

Kenna squares her shoulders bravely. "I'll be fine. Help take care of Milah."

Milah jerks her head up, almost stabbing herself in the eye with an eyeliner pencil. "What do you mean, take care of me? I've already got two babysitters!" she demands. "Are there more creepers outside, or what?"

"Worse," I say grimly, barely out of earshot. "Just stay here until it's your turn to go on. If you're lucky, the only thing you have to worry about is Kenna ripping your falsies off."

She stares at Kenna. "Your name is Kenna?"

Kenna eyes Milah. "Did you think C-cup was on my birth certificate?"

Skylar looks up from the corner, her cold eyes shining like pale steel. "I like her, boss."

Milah sniffs. I snort, then hook my arm around Kenna's waist and drag her closer.

I need her to fortify me. Need to know she's still mine, even after everything I've fucked up. Need her to know the words I can't say right now, not with Milah pouting at us and Skylar gawking and James right outside the open door. I need a lot of things, and they're right there in those widening eyes and the way she flushes and clings to my arms and falls against me instead of pulling away.

"Wait for me, Reb," I murmur, then dip my head and catch her mouth in a kiss.

I want her pliant. I want her submissive. I want her willing, and I want to know I haven't ruined everything between us, and fuck, yes, I'm greedy for the way she goes soft against me and yields and melts until it's like holding liquid flame. Her body so hot against mine and her mouth an inferno of giving, hungry sweetness.

She lets me in.

She lets me the hell in, lets me take and taste and claim her, and shows it in the way she gasps my name against my lips. And the way her mouth goes ripe and full and needy against mine tells me I haven't lost her.

I haven't lost her, and I still have a chance to save us after I un-fuck everything.

I don't know how I keep being so stupid with this woman, and so lucky she'll still be here for me. Drive all this fucking way for me, risking the demons I'm wrestling with.

Risking the demon I am.

I love her.

After tonight, I swear I'm going to show it every way a man possibly can.

I tear back when I can't breathe, when I can't hear for the pounding of my bloodstream, hot and wild as white-water rapids with the need she ignites in me.

"Back soon, babe. Stay here," I whisper, with one last brush of lips, then make myself tear away and walk from the room before I'm tempted to say fuck the concert, fuck Milah, fuck Dallas, fuck everything. I just want to run away with Kenna somewhere safe.

Too bad that's not a real option.

I have to close down. Have to be cold. Have to be the soldier I used to be to get through this.

First point of order: tell James and Skylar not to let anyone in or out of this room but me and Milah.

Second point of order: find Dallas.

I switch to channel eight on my radio. Dallas' men are on channel four, liaising with mine, but I always keep my own crew on a private channel so we can talk if we need to.

Call it paranoia, or good planning. I call it the smartest thing I could've done, when with a few murmurs I've got all my guys on high alert, slowly filtering out to monitor Dallas' men.

HALF AN HOUR LATER, we're on the verge of Milah going on stage, and my crew hasn't spotted anything out of the ordinary.

Dallas is nowhere in sight.

Milah's fretting in the wings, pacing with high-energy

pre-show nerves, her entire body a blinding mess of glitter and her rhinestone-studded pink boots flashing and clicking as she paces. The woman must've done a thousand shows in her life since she blew up the charts, and it's amazing to see her so freaked out.

"Will you hold still?" I growl.

"I can't," she hisses. "This is my biggest show *ever*. Make or break. Have you ever sung in front of ten thousand people? The President of Transylvania is watching – he's a huge fucking fan!"

I bite my tongue, deciding not to tell her Transylvania isn't a real country. More like part of Hungary or Romania or wherever the fuck. Skylar would know since her grandma's from there.

My train of thought running off the track tells me it's not just Milah's nerves.

"It's too many people," I say coldly, peering around the curtain at the overflow arena crowd. Any one of them could be working for Dallas, sights set on Milah. "We should call this off."

"*Now?*" she halts in her tracks, staring at me. "Are you crazy?"

"I'm worried. Got a bad feeling about this, and it's my job to protect you."

"Then do your job and stop letting your hormones go to your head, idiot," she bites off, folding her arms over her chest and looking at me with a huff. "It's not hard to tell what's going on: your dick's pointing you back toward C-cup. Get your brain on me long enough to finish this show, and then you can go home and play house with your little Plain Jane."

I grind my teeth, but I can't say anything else. She's the client. She's the boss.

"Fine," I mutter. "But first sign of trouble, you hit the deck. Get low, stay low, and wait for me to come for you. No arguing, Milah. We're talking about your life."

"Aw, please. Nothing's going to happen," she says with a flippant wave, then makes an odd little *gulp* sound and presses a hand over her stomach. "Except maybe me puking from nerves. Silly, right? I've done this forever."

But then the announcer is live, voice echoing over the arena, lights going up and sparks showering over the stage. Milah jumps at her name being called, then flashes me the first real smile she's ever shown, breathless and anxious and showing how young she really is.

"Wish me luck," she says, then flits her way out to the stage.

"Break a leg," I mutter reluctantly.

Just hope to hell that doesn't end up being literal.

XVII: CURTAIN CALL (KENNA)

*G*od, I'm glad Milah's gone.

Even if she did that little about-face and showed there's an actual heart beating underneath her silicone chesticles, the half-hour we spent tensely circling each other in her dressing room wasn't exactly the most pleasant.

Thank God for Skylar. That strange, small, statue of a woman kept us in line better than a sheepdog with a few strategic looks. The kind that promised fire, brimstone, and somehow, ninjas, if we got into it again.

We needed it, too. Especially after Landon kissed me in front of Milah – and especially after she claimed he loves me, leaving me locked up inside my own spinning head and not really in the mood for her barbed attempts at small talk.

I really need Landon to make up his freaking mind.

If he keeps jerking me around like this, I'm bound to get whiplash.

Right now, though, all I'm in danger of getting is sleepy.

I never thought a high-stakes chase to find Landon would end in me sitting useless and idle in an empty dressing room, drumming my nails glumly, watching the excited crowd on the wall-mounted TV.

I hate feeling useless. I'm not a damsel, I'm not in distress, and I despise sitting around idle when I could be doing something useful, even if it's just keeping an eye on any persons of interest.

It's hot in here, too. Sweltering. The only reason the heat isn't putting me to sleep is because I'm too keyed up with tension, the real reason I'm sweating and dehydrated.

My mouth is a desert. At least if I had to be stashed away for safekeeping, it was in a starlet's well-stocked dressing room. I drag myself off the plush sofa and over to the snack bar.

I should've known what the selection would look like: fifty different kinds of booze, and only two chilled bottles of mineral water bobbing in a half-melted ice bucket.

As I turn away, I glance over the crumb-littered plate and empty wine glass next to the bucket. It doesn't really register, at first. Just remnants and lipstick prints on the glass, as well as streaks of something down below the rim, but something is just off enough to make me stop and take a second look.

There's some kind of residue.

Making a trail from the lipstick print on the edge of the glass to the bottom. Some kind of grains, like sugar that didn't dissolve quite right, though it's white and looks like it might have been powdery before it got wet.

Weird. Frowning, I pick up the glass, looking at it from multiple angles.

What *is* this stuff? Sure, I know Landon said Milah was drugged up all the time, but last I checked you didn't mix powdered cocaine or heroin with your drink and toss them down like that. I've watched enough bad murder-mystery TV to know.

The sound of gasps – shrieks – tears me away from scrutinizing the glass, interrupting the sound of Milah's voice coming from the television and bringing the music to a discordant halt.

I look up sharply, watching on the screen just in time to see Milah go strangely still mid-performance, her face blanking.

She wavers back and forth, slowly but also unnaturally fast, tottering like she's about to lose her balance.

Only, it's worse.

A second later, she's crashing down on the stage, while the entire arena erupts into screams.

I stare down at the glass. Up at the stage. Down at the glass again.

Poison.

Holy shit. Why did Landon's instincts have to be right?

I have to get to him.

It could mean Milah's life, if the paramedics come and don't realize there's crap in her system.

I'm trying my phone, dashing for the door, but of course Landon isn't answering.

Of course he's not, because I can see him on the TV screen rushing out to help carry Milah off stage, Skylar at his side, and he's too busy barking into his radio to ever pick up the phone.

Damn! I'm frozen, wracking my brain for what to do.

I jerk the door open – only to run face-first into the wall of James' bulk. He stiffens, looking over his shoulder.

"Miss Burke, Mr. Strauss said you're not to go anywhere."

"In case you can't hear all that screaming, *Mr. Strauss* could be in real trouble and I don't have time for this." I glower at him. "I'm a grown woman. Not a prisoner. So, move!"

I expect an argument. But then another shriek comes from the stage, and he tosses a wide-eyed look that way, before his radio crackles at his hip and Landon's voice barks out.

"All hands on deck in the wings. *Now.*" There's a thrilling note of command, cool and controlled, that I've never quite heard before. James snaps his radio from his belt and murmurs into it.

"On my way." Then he favors me with a clipped nod. "Come with me, Miss."

James plows ahead, into the chaos of stage hands, managers, record company employees, event staff, and technicians milling around in a mess that's only an echo of the bigger disaster outside among the screaming, frightened fans.

For a brief second, he's my buffer, parting the Red Sea of people for me with his broad shoulders, but that shield doesn't last long. In less than ten seconds, people cut between us, running every which way and slowing my frantic steps.

Jesus. Cradling the wine glass protectively against my chest, I shoulder on, forcing myself toward the stage, only for someone to bump me so hard I go spinning around and stumbling into a side hallway leading back towards an emergency exit.

I start to right myself and dodge around the person, but they shift themselves into my way deliberately, blocking my path.

I still, looking up, following the line of a dark, smooth tie up over broad shoulders to a neatly trimmed beard and a cool, reflective smile, into hazel eyes that suddenly seem less thoughtful and more cold, calculating, and utterly self-satisfied.

Dallas.

My throat constricts. Adrenaline kicks through me so hard it's like I've been hooked up to an electrical socket. My entire body goes still, tense and ready to bolt, poised on the balls of my feet.

"Hello, Miss Burke," he says, rather congenially, eerily at odds with the ruckus just beyond the mouth of the hallway. I don't like that look. That calm. Not after what Landon said. And especially not when Dallas continues, "Well. You've really made this all come together quite neatly, haven't you? What fortune, finding you here."

I take a step back, gauging the space he takes up, what chance I have of squeezing past him.

Maybe if I scream – but who's going to notice one scream among *hundreds?*

"Move, Dallas!" I say. Maybe if I play it cool. Act like I don't suspect him. "I need to find Landon. It's important."

"Unfortunately, darling, I need you to *not* find Landon. Or Milah. Not right now. I need you right here." He smirks. "Look at you. You're a mess. The story practically tells itself. Love-crazed, jealous little girlfriend chases down her man and poisons her rival. Poor incompetent

Landon. So inept at managing his business he can't even protect his clients from one devious little woman. Think what the blogs and papers will say!"

My eyes widen. Everything recedes to a dull, roaring distance.

That's it then. He's going to use me to frame Landon. Only, that doesn't work if I can tell the entire story and show him up for the snake he is.

Then it hits me: the only way this works for Dallas is if I'm dead.

Cold sweat ices down my spine. I don't waste words.

I'm only frozen for a moment longer before I bolt, darting for the small opening at his side, shoving past him. I barely manage to squeeze beyond his bulk before his arm snares around my waist, an immovable band of steel.

He jerks me back against him in a mockery of a lover's embrace. Even while I kick, struggling and snarling and jerking against him, he bends down and whispers in my ear.

"Don't worry," he murmurs, and my skin crawls at the mimicry of intimacy, at his breaths curling against my ear. "This pill won't kill you...yet. They'll find the other in your pocket, and realize you tried to commit a murder-suicide. You should thank me, Kenna. It'll be painless. You'll slip away quietly in your sleep, and won't have to see your annoying little boyfriend fall."

He reaches around me with his other hand, clasps the wine glass I'm still clutching, and snaps the stem like it's the thinnest twig.

I scream, elbowing back, fighting with everything in me, and there's one satisfying thud as my head crashes back against his face before he snarls and clamps a hand over my mouth.

"Be a good girl," he hisses in my ear, before something bitter and foul-tasting rolls over my tongue.

I fight not to swallow, but he pushes down harder, squeezing against my cheeks, pushing the pill deeper. It goes down in a hard little painful lump.

And then the world goes black, fading away into a wavering, trembling nothing.

XVIII: COUNTDOWN (LANDON)

Something isn't right.

I feel like the only one standing still in a sea of panic, with the paramedics rushing in on Milah, the media angling for a look, the crowd alternately trying to rush the stage and stampede the exits.

Only, I'm motionless, watching as Milah is bundled onto a stretcher, taking in the details as the seconds tick by. She's alive for now. Still breathing.

The paramedics are already saying she collapsed from exhaustion, too much stress, the searing heat from the lights. But her skin is gray and her lips are blue, and she's breathing oddly, her chest hitching up in shallow, strained jerks.

No. No, this isn't right.

And the second I overhear one of the EMTs say "she's going tacky. Might be dealing with a drug overdose," my heart nearly stops before Milah's can.

Fuck.

This isn't really happening.

Drugs? *How?* I was with her almost the entire time, and so was Skylar and James. None of us would've let her slip anything past us. She didn't snort up or shoot up with me. I know her routine by now.

She doesn't coke up right before going on stage. She forgets the lyrics, loses focus. There's no way she'd OD. The girl is all kinds of messed up, but she took this show seriously.

This has Dallas' hand all over it.

I just have to figure out how.

But first, I have to find him.

At least I'm leaving Milah in safe hands. There's nothing I can do for her medically, and several of my guys are clustered around, standing watch over the paramedics.

They'll bring her back.

I have to believe that, but me hovering won't help. I stride out of the wings and into the backstage hallway. It's unnervingly deserted, dark, my steps echoing. Everyone's either vacated the arena or rushed out to rubberneck, leaving the place looking like a disaster zone where people dropped everything just to run. Papers scattered, equipment abandoned.

Every instinct in me screams *be ready*. For what, I don't know, but it feels like an attack.

It's like I'm back in Fallujah, relying on the same sixth sense soldiers develop in danger. A man who's seen combat can sense people's intent riding on the air, this heavy scent of purpose that tells us when an enemy is ready to strike.

And this place stinks of Dallas.

But I can't find anyone. Every room I check is empty,

every hallway vacant, this horror movie atmosphere of silent tension stalking me through every corridor.

I know where all of my men are.

It's telling that I don't see a single crew member with the Crown Security logo on their jacket. I'm about ready to join my team on containment and cleanup, shelving Dallas for a more considered, careful approach, when I trip over something that yields with a rubbery push and then kicks back against my ankle. The hard edge of a sandal, *with a foot still in it.*

Fuck. I drop to my knees, an "Are you all right?" on my lips, only for the words to crumble into dry ash once I realize who I'm bending toward.

Kenna.

I've never known fear like these thorns that cage me now, driving deep into my flesh.

She's unconscious, the same ashen gray as Milah, her lips just as blue. *Fuck!*

Dallas again. The asshole must've gotten her. She's so horribly limp when I lift her up, shaking her. So light, like she's already gone, and this is just a husk left behind.

I'm choking, my eyes blurring, as I check her sluggish pulse, then lean down and press my ear over her chest, listening for the faint beat of her heart.

"Kenna," I gasp raggedly, struggling around the thickness filling my throat. "Kenna. Wake up. Baby, Reb, please, wake up. *Wake up!*"

The last two words rocket off my tongue, sheer panic, ripping me in two. I've lived the past three decades of my life learning self-control, discipline, learning to stay calm. And right now that's falling to shit because the only woman I've cared about is dying in my arms.

No response. No whimper. No movement. Nada.

She's as still and silent as the dead, hanging in my arms, this rag doll without the fire and spirit and laughter and sweetness I love. This is my fucking fault.

I took her wide-eyed, trusting innocence that believed in me so much and I ruined it. I brought my poison to her doorstep, and injected it in her veins. Dallas may have done the deed, but she's here, collapsed, dying because of me.

This is all my selfishness, my shittiness, and it isn't fucking fair.

I should be the one lying here barely breathing, clinging to life. She doesn't deserve any of this.

I clutch her to me with one arm, fumbling for my radio with the other hand. But before I can find words, a raw, roaring scream of sheer anguish pours from inside me, ripping out of my chest. I trail off, gasping for breath, then bark into the speaker.

"I need help, help, get someone the fuck up here now!" I snap off. "Kenna – she's – I'm in the hall near the manager's office, send the paramedics – James? Riker? Skylar? Anyone?"

A sharp bang cuts me off. There's a crackle of confirmation from my radio, but I barely hear it as I snap my head up, toward the door that just rocketed open.

Instinctively, I clutch Kenna closer to me with a lion-like snarl – I'm full animal, protecting my mate. Protecting her as much as I possibly can after I'm the reason she's in this state.

And I have every fucking right to be worried, when Dallas comes strutting in with that smug, hateful smile on his lips, his arms spread as if he's presenting the grand finale to this terrible carnival show he's undoubtedly arranged right from the start.

"Landon!" he nearly purrs. "How's it hanging? The two of you couldn't be playing this any better. Who the hell knew you were such a fine actor? Ready to play Romeo to your Juliet?"

Everything goes red. Every last bit of humanity in me vanishes to leave a raging, rabid beast.

"You!" I snarl, and launch myself at him.

He doesn't even dodge. It's like he's asking for it, as my fist swings in.

I catch a glimpse of myself reflected in his eyes – teeth bared, face crazed with fury – before his head snaps to the side with a satisfying crunch and the painful reverberation of impact shakes up through my knuckles and into the bones of my arm. He staggers back, reeling, before catching himself with an almost incredulous laugh and touching his bleeding lower lip. His fingertips come away red, and he stares at them, looking all too pleased.

I clench my fists, sucking in heaving breaths. I want to fucking kill him. I want to fucking kill him now, but first I need to know what he did to Kenna and how to fix it when I can feel the silver thread tying her soul to mine growing thinner and thinner by the second.

"Talk," I spit. "What did you do?"

"What you gave me room to do, you careless, overconfident fool. So noble." He smirks, swiping his lower lip clean with his thumb. "You play the wounded animal, the tortured soul, but deep down you believe so much in people's inherent goodness that you just don't watch your back. You even trusted me to watch it for you." He arches a brow, cracking his jaw in a back-and-forth motion.

"Have to say, the bloody lip will be the perfect finishing touch."

It takes everything in me not to launch at him and wrap my fingers around his neck. "To. What."

"To the dramatic little story of a Juliet gone wild. And her brass balls Romeo who died heroically, trying to stop the man who discovered her attempt to cover up a jealous murder by committing suicide."

My eyes widen. This fucker arranged this, and then used Kenna's convenient arrival to cap it off.

He poisoned Milah to get to me, to shove me out of the game, and he'll kill Kenna and me both to seal the deal and tie up any loose ends.

Like father, like son.

Apples don't fall far from the tree, and these apples are rotten to the core.

I fling myself at him, operating on instinct – only to stop short like my leash gets yanked as a sleek black Beretta materializes from inside his suit. It pins me with the killing black eye of its muzzle, rooting me to the spot with it trained between my eyes.

"Don't make this difficult, Landon," Dallas says almost pityingly. "You always have to make everything so damn complicated. For once in your life – relax."

"Bastard!" I snarl. I'm already calculating, looking for a moment of inattention, a second to get him in a hold and disarm him.

He smirks. "I've been called worse." Then he lifts his radio to his lips, keeping the gun and his sidelong gaze trained on me. "I have target alpha secured in the manager's office. Let's sweep, clean up, and dispose of the trash. Converge."

Fuck. I have maybe five seconds to overpower Dallas and get away with Kenna before his team shows up to finish the job and mop up the mess. As he lowers the radio to clip it to his slacks, I seize the distraction.

I lunge, throwing myself forward with all my strength, all my speed. He barely even hesitates.

There's a sharp report.

A bright, blinding muzzle flash exploding over me.

Then pain, searing into my side, hot enough to eclipse the entire right side of my body with red liquid fire, like I'm drowning in blood. I stagger, falling to my knees at his feet. There's only a moment to grab at him, struggling, fighting.

Then the butt of the Beretta comes down, pain crashes into my skull, and in a flicker-flash of white to black everything goes dark.

* * *

I DON'T EXPECT to wake up again.

For a moment I don't know where I am. Not when I went down under enemy fire, and the first thing that penetrates the dark is the familiar sound of gunfire exchanged on a battlefield. I expect to wake up in a bivouac tent in Fallujah, surrounded by light the color of the sand that creeps into everything, from your gear to your mouth to the crack of your ass.

Instead I wake up to the cold white light of an overhead bank of fluorescents, James and Riker standing over me with their weapons drawn and aimed toward the door, Kenna cold and barely breathing next to me while the blood from the seeping pit of fire carved into my side

STILL NOT OVER YOU

stretches between us to soak into her clothing and link us like some terrible pact in dying heart's blood.

I manage to lift one arm, reaching across the space between us to touch her cheek. It's so cold, but I can still feel her breaths feathering against my knuckles.

She's alive. But I don't know for how long.

I've got to get her to a hospital.

And then I'm killing Dallas.

I've let childhood nostalgia blind me to that asshole the same way it blinded Steve to the darkness inside me.

No matter how awful Reg Reese was, I'd actually been naïve enough to think his son wouldn't be just as fucked.

Naïve enough to buy all that diversionary shit about finding my old man's killer, about working with the police.

Dallas and I have been rivals since the fucking cradle, but it was always that sort of high school shit with trying to be the better son, two princes vying for the crown. I never thought he'd carry it too far.

He was right about me.

No matter how poisoned I may be, there's some part of me that believes most people are like Kenna.

Inherently good. Worth having faith in.

I've always thought I was the only one who couldn't be trusted, with my father's tainted blood in my veins.

And now, my oversight, my error, is killing my Kenna.

Move asshole, a voice deep inside me barks.

I have to get up. Pain chews up my side like a rabid animal, but I force myself up, groaning, and twist to peel back the rip in my blood-matted shirt. Just a flesh wound, it looks like. More blood than there should be, making it look worse than it is.

Probably nicked a minor artery. Fuck. It hurts, but it won't keep me down.

Another grunt escapes as I push myself to my feet. James glances over his shoulder. "Boss, stay down."

Then he's bolting. He breaks off as the door slams open and a bruiser in a Crown Security jacket comes barging in, firing wildly.

I fling myself instinctively to the ground, going for my own gun, only to find it gone. James and Riker drop to guard position – and in two sharp shots he's down. I hear the gunfire outside dying down, and I only hope that means my team has the upper hand. I selected them all for their training and ability to stay cool in a crisis. If Skylar and her team have got the others pinned down from behind, we're good.

Dallas' men are sloppy.

It's only in the quiet that I realize I instinctively wrapped myself around Kenna's limp body, ignoring the pain to make a shield out of myself. Now I force myself to uncurl, brushing her hair back and kissing her brow. "Hang in there, Reb."

Even I don't know if it's a reassurance, or a plea.

Then, standing, I pull her into my arms. I don't care how much I hurt. I can't let her go. I lock eyes with James and Riker.

"Followed protocol?"

"Cops are already en route after the Milah call. We should have containment soon."

"Dallas?"

"Ran the second we showed up," James says with a sneer.

Fucking coward. Of course he did. It doesn't matter.

He'll get his.

Kenna first.

Riker starts toward me. "Hey – you're hurt. Let me take her –"

"No." I clutch Kenna closer against my chest, even though breathing is hard and my right eye is twitching from the pain. I grit my teeth. "Just lead the way. Paramedics still here?"

"I don't know. People scattered pretty fast with the gunfire, but they've gotta be close."

"Then let's move. She doesn't have much time."

Both Riker and James look at the unconscious woman in my arms with a touch of dread, before nodding and leaving the room ahead of me.

We slip out into the now quiet hallways. Bodies are everywhere. Most of them in Crown jackets. I can't stand to see if any of the faces are familiar, and I don't want to think about how to explain this to the police. There are cameras that will tell the story better than I could.

All I really care about is Kenna. We step over bodies, James and Riker forming a protective frontal phalanx, peering around every corner. I hover a safe distance behind. If anything happens, I need to be able to drop and guard Kenna –

Something snaps around my throat, cutting off my air, cutting off my voice, forcing me to immediate silence as I'm dragged backwards.

Blood loss makes me weak, off-balance, leaving me twisting and struggling as I'm garroted into the dark, pulled into the off-stage shadows in the wings, grappling to keep Kenna close and not drop her.

Her legs fall to the floor, her body clutched to me as I

scrabble at the slick thing around my throat with my other hand, straining to find my voice, to call James and Riker back, but I barely manage a wheeze while my fingers slip off the electrical cable cutting into my windpipe and making my vision burst into oxygen-deprived stars.

"Did you think I would let you fuck this up for me so easily?" Dallas hisses in my ear.

Bitter, black rage explodes inside my chest, flooding my veins until I can't feel the pain.

I can't feel anything but the pure destructive power flooding through me, whispering that I can't die here. *Not like this.*

Not silent in the smothering dark, while Kenna slips away in my arms because I couldn't save her.

Instinct takes over.

I whisper a soundless apology as I let her go, sending her slipping gently to the floor.

Then I smash my head back, ramming straight into Dallas' face. There's a deafening crack.

The cable in my throat loosens. I suck in a quick gasp of air, instantly clearing my head, and snap my elbow back before he can recover, jamming it into his ribs.

The moment his grip eases, I snare the cable, yank it away from my neck, duck out from under it, and twist to throw myself against him.

Dallas doesn't have a chance to struggle before I've got him against the wall, pinning him with my body, my forearm rammed against his throat.

We're eye to eye, almost nose to nose, two wild animals locked in a struggle for dominance, teeth bared.

He's losing when I crush down on his windpipe with

all the force of the built-up anger inside me, the years of rage and betrayal, the fresh sharp cut of fury that he *dared* lay a hand on my Reb, my woman, my life.

His eyes roll with fear, whites showing all around. He gasps, struggling like a beached fish.

"How does it feel?" I hiss, pressing down harder, just to see him squirm. "Not as much fun when it's your turn, is it?"

"L-Landon, don't," he pleads, words coming out in choked guttural gasps. "You h-have to u-understand –"

"Understand what, shitface?" I barely growl it through my clenched teeth, adrenaline pumping through me until I feel strong enough to snap his neck in one blow...and I want to.

Murder is hot and dark and in control of me, a drug as heady as lust. "You tried to kill me, asshole. Tried to kill Kenna. You even tried to kill Milah. For what? Just to get ahead? Is money that important to you?"

"You were in the way!" he flares, voice finding strength. "You were always in the fucking way. You and your idiot father. You could never just let things be easy. Always had to fuck everything up, too stupid to know what was for your own good and ours, and –"

Enough.

I cut him off, clamping my free hand against his jaw, slamming his head back against the wall. There's something deadly quiet in me, trembling and ready to snap. "What about my old man? Try the fuck again."

Dallas' eyes glitter. He lets out a wild, manic laugh, mocking. "You've been looking for his killer for so long. Chasing every trail I sent you down like the good puppy you are."

A roar bursts out of me. White-hot madness takes over, and I crash my fist across his face.

Once. Twice. Three vicious times.

Blood bursts out of his mouth. "What did you do?" I snarl the question again, barely even sounding human.

That fear is back in his eyes, and I love it. That sick black part of me loves it, loves seeing him cower and squirm. He shrinks against the wall, dangling from my grip. "We...we didn't have a choice," he whimpers. "Your father was going to ruin Crown Security refusing to play the game. You don't survive in this business without paying the big players, and he was...he was going to get us all killed! We did it to protect you and your mother from his damned stupidity, too!"

"You did it to protect yourselves," I snarl. "You did it to have it easy and line your pockets. You're disgusting. You and Reg. You sat back and let Reg murder my father, and strung me along all these years."

There's a moment. Cunning and dark, something flashing across Dallas' face that tells me exactly how crazy he is, this two-faced demon born in blood, thriving on others' misery.

"Oh, no, Landon," he sneers, a wide, leering grin turning his face into a horrible mask. "You don't understand. I pulled the trigger myself, darling boy. I killed Micah Strauss."

Everything inside me breaks.

If he'd thought that revelation would make me weak enough to let him go, he misjudged. Fatally.

All it does is drive me into a pure berserker state.

Everything smells like blood.

Everything turns the color of death.

I'm dark inside, a shadow full of hate, this driving purpose inside me finally having a target. And that target flops limply from my grasp as I grip him by the front of his suit and whirl him around to smash his flesh and bones against the wall with all my strength, bouncing his head off the hard surface, and then driving him down to the ground, following him with the full force of my killing need.

Dallas is a rag doll as I pin him, straddling him, smashing my fist down into him.

His face bursts with bloody ribbons as I ram my knuckles into him again and again, knocking his head back and forth between one blow after another as he turns red, then purple, then black, his face pulped and bruised and swollen.

Every blow is a balm on the bleeding wounds inside me. Every weak, sniveling cry is a triumph.

I'm finally going to end him.

It's what I've lived for all these years. This moment, finding the man who killed my father, and his life in my hands, dangling by a thread I'm only too willing to snap after everything he did to my father, to me, to Kenna.

I hate him. I hate him as much as I hate my old man, except all my hate at my old man was a lie, Kenna was right, Kenna knew...

Kenna.

Fuck.

I still mid-punch, staring blankly down at the ruin I've made of Dallas' face. A few more blows and he'll be gone forever.

A numb, cloudy feeling falls over me. I did that?

I did, turning savage, becoming the monster I always told her I am. And it turns my stomach.

Kenna believed in me. Kenna believed in me and she's dying for it, and I think even if I killed Dallas right now she'd never say a word and still quietly accept me, and yet...and yet...

I can't stand the idea of being someone other than the man she believes in.

I can't stand being a man who cares more about killing Dallas than about saving her.

My heart hurts. My heart hurts in the most awful ways, and the urge to snap his neck is still trembling in my fingers, but I can't. *I fucking can't.*

Not for Kenna, and not for me.

He looks up at me, barely conscious, his eyes just tawny slits through puffed eyelids. He lets out a groan that might be a word, tongue moving limply in his battered mouth.

I curl my upper lip and spit at him. "You're not worth it," I mutter, lifting myself off him just as James and Riker come clattering back, reeling around the corner.

"Boss?" James gasps.

"Get him in cuffs," I say firmly, jerking my head toward Dallas.

Then I bend to lift Kenna into my arms again. "And get me a car. If we can't find the paramedics, I'm taking her in my fucking self."

XIX: FALLING WITH YOU (KENNA)

I haven't felt this awful since the first and last
time I tried tequila.

I'm not sure where I am. Everything smells like Lysol,
my head is killing me, and my mouth is sticky and gross.

I hurt and feel oddly hollow, and there's a scared quiet
impulse inside me telling me to stay still as a rabbit hiding
from a wolf, because the last thing I remember is danger,
fear, something disgusting on my tongue, the knowledge
that I was going to die.

I'm not dead, though.

Am I?

How can I be dead, when the hand in mine feels so
very warm?

Carefully, warily, I crack one eye open. I can see...an IV
tube stretching from my arm to a pole, pale blue walls in
the off colors only hospitals ever have, and a brawny,
tattooed arm next to a rib cage wrapped in layers
of gauze.

I *know* those tattoos. I know that skin I've traced lovingly again and again. I know that arm that's wrapped around me so many times, and that fear vanishes in a heartbeat when I know as long as he's with me, I'm safe.

Landon.

It's his hand in mine, clasped tight. A reassurance that pins me to earth and tells me I'm very much alive. As hard as it is to believe.

I open my other eye, just watching him for a moment. He's sitting shirtless in a chair next to my hospital bed, his waist bandaged and a few bruises darkening his skin. There's an oddly naked expression on his face, vulnerable and lost and heavy, fear etching lines around his eyes and exhaustion casting shadows in the beautiful hollows of his cheekbones.

"Come on, Reb," he whispers, pressing his mouth against my knuckles. "Come on."

"Why?" I manage to croak out around my dry throat. "We going somewhere?"

He jerks his head up, eyes widening. He stares at me, and I have a second or two to feel the hammer-sharp thudding shock of faint tears glimmering in his eyes before he's on his feet, gathering me carefully to him, burying his face in my hair and kissing me over and over.

"Kenna, fuck," he gasps raggedly. "Kenna, I was so worried."

I manage to lift my arms, clinging to him weakly. "Landon. We're fine now."

I can't believe I'm saying those words. We really are, aren't we?

Relief floods through me. This is real, and I'm really okay.

But urgency pushes heavy on my brain, reminding me what happened, memory rushing back in a fierce pull. I have to tell him.

"Landon, Dallas...he poisoned Milah. Slipped something in her wine. He's trying to –"

"Tried to," he cuts in, growling the words gruffly into my hair, his hold tightening around me. "And he tried to poison you. Strychnine. Low dose so it'd kill you slowly, and wouldn't show up too obvious in your system. Asshole thinks he's a Bond villain."

My heart seizes. Holy hell. It's hard to believe how close I came.

I could be dead right now. I swallow something huge and bitter. "And Milah? Is she..."

"She'll be fine, Reb. They got to her in time. Same as you." He strokes my back soothingly. "Low dose meant there was enough time for the medics to get antidotes into your blood. You just need time. Rest."

"And you," I whisper. "I need you."

Fighting back tears, I bury my face in his chest, never wanting to come up for air again. "You saved me, Landon. Saved my whole life."

"No." He pulls back, clasping my face in his warm, coarse palms, looking at me with those bright blue eyes open and raw and so honest. "You saved me."

"You?"

"Dallas killed my father," he says, words coming off his tongue hard and bitter. "He told me. Right out confessed that my old man was innocent, and he and Reg Reese got rid of him because he was fucking up their dirty work. Dallas was throwing me off the trail the entire time, pretending to work the investigation. Instead he's been making sure I don't get too close to the truth – and I wouldn't be surprised if he sent that prowler around just to make himself look like a hero. Someone you could trust."

A chill runs up my back. I burrow my face deeper into his chest. Even after a man's hand shoved poison down my throat, I'm still creeped out by Mr. Hoodie. "You're sure? I can't stand the thought that this might not be over. That we might go home and –"

Crap. I catch myself, calling his home mine. It's too soon for that. But is it?

Landon smiles, a faint smirk bending the edge of his lips. "Totally sure, Reb. A couple Crown guys survived. They're singing like canaries for the cops and the FBI. One of them confessed to trespassing on my property, not long before Dallas showed up that night."

Thank God. I squeeze him tighter, then attack his lips with a dozen little kisses until he breaks off, laughing. I'll never stop loving that dense, baritone vibration in his chest, his bones, filtering into mine whenever Landon freaking Strauss breaks into his manly laugh.

"Hard to believe, I know," he says. "Guess Dallas was hoping to catch me off guard and get away. He wanted us both gone, and Enguard broken, so he could sweep up the loose ends and position Crown to control the whole fucking SoCal market, still making plenty of blood money on the side."

"Horrible," I whisper, pushing my hands into his.

Landon cocks his head softly. "I almost killed him, Reb. I had that asshole's life in my hands and it would've just taken one more little ounce of pressure to crush him.

Snuff him out like I wanted to all these years. And I couldn't do it. I couldn't be that man. I couldn't murder. Because that man isn't the one you believe in."

This time I can't choke back the tears.

I can't even say why I'm crying. There are too many questions hitting me at once.

Relief that Landon didn't do something so horrible?

Happiness that he really is the man I've loved all these years? Even if he was buried underneath his own pain?

Joy that this is over, and maybe now we can both be safe?

Yes, yes, yes, and yes.

Call it sheer, beautiful love and admiration for the beautiful soul inside this beautiful beast.

I lean my brow into his, sniffling and fighting to stop the tears streaming down my face. "You're the man I believe in, Landon. I love you. I love you, I'm proud of you, I..."

"Shhh." He only gathers me closer, gently kissing the tears from my cheeks. "Just rest. We can talk about everything else at home."

"Home?"

"If you'll come with me. If you're ready to call my home yours."

"Do you even have to ask?" I smile through the haze of my tears. "I wish we could go now."

"Soon, babe. Real soon. I'll probably have to talk to a dozen police officers first, if I don't want to walk out of here in handcuffs. And you need to stay here until we're sure you're out of the woods."

I squint. "Why would you end up in handcuffs?"

He looks at me blandly. "My crew ended up in a fire-fight with the Crown team. Not to mention I beat Dallas to a bloody pulp." At my gasp, he smiles innocently. "I said I didn't kill him, remember? Never said I didn't beat the ever living shit out of him."

"Oh my God, Landon." I shouldn't laugh, but I do, though it trails into a wince as my body protests the shaking. Hissing, I sink back against the sheets. "Ow."

"You okay, babe?" He's instantly conciliatory, sweet, hovering over me and brushing my hair back. "You need the doctor?"

"No." I shake my head with a faint smile. "I'll be fine."

"Just promise me you won't pass out."

Another raspy chuckle shakes my body. "I'm *not* passing out."

"You sure? I'm not."

"I'm not going to pass out!"

He laughs. "Still don't believe you, Reb. Look down."

He curls his hand around mine again, drawing my attention to it.

I look down, wondering how numb and broken my body must be. Because it's taken me this long to notice the new weight against my finger, heavy and warmed by body heat.

A ring.

Attached to the largest diamond I've ever seen in real life – hell, the largest I've ever seen on TV – princess-cut in a glittering, multifaceted gold setting. It gleams against my finger like it belongs there, and my heart does the strangest little flutter, like it's a sparrow cupped in my palms and beating its wings.

"L-Landon? Holy shit." I suck in a few rasping breaths. "Where –"

"Hospital gift shop, babe." He's flushed, grinning. "Apparently, they sell engagement rings. Who knew?"

Engagement rings.

Engagement.

Rings.

There's no doubt left about what he means. Especially when he gets down on one knee, hunkering next to the bed with a faint wince that still doesn't dim his boyish, hopeful grin. My head feels light, and I don't think it's the poison.

But I can't pass out, or it'll be proving this lovable asshole *right*.

He clasps my hand in both of his, the ring growing even warmer in the body heat between us, and looks up at me with his eyes dark and earnest. "Maybe this isn't the best place to do this," he says, "but it's something I should've done years ago. Long before I let my pride and stupidity get in the way. I've given you too many reasons to doubt me, Reb, and I won't do it anymore. So, I'm asking you, right now, for a promise. I'm making a promise to you. If only you'll say yes." He swallows hard, his eyes a different Neptune storm I've never seen. "If you'll just be my wife."

Holy hell.

I don't know how he even needs to ask.

How he hasn't known my answer our entire lives.

How that rough, joyful, long-time-coming *yes* has been waiting between us since the day he ruffled my hair and told me I was a rebel, and I'd have boys lined up across the coast waiting for me, when the only one I *ever* needed was always right here.

But I want to say it. I want to make it real. And I feel like my smile will crack my face as I gasp out "Yes," before nearly ripping my IV needle out to tumble into his arms.

He sweeps me up close, laughing and kissing me wildly.

We're a mess, clinging and clutching and trading kisses and nips and laughs until it's hard to breathe and I don't think I'm the only one crying.

It's perfect. It's wonderful. It's so typically Landon, to finally decide what he wants and to be so impatient that he'll claim it with a hospital gift shop engagement ring if he has to.

I'm just happy that what he wants is me.

It's giddy – so giddy to know he loves me as much as I love him. And I whisper those words again and again as I seal my mouth to his more firmly, kissing him, tasting all the beauty and wildness and darkness that makes Landon so special.

I could love him through anything, I think. Past any pain. Past any shadows. Past hell itself.

I'll love him through everything, no matter what changes may come.

His mouth blazes on mine, his kiss so deep – before abruptly breaking back as he lets out a pained hiss, jerking and looking over his shoulder peevishly. "Ow, jackass."

My brother stands there after smacking the back of Landon's head lightly, Melanie at his side, his hair wild and disheveled and his face drawn with worry, but the most enormous grin on his lips.

"You deserved it," he tells a glowering Landon, before his gaze softens. "I get it now. Finally," he says, looking between us. "It's all over the news. Your father, Dallas, *everything.* If you were going to break that story, maybe don't do it at a concert where there must've been a million reporters around."

Landon winces guiltily and gathers me closer, as if he'd protect me from prying eyes. "Yeah."

"I get what you couldn't tell me," Steve says, and I realize now he knows. What Landon lived with all these years, the hatred and purpose driving him.

His gaze transfers to me, looking intently with that brotherly warmth and love I've missed. It's clear that he knows what secrets I kept, too. And why.

"Both of you," he murmurs. "I get it now. You were trying to protect each other."

"And you," Landon says. "You didn't need to get pulled into this, Steve. It was bad enough Kenna knew."

"Hey." I swat his chest lightly. "If I hadn't known, Dallas might've killed you."

"And I owe you my life," Landon replies softly, those dark blue, heated eyes burning into me. "I owe you my everything, Kenna. I love you."

My heart is going to burst. It's breaking. Repeatedly. In all the best ways.

But before I can say anything, Steve grins and slings his arm over Landon's shoulder.

"Welcome back to the family, Landon."

"Back?" Landon asks, looking almost lost.

"Back." Steve echoes with a firm nod. "You've always been one of us."

"And he always will be," I say, lacing my fingers with my fiancé's, my beloved's, my beast's.

My Landon.

The man I've always believed in.

The fire I never extinguished.

The only hero I'll ever need.

XX: SOMETHING BLUE (LANDON)

Six Months Later

I NEVER THOUGHT this day would come.

I also never thought my easygoing, sweetly playful Reb would turn out to be the ultimate Bridezilla, but I gotta say at least she keeps me on my toes.

She really hasn't been that bad.

Mostly just neurotic, wanting to make sure every last detail of our wedding is perfect. I don't know how to make her understand: we could get married in burlap sacks in a back alley, and it'd be perfect as long as she's there.

She's all I need. She's perfection itself. She's everything.

Marrying this woman is several dreams come true. Pure euphoria. Bliss.

And she's the reason why I feel so light, standing here

on the sand, looking down at her with flowers tucked in her hair. The salty sea air tosses those chestnut tresses swept against her bare shoulders, drawing my eyes to places I can't let distract me.

Not fucking now.

For all her planning with the invites and scheduling, our wedding is a simple thing. Informal, fresh cut flowers scattered across the beach. Everyone we love present – and a few people we tolerate, like Milah Holly herself – perched in folding chairs. Reb's wedding dress is in the same style, a simple white sundress that suits her better than any layer cake of frills ever could.

I told her I didn't want to see a stranger caked in makeup and suffocated in Victorian layers on our big day. I want to see *her,* beautiful as ever without any gloss. My sweet, natural, sexy as hell Kenna, with her magic ability to ignite my blood with nothing more than a green-eyed glance.

This is us. The future. This is how it should be, and will be.

Me and my wife, doing things our own way. Finding out what works for us, just like we always have.

Sometimes, it's chaotic. Sometimes, it's peace.

But it always, always makes me happy. Because she's changed my life several times over. She's changed *me.*

And I know I wouldn't be here without her. Hell, I'd barely be human.

I'm so deep in my own head I'm hardly listening to the priest. All the "dearly beloveds" and "we are gathered here todays" are nothing against the roar and crash of the foamy sea at our backs. Like Mother Nature herself is standing witness, saluting us – and this lovely little kitten of a woman looks up at me with a shy, dorky smile that makes me think of that girl I used to know.

That girl who brought me back. That girl who never left me, even when I left her.

That girl who's been my greatest right and wrong, and my biggest, brightest promise.

God as my witness, I'll never, ever leave her again.

Come hell, come fire, come storm, come the world heaving itself apart...

I'll never leave her side.

The stars are just coming out against a sky of violet and indigo twilight, looking down on us with their glittering eyes when the priest asks for our vows.

My gut knots. I've been holding off on figuring mine out for so long, unsure of the right thing to say.

But as I look into her eyes, I know. It's spontaneous, it's harsh, it's right.

The words just come, as if I've spilled them out in heart's blood.

"Kenna," I murmur, then grin. "Reb." There's a laugh from the peanut gallery, and I recognize Steve's voice but don't care. "I learned who I was years ago when I watched the stars with you, then lost myself when I forgot where they were. You brought the sky back to me again, and taught me how to be the kind of man I want to be. The kind of man I believed my father could be." His ring is heavy in the pocket of my shirt, reinstated along with his reputation. "The kind of man who can cherish you. Love you. Protect you. Fight like hell for you till the day I die. And I want the stars that always drew us together knowing I'll love you. Always. Love you till their light burns out, the earth falls apart, and beyond."

Her eyes are glistening, glittering bright as distant green starlight themselves. She lets out a shaky laugh, her cheeks flushed. "I thought I was the writer," she whispers.

"You're the muse today," I tell her, drilling my gaze into hers. "You draw it out of me. My best, Reb."

She laughs, ducking her head, but clasps my hands tight in hers. "Careful. You're going to make me forget my lines, Landon!"

I wink. "Hurry. We're waiting."

Ass, she says with a smiling glance.

Then she trails into a sigh, those captivating green eyes so warm, so open, brimming with the emotion I'm so lucky she's willing to trust me with.

"Landon...you were always beautiful to me," she says, her voice thick. "Even when you thought you were at your ugliest, your worst, past the point of no return, I saw the same man. The one I fell in love with one day after school when he told me I could be myself, and take the world by the horns. Whether your heart smolders with darkness or burns with light, you were gorgeous. You were strong. You were beautiful. And you still are. So flipping beautiful I can't help but love you, Landon, and all the wild, chaotic whirlwinds of emotion that's become us. You have a beautiful heart...and I'm so, so glad to finally call it mine."

Fuck.

Fuck, this woman might destroy me, baring herself like this. But maybe I'm not afraid because we've already done that once. Exactly what I needed.

Destroyed and rebuilt into something and someone better, the rubble of that hateful, broken thing I was left behind.

"That's it, babe," I whisper, leaning in where no one

else can hear, grinning like a fool. "Because if you make me go all bleary-eyed in front of all these people, you're in so much trouble tonight."

She grins back. "Looking forward to it," she teases, only for the priest to clear his throat and pull us back from our absorption in each other, back into formalities.

The rest is a sugary sweet blur.

There's a *do you, Kenna? A do you, Landon? A with this ring, I thee wed.* The rings, transferred from my pocket to our hands, slid reverently onto mutually shaking fingers. I do. *I do.*

I do, I do, I do.

Then an *I now pronounce you.*

Husband. Wife. Till Death do you part.

And then she's in my arms, and our families are cheering and crying and laughing and shouting, and I'm kissing my wife for the first time.

Hot fuck. The first little flick of her tongue against mine does terrible things to the animal inside me. I have to restrain myself, remember not to grab her ass in public. I stop at the small of her back and just pull her in, attacking her mouth, the mouth I've claimed forever, pulling her into me.

She's mine, mine, gloriously *mine.*

Every day for the rest of our lives, I'll remember.

I'll cherish.

I'll believe.

I'll love like madness.

How she falls into my arms with such absolute trust, absolute love, and kisses me with a joy and passion and promise that says no matter what rocky roads we may face, no matter how we may clash and push apart and pull back together...

She loves me.

And she knows I love her.

And I show her again and again and again, with every fiery pulse of lips to lips and dancing, swirling souls.

I want her to myself. Right the fuck now.

Unfortunately, the biggest problem with a wedding party *is* the wedding party.

High on dizzy joy and clinging to each other nonstop, we hold court. Bide our time. And I force my throbbing dick to behave for a few more hours.

Mothers suddenly become mothers-in-law, hugs and tears all around. Another smack upside the head from Steve, who introduces me to their Gam-Gam, a ninety year old woman who pinches my cheek like Goliath. She tells me and Kenna we've given her the best late birthday present she could ever ask for – unless we're planning on giving her a grandbaby next year?

Fuck.

Pouting from Milah, who tries her damnedest not to show that she's red-eyed from crying and forcing down the biggest grin. She's pretending to be her usual sourpuss screw-the-world self, but the fact that she's here at all tells us there's more under her perfectly tanned skin.

When she hugs us both, it's fierce and genuine. None of the smarmy act she puts on, and everything of a girl who's slowly finding her way in the world, one mistake at a time. Incredibly, she doesn't even touch a drink the whole time I glance her direction.

She sniffs at us with mock hauteur. "You guys are so

predictable, having a cheap wedding. It was quaint, I suppose. Charming."

Kenna grins and tucks herself into my side. "Do I need to remind you I will end you?"

"Landon wouldn't let you," Milah fires back, though there's no flirtatiousness behind it. She hesitates, then gives me an uncertain look. "I...fuck, I don't know how to say this."

"Say what?"

She looks away, rubbing her arm uncomfortably. "Just...thank you. Thank you both. For realsies."

I grip her shoulder gently. I get what she's not saying. What could have happened to her, how frightening it must have been, coming face-to-face with the Reaper without a split second of warning.

"Hey. I was just doing my job," I tell her.

"Yeah, well, you're kind of okay at it." She pulls back with a toss of her hair. I let her.

It's bravado, clinging to her dignity, and it's not nearly as grating as it used to be. "Since you had to have such a *cheap* wedding, I insist you splurge on your honeymoon."

Kenna laughs, rubbing her cheek on my arm. "We already did. A week in Mexico!"

I love how her voice lights up. Hell, I'm feeling it, too, my mind instantly going to spicy micheladas and long nights on the vacant, warm beaches with Reb. Completely naked.

Milah smiles. "Mexico's perfect! I have like, six houses there. Or is it seven? You simply *have* to stay at one of my properties. You'll be pampered better than any hotel."

Kenna parts her lips to protest. I elbow her gently, and we exchange a glance.

Somehow, we've developed our secret language of silences we used to have when we were kids, and could read each other with just a look – and what I'm telling her with my look right now is to let Milah have this one.

Kenna sighs indulgently, eyeing me with a wry smile, then turns that beaming look on Milah.

"We'd be honored," she says. "Thank you."

"It's settled. Awesome. Right now, though..." Milah looks at a cell phone she doesn't bother to pull out of her purse. "I have a plane to catch. My new career's taking off thanks to a certain knight in shining armor, and I'm due on a flight to Paris tonight." She giggles, tosses us both a flirty wink and a blown kiss, and turns to flounce off. "Ta for now."

Kenna and I stand on the sand, looking after her bemusedly. Kenna tilts her head. "Jesus. That girl..."

I laugh. "I know, Reb. But she kind of grows on you."

She mock-punches my arm. "As long as growing is *all* she's doing on you."

"Not my type, and you know it."

"Oh?" She angles her face up sweetly for a kiss.

"My type's right here. Only type I'll ever need." With a growl, I lean down to capture her lips. Just a quick taste, like sugar on my tongue, but I'm already sparking hot and needing to be away from this ruckus.

With one nibble of her luscious lower lip, I break away. "We had our fun gabbing yet? Think we can sneak away early?"

She's breathless, flushed, her eyes dilated, but she laughs. "Not unless we want to hear about it from our mothers for the next thirty years."

"Heaven forbid." I grin, desire curling dark in the pit of my stomach. "But after dinner, you're mine."

And I can't stand the wait.

But I endure it, and even enjoy dinner. Even if I'm eager to have her...there's a part of me that wants to slow down and enjoy this, too.

I feel like ever since my father died, I've been hurtling at breakneck speeds toward a crash. Now, though, I've come to a screeching halt just before hitting a brick wall head on.

Disaster averted, thankfully. Now, everything's coming up Landon.

Dallas is in jail, rotting away in a cell probably not too far from his old man's. The trial will be wrapping up soon, but he's already not my problem anymore.

Kenna and I already testified as witnesses for the FBI. They're done with us as long as they can reach us if they need to.

Reg in jail for tax evasion and underworld human trafficking atrocities. Dallas in jail for murder, and more.

Frankly, I'd rather leave them suffer than see them dead.

It only makes the happiness I feel as I toast my new bride before our friends and family at our reception dinner that much sweeter.

Everything's damn perfect.

Correction: damn *near* perfect, I remember, when we stop by the table with my main Enguard crew. I see Skylar nursing a coffee drink, her eyes anywhere but our wedding.

"What'd I tell you about tonight?" I say, breaking away from Kenna to pull up the empty seat next to her.

She looks at me and blinks. "I know, I know. Enjoy myself. I'm trying, Landon. Had the bartender throw some Kahlua in this thing."

"After this craziness dies down, I'll help you find her. I promise." I watch her till she nods, sheepishly gnawing her lip, hating to accept anything. "You can't do it all yourself, Skylar. I know you want to keep it in the family, going after Joannie, and I'm not here to cross any line I shouldn't. But, shit, you tell me what you need. Resources? Time? Manpower? It's yours. You're at my wedding because you're practically family, same as these other two party-crashers."

I knock my fist against the table gently, catching smiles from both James and Riker. They're both busy chatting up a few of Kenna's old friends, and they know better than to start any shit that'll only cause trouble when they see the flash in my eyes.

"Thanks, boss. You're a good man and I'm seriously happy for you." Skylar smiles, taking another loud slurp of her coffee. "You've got to get out of here, now. The last thing I want my crappy situation to do is drag down your wedding day."

I throw a hand on her shoulder and squeeze one more time, and then I'm gone, finding my wife in the crowd again.

Although there's a warmth, an afterglow, to feeling like I'm part of something again after the joy and rush of marrying Kenna, it's a relief when time catches up. We watch the last car pull out from the driveway and leave us alone among the tables lined up along my private beach, just skirting the edge of the waves in the strip of sand between the ocean and the newly reconstructed beach house.

Kenna's looking out across the water; the sky's a deep velvety blue, the waves black silk, and they meet where the stars and moonlight throw down their reflections to make glinting edges on the waves. I slip up behind her, wrapping my arms around her waist, and then pressing my lips to her sun-freckled shoulder.

"Ready to go home, Mrs. Strauss?"

She smiles, soft and thoughtful. "I'm *already* home." She turns in my arms, slipping her own around my neck. "Home is where you are."

"Then come with me, my beautiful bride."

That's the only warning I give her before I lift her up in my arms, sweeping her against my chest. She lets out a yelping laugh, clinging to me, and rests her head on my shoulder as I carry her toward the beach house, stepping over two drowsy cats dozing on the front pathway.

They've had a big day, too, with all these people milling around. For once, I'm happy Velvet and Mews will be too tired to bother us tonight.

There's a deep satisfaction carrying her over the threshold, as if honoring a time-worn tradition makes this final.

Makes this *real*. And there's a sense of breathless antici-pation as I carry her through the open, spacious rooms, into a new addition I had built into the reconstruction just for her.

The solarium is almost pure glass, and the curved dome of it turns the room into a glittering globe of the heavens captured just for us, a pocket of silver and shadow pulling the night into our own private heaven.

Reb looks ethereal, more like an angel than a living woman, as I lay her down on the bed tucked into one corner. She's all pale moonlight and sea-green eyes and chestnut hair and tiny flowers scattered all throughout those spreading locks, looking up at me like some wild sea-nymph I managed to coax up to shore.

That filmy, soft white sundress is beautiful on her. *So fucking beautiful.*

I'll always remember her like this: natural and perfect and mine, watching me with her eyes dark and dilated, pink tongue caught between her lips, as breathless and soft as if it's our first time.

In a way, it is. A new beginning. A promise we made months ago fulfilled.

The first time I'll touch her as my wife, claim her body as her husband. Kiss her as my one and only truth.

Take her, and then take her again. Binding her to me in flesh as well as in word.

This feels like an act of worship. The heat that burns in me is as slow and deep and scorching as magma, and I can't even find words for the emotions racing through me as I strip out of my shirt, then sink down to cover her body with my own.

The way she fits against me is just right – as if we were *made* for each other, crafted from the same primal clay. Meant to meld.

She arches to me with a sigh as I skim her body with slow touches, letting her shape guide me, memorizing her with my palms. I lose myself in the rhythm of her sighs, the music of her soft, low sounds.

Face, hair, skin, tits, and cunt. They make me more frantic the more I have.

I devour every arch of her body, every flutter of her pulse against her throat, every part of her lips and flush in her cheeks. She responds to me with such delicacy, such perfection, such perfect rhythm.

We're no longer two separate beings, but one.

Kenna is, and always will be, my heart made flesh.

She lifts her arms over her head as I strip the sundress away – then gasps as I tangle the dress around her upraised wrists, keeping them trapped, pinning them there.

Her pale, smooth skin is a feast for my lips. Her taste so lush with that faint hint of sea salt clinging to her as I kiss her shoulders, then the upper curves of her tits, then her soft, sleek belly, and then her inner thighs.

Her moans slip out and I submerge her into a delicious torture.

Nibbling along the curves of her bra, the line of her panties, teasing her just to hear her whimper, just to watch her writhe in anticipation.

When I tug her lace cups down over the tempting, plush mounds of her tits, those strawberry-pink nipples are already hard and begging for my mouth. And when I wrap my lips around one, tracing it with my tongue, the way she jerks beneath me and the soft cry that rises makes my cock throb with a raw, potent, animal need.

I want to taste every fucking inch of her. Touch it. Bite it. Own it.

From the soft underside of her knee to the crease inside her thigh, from the soft sweat-misted valley between her tits to the hot, soaked folds between her thighs.

She's already wet, so wet for me, and there's something deliciously dirty about leaving her drenched panties on and only tugging them aside to bare her to my tongue.

Fuck. Yes. *There.*

"There, baby, there," I growl between licks, sending a quiver through her body.

I can't get enough of her taste. She's tart and sweet and creamy all at once.

I lick every last slick drop from her skin – circling her clit, delving inside, finding every place that makes her shrill whine hit the peak that just fucking ruins me before it breaks and she nearly sobs out her pleasure, digging her fingers into my hair.

"Landon!"

I want her like this.

Always like this: open for me, wet for me, begging for me.

I'm not exaggerating when I say I could spend hours buried between her thighs, kneading my fingers into sweet yielding flesh, fucking my tongue into the sweetness of her cunt till her back arches and she spasms hard.

But Reb clenches her knees against my waist, pulls me up, and kisses me too soon, distracting my mouth.

This sweet wanton woman who's as delicate as a virgin and as willing and wanting as the most experienced lover. How could I ever resist the electric tease, the need building in my balls?

I give her the taste of her on my lips while she tells me what she wants without words, moving her body against mine until her slickness glides against my cock and I throb from root to tip with the violent caveman urge to be inside her.

So ready to fuck. So ready to take. So ready to pump

everything inside me in her.

A few more teasing strokes. A few more moments of delving, deep, soul-melting kisses, and then our bodies glide together.

The moment comes when we fit perfectly, my cock poised just short of finding home, her wet, heated folds wrapping around my cock head. Gasping, I part our lips, resting my brow to hers. "Kenna."

"I know," she whispers, so many wordless things between us. "I *know.*"

She coaxes me into her pussy, drawing me deep with the clench of her thighs.

Groaning, I bury myself in her body, slowly, drawing it out till we're mated in tandem with strained cries and tortured breaths and the trembling flex of our muscles.

Moment after moment, I hold and savor her sweetness. I engulf my dick in her silk, resisting the urge to slam her into the mattress with powerful, beastly jabs of my hips. I hold out just a few seconds longer, before taking her deeper, *deeper,* even as her fire torches down my senses, my control.

And by the time I'm fully inside her, enveloped in a wet and giving lushness like a deep and burning sea, I'm lost.

Happily undone.

I lose myself in her, thrusting like a madman, driving deep again and again, moving to the crash and roll of the waves outside, the turn and sway of the constellations overhead.

There's pleasure and then there's this – this insane thing where every time my body cries out in torment, my heart and soul answer. Ringing affirmation.

Drawn into this wicked primal rhythm. I can't even breathe without tasting her.

My balls keep time, smacking against her skin, my dick swelling as I fuck her straight through one spastic release and into the next. Her body is my dream, my ambrosia, my vessel.

This is our true wedding vow.

Here, joined together, buck naked and writhing like wildcats in heat.

This moment, our moment, witnessed by stars and sea. Promises made in breathless, strained exaltation, heard only by sky and sand and our own pounding ears.

I clutch her to me, crushing our bodies together. I need to fucking come.

We're melded in sweat and tangled limbs, in desperate kisses and needy grasping hands. Kenna rises up to meet me again and again, faster and faster, until we flow, until we're liquid, until we're falling apart.

"Fuck, Reb, come with me. Come. Right. Now."

I burst. I dissolve. And so does she.

My balls twitch, pouring sheer fire, my whole spine going electric. For a second, I really am an animal, claiming and mating and marking her as mine.

It's rough. It's raw. It's sharp and strange and biting, that quiet twilight magic turning into wild bestial sorcery, and as we crash together one last time I lose control.

Lose it, yeah, but never lose my hold on her, even as I spill myself into her gushing, sucking cunt and breathless screams, feeling that tightness that comes when she takes me for every drop and gives back her own and begs for more.

Kenna's mine tonight, as long as the stars shining down on us last.

No, longer.

She's mine, heart and soul, and nothing will ever make me let her go again.

* * *

WE LIE in the muggy summer heat, tangled together, naked and stuck together by sweat.

She's half asleep; I'm not far behind.

Something about our first time as man and wife broke something inside me.

By something, I mean my fucking self-control. I turned into a goddamn animal in heat and took her every which way I could.

Up against the headboard, her fingers clutching at the edge of the wood and her ass thrust back against me while she taunted me with little grinds of her hips.

On her hands and knees, fingers tangled in her hair. The noise Kenna made when she came branded itself in my memory. So did the way her sweet cunt shook every inch of me, pulling the heat from my balls with every whimpering twitch of her skin.

On my back, her body plunging down over me, glorious and beautiful and wild. Her hips tempting me to dive deeper into her. Her mouth molten on my cock, making me writhe.

I made noises straight from the Caveman Lexicon. Feral, sandpaper sounds, like my own rough pleasure scratching at my throat as it left me.

Her legs over my shoulders, her hips bucking, jerking

and thrashing and coming real sweet for me again while I licked her clean with my tongue. I gorged myself on her greedily, and I feel no shame for it.

How she'd suck me nice and hard between each round. She's an angel when that mouth speaks, but the woman is *all devil* once her tongue touches my cock. Her delicate tease up and down my length ends with her circling my swollen crown, focusing her soft licks under it, finding the spot that makes me want to shoot off in her mouth if I wasn't so crazed to fill her pussy.

I've taught her too damn well.

If I can't walk in the morning, it's entirely her fault for being this gorgeous.

I can't stop myself from tracing the line of her hip with my hand, following the dip down toward her still slick opening again. She laughs, batting my hand away drowsily.

"Enough, tiger." It's barely an exaggeration. I have to fight to suppress a growl that'd make a saber-toothed beast do a double take.

"Rest, babe. You've earned it," I say, kissing her bare shoulder.

With a contented sound, she snuggles against me, spooning herself into the curve of my body with that delectable little ass rubbing right against my cock. "I feel like I've been beaten with a meat tenderizer."

"That's not something my cock's ever been called before. Nice compliment." I wink.

She laughs, twisting in my arms and facing me, resting her hands against my chest. "You *know* what I meant. You're awful, Landon. Why do I love you?"

"Because you do. And because I love you. And because

you'll want this dick again in the morning, and I'll want to give it to you so hard you'll come up with fun new names for being fucked."

"Landon." There's a playful warning in her voice, her eyes narrowed.

I run my fingers through her hair, pushing her against me, taking my sweet time burying my lips on hers. "You heard me, Reb. Don't act like you didn't. I love fucking you like a man possessed because I just fucking love you. Period."

Kenna's gaze relaxes. She lets out a soft, contented sigh, her green eyes bright in the darkness. "Nice save. I'll never get tired of hearing that."

"Good. Because it's gonna be your background track from now on." I brush my lips to hers, tasting the sweat of us on her lips.

Fuck, do I love it. Just tasting us together. Another sign we're inseparable.

I sigh, gathering her closer. "I've known we were connected since the moment I met you, Reb. Call it fate. Like the gravity in the stars. I was lost then. Spent so long looking for the constellations to guide me home...when I always should've known they were here, right in front of me."

"You've found your way. Home," she whispers, while I brush a lock of sex-kinked hair away from her eyes.

No word on her lips has ever tasted sweeter or truer than that last one. Home.

And I'm still thinking about the kind of eternal home we'll make for ourselves when I silence her with another hungry kiss.

XXI: EXTENDED EPILOGUE (KENNA)

Three Years Later

I'M GOING TO SCREAM.

Wait. Scratch that.

I *am* screaming.

Careening down the stairs, emitting a high-pitched noise that I'm not sure is a shriek or a laugh but it's full of pure joy as I shout, "Landon! Landon!"

He leans out from the kitchen, mock-grimacing at me. "What have I told you about screaming in the house, Reb?"

I wince, stopping with a sheepish smile. Twining my hands together behind my back, I look up at him with mock contrition. "That it puts you on high alert? And your first instinct is to hit the panic button and call the cops?"

Chuckling, he sets down the mixing bowl and snares an arm around my waist, pulling me closer with that delicious strength I love so much. "That was before, babe. Now it's because you'll wake the kid."

This time my wince is more real, and I glance over my shoulder toward the nursery, dropping my voice to a whisper. "Oh, crap. Did you *finally* get him down for a nap?"

"Yeah. About five minutes before you started doing your best impression of a civil war soldier in full bayonet charge. What'd they call that shit again? The *rebel* yell?"

I swat his chest playfully, but we both hold tensely still. "I'm gonna make sure you remember that history lesson for when he's older."

And our baby boy is growing up too fast.

You don't know tension and fear until you've been a parent with a fussy four-month-old baby who will only nap when the moon aligns with Venus and it's raining over a specific obscure mountain village in the Himalayas. I'm only exaggerating a little about zodiac signs helping him to sleep.

Seriously, those endless waits are the longest of your life, wondering if you'll hear blessed silence, or the irritated wail of the cutest little monster in the world.

No, actually, I've thought it over and his utter adorableness doesn't change the fact that little Micah Steven Strauss is, in fact, a complete tyrannical monster.

Just like his father.

Except my tyrannical monster happens to be an amazing dad, too. We've developed a great routine, swapping shifts between my writing and his work, making sure one of us is always with the baby and somehow we still find time for each other.

I don't know how, after so many years, the love can still feel just as fresh, just as natural, just as *real* as it did the first time he pulled me down in the grass in Steve's back yard.

But it does.

It does, and I'm content to snuggle myself into the crook of his arm as the countdown passes without that warning wake up scream coming from the nursery.

"Phew," I exhale.

Landon chuckles and rests his chin to the top of my head. "So, you want to tell me what exactly that was about?"

"Oh!" I perk up, remembering, bouncing on the balls of my toes. "Right. The third book in the Royal Nuisance series just hit the New York Times list!"

He raises his brows, but there's repressed laughter in his eyes. "Again? How long is it now?"

"Five weeks in a row." I drape my arms around his neck. "Who's the best author in the world?"

"Philip Roth."

"Asshole."

He breaks his stony façade with a grin. "Sorry. I meant to say *McKenna Strauss*. Didn't think I should lead with my strong fucking personal bias for her." He leans down and kisses me gently, melding with my smile. "Knew you could do it, babe. I always knew."

I nip his upper lip. "Yeah, wise man?"

"Hell yeah." His hand strokes down over the curve of my hip. "I know something else, too. Soon they'll be making movies about your characters. No bull."

I roll my eyes. "Oh, God. You can keep that one to yourself, thanks. My books are too crazy to translate to the big screen, and you've already done enough crazy for us both."

He winks, pulls away, and takes up the mixing bowl again, starting to whisk while I settle on a barstool to watch. "Have you even seen the last one about me? Luke Shaw did a damn fine job playing yours truly, but the rest...shit."

I arch a pointed brow. "If you recall, you had to physically restrain me from going after the director for implying you and Milah were in love and worked together to bring down the mob. That's *not* a documentary, that's a really bad romantic suspense. So, yeah, I'd say Shaw the famous actor was about the only good part."

"They're just sensationalizing for television, Reb. Creative license turning into creative stupidity."

He says it so offhandedly, like it doesn't matter, but he seems to have forgotten how red-faced he was when he was sent the script after the director asked for the rights to his story.

He's still like that.

A snarling, temperamental beast. This huge over-protective hulk of a man, now with a growly Papa Bear edge filing away the sharper one left by bad history.

Landon's a newer, better man. He saves his temper for things that are actually worth it, instead of using it to shove away anyone and everyone who could ever care about him.

I prop my chin in my hand, just watching him. There's a softness about him now, his jagged edges soothed.

Fatherhood suits him. With baby Micah, he's all

warmth and laughter, and it melts me every time I see him sprawled on the bed playing jet plane with our little boy. Or tickling him until he dissolves into giggles.

He's got his father's blue eyes and my brown hair, and he just might be the most beautiful thing I've ever seen aside from the very man who fathered him.

Landon glances up. "What?"

"Nothing." I laugh, leaning forward to peer into the bowl. "Whatcha making?"

"Mixing marinade for ribs." When I blink at him blankly, he frowns. "The barbeque? You *did* remember Steve's coming today, right?"

"Um. Right. What day is it again?"

"Sunday, babe."

Holy hell. He's serious.

"How long have I been in the writing cave?!" I ask.

He gives me an amused, indulgent look. "Only two days." Then he points a dripping spoon at me. "This time."

"Sorry." I wince with an apologetic little smile. "Let me go get cleaned up, and I'll help you with the food prep."

I dash upstairs and grab a quick shower, wondering how he puts up with me.

Sometimes, if I hit the zone on a good writing streak, I might forget about things like food and water and not smelling like a used gym sock.

I'm a lucky, lucky woman to have him.

It doesn't take me long to scrub myself fresh, toss my hair out into a pretty windswept mess, and dress before I'm downstairs in the kitchen, helping Landon prep meat and sides for the barbeque. We dive into making potato salad and coleslaw and desserts, working together with an easy familiarity born of practice, time, and the love that has us stealing kisses every time we bump each other in the kitchen.

We're not even halfway through before two cats come striding into the kitchen. Velvet and Mews both have their tails up in curly question marks, sniffing at the air.

"How could I forget?" Landon smiles, grabbing two small bowls of meat off the counter, pushing them at their greedy mouths.

I slide down the counter next to him, both of us smiling, stroking between their ears.

Later, I'm just laying out place settings on the patio when Steve's big hulking Durango comes cruising down the drive, the closest he says he'll ever come to a minivan.

He might want to rethink that, I realize, as Melanie slips out of the passenger's seat and I recognize the beginning of the pregnant waddle I know all too well myself, even if she's hardly starting to show.

Their two-year-old, Jessie, hangs on her hip, sucking on her thumb, watching me and Landon with the wide, wary eyes of a little girl who knows we're not strangers but doesn't yet know us well enough to trust.

But she comes to me easily enough when I reach out my arms and pull her in close, breathing in her sweet little-girl scent and nuzzling her hair. "There's my big girl," I murmur. "You're growing up so fast. Are you too big now to play with your little cousin?"

Jessie shakes her head mutely, then giggles and hides her face in my shoulder.

I'm already wondering if I want a daughter next, my insides twisting up sweetly, when Steven rounds the car and pulls both me and his little girl into a big bear hug. "Hey there, baby sis."

"Hey yourself." I stretch up on my toes to kiss his cheek, then transfer his daughter – so young and already a daddy's girl, snuggling into his barrel chest – back to him. "You're a little early, but we're about to throw the meat on."

"No rush. You know we don't come here for Landon's shitty cooking."

"I heard that," Landon calls from behind the grill.

"I know you did, asshole," Steve fires back with a fierce, friendly grin.

"Steven!" Melanie chides, reaching over to cover little Jessie's ears. "Language."

I laugh and beckon them toward the table. "I think she's gonna have to get used to it in this family."

Melanie sighs, long-aggrieved, still giving her man the evil eye. "I just don't want her first concrete sentences involving the f-word."

"Fa?" Jessie repeats curiously.

Melanie makes a strangled, disbelieving sound. I clap a hand over my mouth, struggling not to laugh. Steve looks guilty for a moment, while Landon grins, devilish and unrepentantly amused.

"Love having a niece after my own heart," he says.

"*Ahem.*" Steve clears his throat noisily and quickly trundles back toward the car. "I brought something for you."

I smile, recognizing a diversion when I see one. Still biting back a laugh, I trail Steve around his car, where he fishes out an old, battered wooden box from his back seat.

I recognize it immediately. It's the same little box where I used to keep bits and bobs and trinkets I'd picked up all over the place, storing them away like bits of stories I'd weave into my books later.

Including the old, scratched-up pair of tan binoculars, resting there among the bottle caps and dried flowers and bits of braided string.

My heart goes soft and wild all at once with the sweet bloom of nostalgia as I reach in and pick them up. Landon leaves the grill, crossing the grass. "What've you got there – *oh*." He smiles with a softness I'd thought was dead for the longest time as he reaches out to trace the edge of one lens with a fingertip. "Holy shit. Long time, no see. Can't believe you kept these."

"Of course I did!" I say, hugging the binoculars to my chest. "These were how we used to see the stars."

His arms slide around me, pulling me close, capturing me in the warmth of him; in the warmth of being surrounded by my family, of having the life I've always wanted.

"I see the stars in you," he whispers low in my ear, just between us. "But we can break them out tonight, if you want. Re-live old times. We'll find our constellations again and again. Every night, babe, for as long as you want."

"I *do* want," I murmur, leaning close into him and taking in his scent, as wild and dark as the sea. "I'll always want."

Because I know that when he says find the constellations, what he really means is finding his way ever deeper into the caverns of my heart.

* * *

THANKS FOR READING! I hope you enjoyed Still Not Over You. Look for Skylar's story coming soon!

READ on for a preview of another bestselling protector romance of mine, Accidental Hero.

ACCIDENTAL HERO PREVIEW

I: Walking Masterpiece (Izzy)

I have to bite my lip at how the silence excites me.

This is *exactly* what I've dreamed about for years. A room full of talent. Bright eyes and young souls eager to impress, bleeding creativity.

Every student deep in concentration, glancing towards the drawing on the easel next to my desk only long enough to confirm the next swoosh of their pencil. I hadn't known what to expect when I accepted this position, other than it would bring me one step closer to my goal. Plus a little more money.

Oh, and it's the perfect escape from the weekly family dinners. Losing those gossip-fests is worth more than the income boost any job brings.

Working with this room full of remarkable young artists is way more fun than listening to mom's tongue-in-cheek 'encouragement.'

Or entertaining cousin Clara's dire warnings about

how I'm destined to wind up with a house full of cats and die in my eighties, still a virgin.

That's my future. Isabella Derby. AKA crazy cat lady.

The fact that my family believes that's the path I'm on and insists on reminding me so often never fails to piss me off. No matter how many times I hear it.

This is the twenty-first century. Supposedly. I don't even own a cat, and I'm twenty-three.

Twenty. Three.

Not fifty-three, and pining about what might have been. I have *years* before I need to worry about getting married. I have ambitions. Always have.

If only everyone else in my life would see that and leave me the hell alone.

If only they'd notice accomplishments besides landing men and wracking up babies.

"Ms. Derby?"

I rise from my chair and walk around my desk, happy to have something else to focus on besides my sad, nosy relatives.

Stopping next to her, I look down at the girl and smile. "Yes, Natalie?"

She's what some would call a child prodigy. Only ten, she has the talent of some people five times her age. Not just in fine arts either.

Her enrollment papers says she's in eighth grade. Most kids her age are still fourth graders. I kneel next to her. "What's up?"

She gestures to my drawing at the front of the room. "Um, I just noticed...the dog you drew doesn't have any eyelashes." Her shy voice comes out in a whisper. "Is it all right if I add some on mine?"

"Of course! Your personal muse is always welcome in this class." I look at the drawing on her easel, picturing exaggerated Minnie Mouse eyelashes.

Wrong idea.

My breath literally stalls in my lungs at the detail in her creation. This little girl wouldn't be caught dead making anything unrealistic. The collie she's drawn looks like it's ready to leap into the room. Just like everything she does.

It's more like a black and white photo than a drawing. Especially one done by a child.

Every feathery line she's sketched brings the dog to life in ways I can't even describe.

Hell, it's almost better than *mine*. And it took me a Master's degree and years practicing to get where I am.

I glance between her dog and mine. Forget *almost*.

Hers is far better. A masterpiece.

I choke up as I watch the eyes on her dog come to life as she carefully pencils in a few soft lashes. "Keep going. You're doing a great job!"

"Thank you," she whispers.

The way she's biting the tip of her tongue demonstrates how fully she's concentrating. I smile again, then stand, making a round of the whole room.

Only six students here this evening. The others are all high school kids. Natalie's dad had to pull some strings to get her into this class, meant for kids at least in their freshmen year.

That's what I was told. Since this is my first year with the district, I'm as unfamiliar with the students and their families as I am with the staff. That'll change in time, I'm sure. We're only three weeks into the school year.

The other five drawings look much like I expect. They demonstrate passion and promise, but honestly, there isn't another one that comes anywhere close to Natalie's.

I wonder if her talent comes from her father. The man I try *hard* not to think about every time she steps foot in my class.

If the last two weeks are anything to go by, he'll be here soon. A good twenty minutes before class ends. He'll stand in the back of the room with a spiral notebook, open it up, and let his big, rough hands touch the paper.

The first night, I thought he was making a list or notes. But last week, I had a strong feeling he was drawing. Sketching right along with his daughter and the rest of the class.

We'd started the dog last week, drawing the base after I'd gone over my quick anatomy lesson for animals. Tonight, I showed the students how to make the fur have shades of white, black, and gray.

A small, senseless part of me wonders if Natalie's dad will join in without even hearing my lesson. An even crazier part wants to see his drawing.

It could be a masterpiece like hers.

He certainly is. And that's the problem.

Mr. Tall-Dark-and-Brooding is every forbidden male archetype stuffed into one ripped package.

Mysteriously sexy by default. Imposing by gravity. Protective by virtue.

He's the kind of man I'd love to bring to a family dinner.

Just once.

That's all it would take. He'd render Clara speechless

and end mom's needless sympathy looks in one blow. He'd shut them down and then some.

Every Derby woman would be too busy gasping for breath and fanning themselves to give me any crap.

Honestly, I know the feeling. It was my reaction the first time he walked in. And the second.

At least I hid it well.

The military patches on his black leather jacket were no surprise. He has that air.

Straight back, chest forward, chin up. Disciplined. Hard.

Every move he makes, every glance, has a purpose.

Remember what I said? Every *forbidden* archetype.

The ones good girls are warned about, but never stay away from.

God. I shouldn't be having these thoughts.

Not about a student's father. He's probably married. And if he isn't, *why the hell not?*

But I didn't see a mother listed on Natalie's emergency contacts. That makes me feel slightly less guilty about the impure thoughts stirring in my head. It also concerns me.

I hope she isn't being pushed beyond her limits. Flogged on to greatness by a headstrong father who believes his child should succeed in everything, no matter the cost.

I know the burden.

Just as I arrive back at my desk, the hair on the back of my neck tingles. It's almost like there's a sixth sense before the Walking Masterpiece shows up. I close my eyes briefly, preparing myself for the sight I'll see after the door creaks open.

My heart jackhammers by the time I turn around, air stalling in my lungs.

Right on time. Sure as shit.

It's him.

Brent Eden. His hair is the same wavy black as his daughter's. Natalie has his eyes, too.

Emerald green.

His are colder, though. More seasoned. More cautious.

His features add to his presence. A tiny faded scar here, an inked muscle there, a calloused hand. Things a normal person wouldn't notice unless they're gawking at him like me.

Beautifully rough finishes for a man cut from Heaven's most twisted fabric.

The thick trimmed beard circling his jaw must feel as dangerous as it looks. Delicious torture on any woman's skin. Especially mine since it's as virgin as the rest of me.

Fucking-A. Last week's after-dinner talk with Clara clearly messed with my mind.

Left me focused on things I've never worried over before. Namely, finding a man to take home to mother. And maybe to bed while we're at it.

What the hell am I doing? I pinch my thigh. Ogling a man who's nothing but trouble, apparently.

He eases the door shut and quietly moves along the back wall, taking the exact same spot where he's stood the past two weeks. Leaning against a desk, he unclips a pen from his notebook's cover and then flips it open.

Look away, Izzy.

I sense he'll look up any second. Naturally, I can't. It's like someone telling you to not think about a pink elephant.

There's too much gorgeous mystery in front of me. Too much temptation.

The heat rushing to my cheeks tells me I've been caught staring even before my eyes travel all the way up to meet his. *Damn!*

"Ms. Derby?"

Tad Gomez calls my name, one of the older students, but a snail could beat me turning around.

Brent's gaze is intense. Heated. Almost like he's challenging me not to look away.

I'm not a daring person. I just don't want to lose this staring contest. But duty calls.

Lifting a brow, I rip my gaze off his, and scuttle towards Tad's seat.

I'm grateful for the few seconds I have to find my voice. "Having trouble?"

"Yes, ma'am. I can't get the nose to look 3-D. Not like yours."

I point towards Tad's drawing, which is good, but as he said, a little flat. "It's the angle. Here, let me show you."

He nods, handing me his pencil. I lightly outline how to angle the nose downward in order to give it depth. "See? One little change works like magic."

"Yes, Ms. Derby. Yes, I do. Thanks!" He takes his pencil back and continues filling in the outline.

"Light strokes, remember. They'll flesh it out even more."

Barely touching the paper with the edge of his pencil, he nods bashfully. "Thanks."

"You're welcome, Tad. Keep it up. You're off to an awesome start."

He pushes his thick glasses up his nose. "I really like this class, Ms. Derby."

Such a sweet boy. How could I do anything but smile? "We all do."

The door squeaks again. This time, it's Ester Oden's mother. She works as a custodian at the school and stays late in order to drive Ester home after class. I smile at her as I make my way around the room, checking on the progress of each student, offering a helpful hint and words of encouragement.

It feels good to do my job. And to find a perfect distraction from the man I shouldn't be staring at.

"Five more minutes," I say, once I'm back at my desk.

There are no audible groans, but I can sense each student's disappointment, knowing this week's class is almost over. I'm honored they don't want to leave.

This, right here, is the reason I sunk a lot of time and money into getting my credentials. It's why I spent years doing every part time job in the known universe. It's what I've dreamed about, working at the most prestigious academy in the Phoenix area.

"Ms. Derby?"

"Yeah, Ben?" I reply. Ben Pritchard is a typical teenager. Tall, thin, and a bad case of acne.

"Is it all right if I snap a picture of your drawing at the end of class so I can work on mine later?" he asks, holding up his cell phone.

"Go for it! But no Snapchat filters on me, and you'd better believe I'm watching. Only warning I'll give." I bite my lip and shake my finger, making them laugh.

I nod towards the others in the class and step out of the way, assuring them they can all take pictures. I hear the digital *click-click-click* of their phones and a few snickers.

Then my gaze, all on its own, drifts to the back of the room. Brent's head is down this time, thankfully.

He's sketching again. Furiously.

I have a different reason to bite my lip. This time, not so playfully.

There's something admirable in his focus. Something sexy.

I'm waiting for him to look up, after the older kids are done taking pics. At ten, I doubt Natalie has a cell phone. I assume he'll want to get a picture for her.

He never looks up, though. Never throws his eyes my way. Even though I sense him wanting to behind his determined, subtle smirk.

I suck a deep breath and hold it, hoping it eases the heat coursing through my system. I glance at the clock and then smile at my students. "Okay, guys and gals! Time to start putting your stuff away. Please bring your completed drawing back to class next week."

Every student, except Natalie, finishes taking pictures of my drawing, either before or after they've packed up their belongings. While saying goodbye to each of them, I start gathering my things, too, but leave the drawing on the easel.

What gives? Why isn't Brent getting her a picture?

He's still lost in his own world. Sketching quickly. Frantically. Like he's desperate to finish something before leaving. My curiosity turns into pure adrenaline.

I can't stop myself. "Mr. Eden? Would you like a picture?"

When he looks up, his gaze is so intense my heart nearly stops mid-beat.

"Oh, I'd like that! Please, can you, Daddy?" Natalie asks, turning to him.

I'm glad she doesn't witness me melting into a puddle of nerves.

His bright eyes shift. The smile transforming Brent's face is for his daughter, but it steals my breath.

I've watched lots of men smile. I've seen it, sketched it, noted how a thin quirk of the lips can change a full appearance.

But this man, this beast, goes from hardcore army badass to giant teddy bear in the blink of an eye.

He can't hide the adoration lighting up his eyes the second Natalie calls him Daddy.

At least I've learned one thing tonight: this man lives for his daughter.

Guilt twists in my guts again when I remember my earlier worries about him being overbearing. Not now. It just doesn't seem likely.

"Sure, sweets. One second," he says, closing his notebook.

My heart starts working again. It beats harder with every step he takes toward the front of the room.

I've been this close to him before. Once. The first night, when he'd dropped Natalie off and introduced himself.

I tried like crazy not to freeze up, and failed miserably, barely muttering my name.

Can't let that happen again. I won't embarrass myself a second time, no matter how many feels this handsome enigma shoots through me.

Pretending I'm unfazed by his presence, I say goodbye to Ester and her mother before they walk out the side door. Then, in my scattered state of mind, I accidentally knock a stack of papers off the corner of my desk.

"Oh, f – fiddlesticks!" I say, catching myself.

God. I'd nearly dropped an f-bomb in my flustered state. My tongue is my biggest vice sometimes. I'm still sanding away the rough language I picked up too much of in college.

Natalie shoots forward. "I'll help, Ms. Derby!"

I kneel down beside her and start gathering the papers. "Thanks, Natalie. I certainly can be clumsy sometimes. Must be getting late."

Must be. Or else I'd totally have to admit I've been drooling over her father for the better part of the last ten minutes.

"We all have accidents," she says. "Don't stress."

I smile, nodding slowly. This girl sounds far too old for her age, which causes me to glance up at her father.

He's raised her to be polite. Kind. Intelligent.

He shrugs when he sees there isn't room to step in and help, walking over to pick up the backpack she's left on the floor.

I take the papers Natalie collects and stack them on top of the pile I've formed. "Thanks for your help again, Natalie. You're too awesome."

"Ready, sweets?" Brent asks.

"Coming!" Natalie flashes a big grin. "See you next week, Ms. Derby. Can't wait to finish my drawing."

"Looking forward to it," I answer, flinching slightly at not being able to come up with something more original.

Brent nods at me while laying a hand on Natalie's shoulder and guiding her towards the door.

I nod back. I think. I'm too embarrassed to say for sure.

Woof. I'm so ready to slump into my chair before I leave the building.

I need five or ten. Just a few precious minutes to let my body, mind, and pulse find their baseline.

I doubt there's any time. This is the only evening class near closing time. Oscar Winters, the janitor, who doubles as our evening security guard, is already waiting for me to leave so he can lock up and go home.

Sighing, I set the stack of papers on the corner, hoping the regular teacher in this room, Mrs. Wayne's substitute, isn't overly upset tomorrow morning that they aren't in the same order. Then I start packing my things in my carry-all. I'm so busy trying to get out of here I don't even see him enter.

"Finally! Why the hell have you been ignoring my calls and texts?"

The voice vibrating in my ears makes me shudder like a spider crawling up my spine. A huge, unwanted, hairy one.

Crap. Not this guy again.

I huff out a breath of air before glancing up. "What are you doing here, Preston?"

All five feet and nine inches of Preston Graves stands just a few feet away like he owns the place. He probably thinks he does.

He's that arrogant. If you could take a picture of a blind date gone bad, it would look like this man.

Bleached blond hair, blue eyes, and obscenely rich. He's also the biggest prick I've ever met.

He looked better in the pics he'd uploaded to the matchmaker app. I was actually excited when it said we were compatible, mainly because I knew mom would approve. Well, and because he didn't look quite as phony with a good filter.

Then we met, and he opened his dumb mouth.

"Isabella, don't play coy. You know why I'm here: you haven't responded to a single one of my messages. You're ignoring me." He leans a hand on the corner of the desk. "For your information, Preston Graves does not like being ignored."

That's how he talks. Third person. It's overly unnecessary and fucking annoying.

Correction: he's overly fucking annoying.

"I've been busy," I say.

I mentally wonder how crazy my intruder is. Could he stop me from reaching for my phone if push comes to shove?

"Excuses, excuses. Who do you think you're dealing with, dear? No one's ever too busy for me. What's the real deal keeping you away?"

Gag me with a fucking spoon. "The school year just started."

I force a weak smile. It does nothing. Call me an idiot for letting the dating app scan my real employer. I'm an even bigger fool if I think it'll help get me out of this madness.

"And?" Preston taps his polished shoe impatiently, scratching his head.

Ugh. Is he dense or just insufferable?

I'd told him when I cut our date short that I didn't have time to see him again, but he obviously thought I was lying. Why he'd want to chase a liar, who knows.

Time to take a different route. "Preston, look, you shouldn't be here. It's a secure environment, this academy, whether it's school hours or not. We have rules."

"Nonsense. Nothing's too secure for Preston Graves. My Uncle Theo sits on the board of the largest banking chain in Maricopa county. Security's practically my middle name. It's lovely you follow the rules, Isabella, but you've got nothing to worry about as long as –"

Oh, please, *shut up*, Gaston. It's too much like my favorite fairy tale with none of the charm. I stop listening.

It's time to end this right now.

"Do you have a pass, Preston? Did you show it to the guard in the hall?"

"The janitor, you mean? The man who's vacuuming a few classrooms away?" He turns his nose up, walking around the desk, dragging a manicured hand along the edge. "Very funny, Isabella. You're on fire tonight. Why would I waste the time? When Preston finds something he wants, *nothing* stands in his way." He stops right in front of me. "Nothing and no one."

My heart leaps into my throat. This puffed up joke of a man is getting old and weird fast. I don't like the glint in his eye. He's a mega-creep, too. Not just socially clueless.

I think I know a psychotic asshole who was born with a silver spoon in his mouth when I see one. Knew it from the night I was dumb enough to go out with him.

I just didn't think he'd go to these lengths for another chance. Never imagined he'd bother me here.

I freeze, trying to think without making it too obvious. I don't dare glance around.

That would be the worst thing: letting him think he has me scared.

But he does.

This looney tune has my heart crawling up my throat.

"Are we done playing now?" He steps closer, an eerie warmth on his face. "I know you like Preston, Isabella. Everyone does. You just have a rather curious way of showing it."

A shiver ripples through my entire body. I have nothing to defend myself, and shoot a sideways glance at the desk, scanning for something that might work.

Nothing. Not even a sharp pencil.

I'm screwed. Estimating how loud I can scream when everything changes.

Preston falls backwards, grabbing the edge of the desk so hard it moves, scraping the floor. Then I see Brent Eden. Nostrils flaring, he has a hand on the back of Preston's starched shirt collar.

Preston twists his neck, taking in the man holding onto him. "W-Who are you?"

"Nothing and no one," Brent says, echoing his earlier words.

Though I never condone violence, right now I wouldn't mind seeing Preston knocked on his ass.

He tries shaking off Brent's iron grip. "You're making a big mistake! I'm Preston Graves the third and –"

"I don't give a fuck," Brent growls, tightening his hold.

Wow.

Preston squirms, panic in his eyes. "But...this is crazy! Isabella and I are dating."

Brent's green eyes settle on me. My heart's still in my throat, but I manage to shake my head for a split second.

This courtship ended after the first and only date Preston Graves will ever get from me. One date too many.

"I don't think so," Brent says, eyeing me suspiciously.

"Yes, we are," Preston insists. "Tell him Isabella!"

Even if I could find my tongue, that's the last thing I'd admit to.

A mischievous glint flashes in Brent's eyes. "She can't be dating you. She's dating me."

Wait. What?!

I nearly choke on my own breath.

Preston tries harder to get loose. "Impossible!"

Brent spins Preston around so they're face to face. "Then you probably also believe it's impossible we're engaged. And that I'll beat the fuck out of any man who comes within twenty feet of my fiancée."

I'm no stranger to F-words, but that one, on his lips, makes me want to pass out.

He gives Preston another shove and before I know it, Brent grabs me, one hand on the back of my head, and smashes his lips against mine.

I'm gone.

Heat consumes me so swiftly the world melts. His lips are all fire. The blood surging through my veins might be lava.

My lips part – they never have a chance – and his tongue sweeps into my mouth.

Hot. Bold. Amazing.

Brent's other arm wraps around me, holding my body tight against the length of him. It's like an ice cream cone up against a space heater. My entire body melts down from the inside out.

Holy hell. This is the kind of kiss every girl dreams about. The take-me-out-of-this-world kind.

I'm so engrossed several moments flit by before I remember he shouldn't be kissing me.

We aren't alone. I barely know him. He's my student's father.

A dozen other realizations bum-rush my dizzy brain, including Preston's voice.

I pull out of the kiss – regretfully. Still too worked up to stand on my own, I lean against Brent, taking a few seconds to let the real world return.

"No one dumps Preston Graves!" He says numbly, his anger slowly returning. "And that stupid app guaranteed *three* dates. Three!" He holds up his fingers, as if I don't know how to count.

Hell, after that kiss, maybe I don't.

"I can sue. Sue them, and you. Both of you!" He prattles on, stomping a foot like a child not getting his way. "You've made a big mistake, Isabella Derby. You and your thug boyfriend. I'll take every penny you have and – and her teacher's license. Just watch me. Preston Graves can do that!"

Brent's upper lip curls slightly as he shakes his head. "Preston Graves better get the fuck out of here before he needs to sue for medical expenses, too."

"Hey! Is there a problem here?"

I push away from Brent's side as Oscar Winters and Natalie walk through the door. The poor girl looks bewildered, probably wondering what the hold up is with her dad.

"Yeah. Big problem," Brent replies, pointing at Preston. "Did you let his man in the building?"

"No." Oscar's face falls, realizing the seriousness. He might not have Brent's rogue good looks, but he's a big man. Over six feet tall and two hundred intimidating pounds, Oscar walks towards Preston. "How did you get in here, sir?"

"Dear God, are you *all* clueless? Preston Graves can go anywhere he damn well –"

"No, he can't," Brent interjects. "I don't know how he got in the building, but I saw him sneaking out of the men's room. Didn't like the look on his face. I followed."

"You're in the wrong place. Let's go." Oscar grabs Preston's arm. "I'm truly sorry for this, Ms. Derby. It won't happen again."

"I hope not," Brent says seriously. "Safety's in your hands." He nods towards Natalie. "That shouldn't be taken lightly."

"Never, Mr. Eden. You're absolutely right. Believe me, I'll find out how Mr. Graves found his way in. It won't happen a second time." Oscar tugs Preston towards the door, none too gently.

Preston appears to have lost some of his arrogance as he crosses the room, at the mercy of two powerful men. But he's still wearing a this-isn't-over glare I don't like one bit. I roll my shoulders, pretending to stretch. Really, I'm hiding the shiver.

Brent's hand slides off my shoulder and down my back. Amazingly comforting.

"Get your things," he says quietly. "I'll walk you out."

"I'll take your sketchpad!" Natalie says cheerfully, ready to chip in.

Her smile suggests she saw plenty, probably through the small glass window in the classroom door. It also says what just happened hasn't bothered her in the least.

My cheeks go bright red. I'm more thankful than ever she's mature for her age. At least I don't have to worry about any gossip that could get me in deep, deep doo-doo.

Still fighting off a nervous tremble, I say, "Thank you." Then I look at Brent. "That's not necessary, but thanks. Again. I can find my own way out, Mr. Eden."

"No. You're coming to your car with me," he insists, grabbing my carry-all off the desk. "This everything?"

He's no nonsense through and through. The hint of irony in his glare tells me not to argue. So I don't.

"Everything," I echo, stepping forward and taking my sketchpad from Natalie. "Thank you."

"You're welcome, Ms. Derby." With another large grin, she leans in and whispers, "Thank you, too. Dad likes being a hero. Doesn't get to do the whole white knight thing as often as he'd like."

"Nat." There's a hint of a warning in Brent's tone.

Natalie shakes her head slightly while her green eyes twinkle. "He's a good knight, too."

Unable to disagree, I nod.

"Where's your backpack, baby girl?" Brent asks.

"Oh! I think I left it in the hallway when you told me to go get Mr. Winters," Natalie answers.

"Go get it. We'll wait right here."

"Okay, Daddy!" There's a skip in her step as she hurries towards the door.

Once again, I'm searching for my tongue as I walk towards the door with Brent by my side. I need to tell him thank you, but I'm afraid I'll sound like a bubbling idiot.

"One question: what made you go out with a man who calls himself by his own name?" Brent asks once Natalie's out of earshot.

Kill me. He's trying to lighten this insanity, I'm sure. Still, full-fledged embarrassment burns my cheeks. "Fuck if I know." I flinch then and bite my tongue.

That's *not* how a teacher speaks. Especially a preschool teacher who does evening art classes for older kids.

For a second, he cocks his head. Then, to my utter amazement, he laughs. It's a nice sound. And it breaks the invisible ice surrounding me. "That's a damn good answer, Ms. Derby."

"Well...thank you," I say sheepishly. "I knew I made a mistake. I thought we were done. Tried to let him down easy. Never, in my wildest dreams, did I think he'd show up here."

He lifts a brow as we step into the hallway. "Is Preston Graves in your wildest dreams?"

"Hell no!" I flinch again at my own language. "I mean, *no.* Gross. He was a match-up from a dating site. One I won't mention because I'm *very* dissatisfied."

"How many times did you date him?"

"Once." I shake my head. "Actually, it was more like a half-date. I didn't even make it through reading the menu at the place in Scottsdale before I knew I had to cut things short. It had already been too long."

My comment reminds him we're probably wasting time, too. He starts walking and I follow.

Natalie is waiting by the main entrance door with Oscar. It's a long corridor. Brent sees them, but doesn't seem to be in a hurry.

"What did you do?" he asks.

"I laid a twenty on the table to pay for my glass of wine, gave the waitress a big tip, which she highly deserved, and lied."

"Lied?"

"Yes. Lied. I told him it was nice to meet him, which it wasn't, and then I said I was sorry, but I simply don't have time to date right now."

"When was that?"

"Almost three weeks ago. He stopped texting me last week when I didn't respond, so I'd hoped it was finally over." It's embarrassing telling him all this, but it's the truth, and he deserves that much after coming to my rescue.

Preston's creepy encounter shook me up more than I want to admit.

"I have no idea how he got inside, Mr. Eden," Oscar says as we approach him and Natalie. "The doors were locked. I let everyone in and out and didn't see him once. I always double check. I'm sure of it!" Oscar looks at me, frustration lining his brow. "He's gone now, Ms. Derby. I escorted him to his car and watched him drive away. I'll gladly do the same for you."

"We're good, Oscar. I'm her escort," Brent says. "Did you search him for a key fob?"

Oscar's face falls as he shakes his head. "No, sir, but I'll make a full report of the security breach. As you know, the academy takes security very seriously."

Brent turns to me. "Could he have gotten your key fob?"

"No. It's right here." I pull the badge around my neck out of the top of my shirt. My I.D. card and the key fob dangle off the end. "It hasn't been out of my sight since I got it two weeks ago. Jesus. This doesn't make any sense..."

Brent nods, turning back to Oscar. "I suggest you find out who lost a key fob recently and make everyone aware what Preston Graves looks like. Make sure they understand he's not allowed on the premises."

Oscar nods. "Of course, sir, I'll do that. I'll stay late. Get the report in the system before I leave."

A million questions race through my mind, but I hold them until after we walk outside. The heat still coming off the nighttime pavement makes me want to fan myself. We're off high summer, the hottest time of year, but not to the point where the nights are really comfortable.

Once we're walking down the long concrete walkway leading to the parking lot, I ask another question I've been holding in. "So, uh, Mr. Eden...are you a detective? A cop, maybe?"

"No."

"He works with cops all the time," Natalie says. "He owns his own company."

I wait for either one of them to add more, but they don't, and I'm too tongue tied to keep probing. Or too scared.

Though he came to my rescue, gave me the hottest, most memorable kiss of my life, there are red flags popping up all over. This whole thing is bad news.

He's a student's father. The academy has rules against teacher-family relationships. Pages upon pages of iron-clad rules. As the most elite private academy in the county, the wait list to become a student, or to get a job here, is as long as Route 66.

Landing this preschool position was pure luck. Same as the very part-time accelerated art class I'm filling in for.

I can't fuck it up. Cannot. Will not.

Not even for drop dead sexy men with beast eyes and beards who kiss like they mean business.

"That your car?" Brent asks.

Lost in thought, I glance up, nodding. Classic Mustang convertible. Old. Not at all what anyone would expect a teacher to drive. "It was my dad's."

He doesn't respond physically or verbally, just keeps walking. At the car, he opens the door and looks inside before stepping aside.

"You should lock your doors."

"I usually do." I'd been running late, trying to get back in time for the evening class and hadn't, but won't make that mistake again. I take my bag from him and pull out the keys, then put the carry-all and my sketchpad in the backseat. I make sure to include Natalie as I say, "Thank you both. For everything."

"Nah, it was our pleasure, Ms. Derby!" Natalie talks like she's forty instead of ten. I smile like mad. She steps forward and wraps her arms around my middle. "Please don't be embarrassed. We were really happy to help tonight."

Something inside me flutters as I hug her back. It's not everyday you run into good people.

Our hug ends, and as she steps away, she twists to look at her father. "Weren't we, Daddy? Happy to help Ms. Derby?"

The transformation on his face happens again. "Yes, baby girl," he says. "Thrilled." His smile fades as he looks at me. "Our truck's right over there. We'll wait until you drive away. Unless you want us to follow you home?"

"No!" I flinch at my immediate response. "I mean, that's totally okay. You've already done more than enough. Much more. Thank you."

Completely unsure what to do, I take a step forward, but pause, not sure if I should shake his hand, or, well, hug him. Some crazy part of me shouts *hug.*

Fine. I step forward and give him a quick thank you squeeze.

His statue stiffness tells me I should've went with hand shake.

Crap.

I really am an idiot. But it's not like I have experience handling gorgeous men who pretend-kiss like it's the end of the world.

"Goodnight, guys!" I spin around and jump in my car, slamming the door shut, before I make this more awkward.

I wait until they turn around to walk across the three parking spaces between his truck and my car before leaning my forehead against the steering wheel. Mortification overwhelms me.

Heat does, too. Inside and out. It's been a brutal summer. Hot and windy, the autumn break can't come soon enough. Southern Arizona isn't a humid place, but the dry, hundred degree plus days wear on a body and soul.

I crank the window for fresh air and glance out the opening. There's a car rumbling up beside mine. Not Brent and Natalie's.

My heart leaps in my throat, but then slides back down where it belongs when I realize who it is.

Clara. *Damn!*

After everything went haywire tonight, I spaced on our plans to meet here so she could drop off one of her famous pies.

It's too late to stop the chain reaction. I see Brent gesturing furiously at Natalie to get in his truck as he starts walking back towards me. Opening the door, I climb out, hands in front of me. "Whoa, whoa, it's okay! Nothing scary. This is just my cousin, Clara."

Clara doesn't miss a beat. If she was a curious cat, she'd have lost about all nine lives by now. "Isabella Derby!" She's already shaking her head.

Oh, God. Here it comes.

Holding out her hand, she walks straight toward Brent. "Who on Earth is this fine specimen?"

I run. Around the back end of her car, to her side.

I'm too late to stop anything. Natalie is already answering, "He's our hero tonight!"

Seriously. Where's the hole in the ground? The kind that can swallow a person whole, when we need one?

"Hero?" Both of Clara's eyes are wider than an owl's as she looks at me and blinks. "Isabella *Derby!*"

Forget the hole in the ground. The brutal smile on her face makes me wish I had one in my head.

This night truly can't get any worse.

I love Clara, but she's the biggest gossip in the family. And I'm not sure Derby blood was ever compatible with privacy.

"He's just...the father of one of my students. Nothing

to worry about," I say, adding so much emphasis it hurts my tongue.

Her smile turns coy as she turns back to Brent. Sticking out her hand even further, she says, "Well, well, it's truly a pleasure. Clara Derby, Big Daddy. How do you do?"

Brent shakes her hand with an uneasy smile. I just close my eyes and pray for this day to be over. It's cursed. From the very second my alarm went off this morning.

"Nice to meet you, Ms. Derby." I hear him say. Then, "I'm afraid I have to run. Good seeing Isabella with a friend."

He gives me a knowing glance. I die once under his striking eyes, and again when I hear how my name sounds on his lips.

"Brent," I whisper. His name, rather than Mr. Eden, tastes wonderful in my mouth, too.

"Goodnight, Ladies."

My eyes snap open and I watch him walk to the truck. Clara's mouth drops.

I want to laugh. As painful as this is, it's so ridiculous it's kinda surreal.

Nerves. Has to be. Yet, in my defense, the way he didn't give Clara what she wanted, a name to Google, is comical.

He climbs into his truck and starts the engine.

Clara turns to me, mouth still hanging open and eyes wide. Her silence only lasts a nano-second.

"OMG!" she hisses. "He's to die for, Izzy!"

I can't agree. Well, I can, but I won't.

I still can't believe I forgot about her stupid pie.

Fuck. This is turning out to be the night of unwanted company to the nth degree.

Clara's long dark hair whips in the wind as she turns to his truck and then back to me. "Where? How? How long? Is he your dating site match-up guy? Why didn't you tell me you'd matched a ten out of ten hunk, lady?"

"What? No, no, no, and no!" I try to wipe out all her rapid fire questions at once.

"You're terrible for holding out on me. I thought we were family! You never said how your date turned out – mighty good by the looks of him. I mean, *it.*"

I shake my head. "Clara, it's late. I should be getting home."

"I brought you a pie! Coconut cream." Clara winks, reaching in the door she'd left open, her car still running. "Your favorite. I made a couple for dinner, and everyone agreed I should drop one off since you missed out. You're welcome, cuz."

Just great. I don't even like coconut cream pie that much.

Like most everything about the family dinners, I pretend I do to keep the peace. Then, a solid escape opportunity dawns on me. "Awesome!" I snatch the pie from her hand, feigning joy. "Better go before this melts. Have a nice night, Clara!"

"You really need a new car, Izzy. One with modern air conditioning."

"Someday, when I can afford it." I hold up the pie and smile as if I can't wait to bite into it. "Mmmm, supper! Thanks again."

I'm half way to my car, when her question stops me.

"Does your mama know about Big Daddy?"

I spin around as my stomach hits the ground. "Nope. And that's the way it's gonna stay because there isn't *anything* to know."

"He's still sitting there. Watching." She smiles, nods toward their truck, and does a small wave.

"He's just being polite." I start walking again. "And we're being rude, Clara. He has a little girl to get home to put to bed. He's waiting for us to leave. Making sure we're safe." I leave it there so I don't have to mention, much less think about Preston again.

"So...no mother? No wife? I mean, if you've got to deal with her, there are always ways around the drama. You can't let that stop you!"

"Clara."

"Okay, okay! I'm just curious."

"Nosy, you mean," I mumble, climbing in my car. As the engine purrs to life, I wave. "Thanks again for the pie."

She gets in her car and pulls away. I follow. Brent follows me. I try to let out a huff of relief, but there's none in me. I follow Clara's tail lights to the highway.

Thank God.

I cringe. Hoping he doesn't plan on following me all the way to my place in Tempe. Knowing Clara, she's already considering how to turn around and follow him home. My mind starts spinning faster than the nighttime traffic whipping down the four-lane highway.

A small sense of relief seeps out of me when I look in my mirrors again. Brent takes an exit. And I don't see a car that looks like Clara's anymore.

Then reality hits home.

Jesus! This night could've been an even bigger disaster.

If Clara ever hears what Brent said to Preston, about us being engaged, I'm toast.

And so is he.

There's no drama in the known universe like Derby drama.

And me, being a single crazy cat lady for the rest of my life, has been the main family tragedy for months.

Who knew the fix could be even worse?

GET ACCIDENTAL HERO AT YOUR FAVORITE RETAILER!

THANKS!

Want more Nicole Snow? Sign up for my newsletter to hear about new releases, exclusive subscriber giveaways, and more fun stuff!

JOIN THE NICOLE SNOW NEWSLETTER! - http://eepurl.com/HwFW1

Thank you so much for buying this book. I hope my romances sweeten your days with pleasure, drama, and all the feels! I tell the stories you want to hear.

If you liked this book, please consider leaving a review and checking out my other romance tales.

Got a comment on my work? Email me at nicole@nicolesnowbooks.com. I love hearing from fans!

Nicole Snow

More Intense Romance by Nicole Snow

ACCIDENTAL HERO

CINDERELLA UNDONE

MAN ENOUGH

SURPRISE DADDY

LAST TIME WE KISSED

PRINCE WITH BENEFITS: A BILLIONAIRE ROYAL ROMANCE

MARRY ME AGAIN: A BILLIONAIRE SECOND CHANCE ROMANCE

LOVE SCARS: BAD BOY'S BRIDE

MERCILESS LOVE: A DARK ROMANCE

RECKLESSLY HIS: A BAD BOY MAFIA ROMANCE

STEPBROTHER CHARMING: A BILLIONAIRE BAD BOY ROMANCE

STEPBROTHER UNSEALED: A BAD BOY MILITARY ROMANCE

Prairie Devils MC Books

OUTLAW KIND OF LOVE

NOMAD KIND OF LOVE

SAVAGE KIND OF LOVE

WICKED KIND OF LOVE

BITTER KIND OF LOVE

Grizzlies MC Books

OUTLAW'S KISS

OUTLAW'S OBSESSION

OUTLAW'S BRIDE

OUTLAW'S VOW

Deadly Pistols MC Books

NEVER LOVE AN OUTLAW

NEVER KISS AN OUTLAW

NEVER HAVE AN OUTLAW'S BABY

NEVER WED AN OUTLAW

Baby Fever Books

THANKS!

BABY FEVER BRIDE

BABY FEVER PROMISE

BABY FEVER SECRETS

Only Pretend Books

FIANCÉ ON PAPER

ONE NIGHT BRIDE

Made in the
USA
Columbia, SC

80660194R00183